THE DEMPSEYS

THE DEMPSEYS

Aiden Castle

Table of Contents

Part 1: 2023

Part 2: 2003

Part 3: 1993

Part 4: 1973

Part 5: 1983

Part 6: 2023

Part 1

2023

Chapter 1

Marcus Dempsey's eyelids opened as a hint of daylight peeked through the heavy drapes. He lay motionless, absorbing the silence that permeated the small room. His office had long ago transitioned from a space of scholarly pursuits to a makeshift bedroom. The walls, still lined with countless academic books, had taken on a more lived-in appearance.

Marcus pushed himself into a sitting position, the bed creaking under his weight. His gaze swept across the desk, where two computer screens lay dormant, their blank faces poised to flicker to life with the day's financial news. A collection of papers lay scattered across the surface, like soldiers on one of the battlefields in his books.

Marcus reached for "The Red Badge of Courage," which was resting on his nightstand. Its cover was worn, and the corners were bent from repeated readings. He picked up the book, the familiar weight comforting in his hand, and thumbed to the dog-eared page where he'd last left off.

As Marcus placed the book down, he noticed how his hands had changed over the years—veins more prominent, skin less forgiving. Standing up, he stretched his arms towards the ceiling as time pulled on his muscles. His reflection caught his eye: silver hair perfectly combed back and a tanned complexion. His light-coloured pyjamas, striped in blue, hung loosely on his frame.

"Seventy-five," he said to himself, a trace of disbelief in his tone. Despite his age, vigour still surged through his veins, defying the years. Marcus bent forward to touch his toes, and a sharp pang raced up his spine. He winced at the unwelcome reminder of his mortality.

"Damn it," he said as he straightened. The pain was fleeting, there and then gone, much like the memories he sometimes tried to outrun. Marcus savoured these moments of solitude, the soft tick of the clock on the wall the only accompaniment to his thoughts.

Marcus scanned the familiar terrain of his room; each artifact and memento reflected a life steeped in knowledge and ambition. His fingers, still nimble despite their wrinkles, glided over the mouse, coaxing the dual screens to life. The stock market's pulse beat across the monitors, red and green arrows darting like warring factions in one of his lectures.

"Fuck, why didn't you buy Bitcoin, Marcus..." he said to himself under his breath, the words laced with a blend of irony and self-mockery. "...because you don't even know what it is, you dummy." A chuckle escaped him as he shuffled papers into some semblance of order. His hand paused over a crumpled sheet—the beginnings of a historical analysis of the fall of Cartage, now as relevant to him as ancient hieroglyphs.

His eyes turned to the window still covered by the blinds. Marcus moved to the window, grasped the blinds, and flung them wide. Sunlight ambushed the room, revealing a stream of dust particles in the air. Outside, the pool shimmered like a jewel set against the backdrop of trees, offering an illusion of seclusion amid the sprawl of suburbia.

Then, she entered his view. He followed her with his gaze. She was a sprite of youth, moving with an effortless grace around the water's edge. The pole in her hands was an extension of her lean form as she scooped the water with the net. Her company shirt was knotted above the waist, revealing a flat stomach marked by a solitary naval piercing. Black spandex shorts clung to her, and her feet were encased in pragmatic black work boots, contrasting the frivolity suggested by the rest of her attire. Strands of blonde hair tumbled from beneath a baseball cap, betraying the ponytail's attempt at containment.

For a moment, Marcus allowed himself to wonder about her life—a narrative filled with dreams and disappointments, loves found and lost. Did she return home to someone who shared in her laughter and fears? Did that person know how easily he could lose it all?

"Hi, Mr. Dempsey!" Her voice, bright and unburdened, severed his moment of introspection. She was peering up at him with an easy smile as she offered a wave.

"Ah—" The word caught in his throat, a strangled acknowledgement. Marcus's hand lifted by reflex, an awkward gesture before he retreated from the window as though his act of observation had been an intrusion. "Damn it," he cursed, the heat of embarrassment flushing his cheeks.

A rush of regret washed over him as he withdrew from the window. It wasn't the young woman so much as the reflection of his mortality in the window—a view no scholarly achievement could dispel.

Marcus shook off the lingering embarrassment from his earlier gaffe, the flush fading from his cheeks as he turned to the task of dressing. His fingers grazed over the selection of shirts hanging on the coat rack before pulling a soft cotton one free. It was a familiar ritual as he shrugged out of his pyjamas, letting the light fabric pool at his feet.

He stood for a moment, clad only in his underwear, facing the narrow mirror that had been his silent witness to the passage of time. Marcus twisted, inspecting his profile. Age had curved his posture but not his spirit. He snapped into a playful bodybuilding pose, muscles flexing in response to long-remembered routines. A chuckle escaped him; vanity had never been his vice, yet he couldn't help but admire the resilience of his frame. "Not bad, old man," he said to himself, the corners of his eyes crinkling with self-deprecation. "The years haven't taken everything."

Clad in shirt and pants, the fabric settling around him, Marcus left the room, the click of the door punctuating his departure. He walked down the hallway, his slippers padding against the hardwood floor. The open space of the living room welcomed him, its large windows offering an unobstructed view of the morning light spilling across the backyard. The stone patio lay still, furniture untouched by the early hour, while the pool's blue surface mirrored the sky above.

The scent of ground coffee beans in the kitchen promised the ritualistic comfort of his first cup. He filled the machine with water and opened the fridge door, letting the cool air brush against his face. He reviewed various health foods—probiotic yogurts, fruits, and green vegetables. "How can someone live off this shit?" he said, his words tinged with bemusement rather than scorn. The lifestyle reflected in the fridge promised longevity but lacked the substance of indulgence.

He retrieved a bagel from the freezer, giving it a cursory 20-second thaw in the microwave before slicing it. As the toaster hummed to life, he leaned back against the counter, the faint aroma of toasted bread soon filling the air. This simple pleasure, at least, remained unchanged and his to control.

While his bagel toasted, Marcus went to the bathroom to complete his morning routine. He squeezed toothpaste onto the brush and tasted its minty scent. As he scrubbed at his teeth, he examined his reflection in the mirror, noting how time had etched lines into his once-smooth skin and how the silver in his hair was more pronounced in the unforgiving bathroom light.

Rinsing his mouth, he splashed water on his face, droplets cascading down his weathered cheeks. A sigh escaped him as he reached for the towel and patted himself dry. His bladder urged him toward the toilet, a reminder of his age's relentless march. The task complete, he stood before the medicine cabinet, his fingers trailing over the various bottles and jars—a catalogue of ailments and remedies. He found the statin and swallowed it with practiced ease, hoping to quell the silent rebellion brewing in his arteries.

Leaving the bathroom, Marcus looked down the hall and noticed the door was left ajar. An invitation, perhaps an oversight, beckoned him to peer into the room. Julia lay nestled in the expanse of their once-shared bed, dwarfed by its size yet somehow filling it with her presence. Her eyes were fixed on the glowing screen of her iPad, shielding her from the world—and perhaps even from him.

"Hi, Marcus," she said without lifting her gaze, her voice carrying a note of distraction.

"Morning, Julia." He said, the name settling on his tongue like a familiar tune.

He cleared his throat, announcing his intention to fetch some socks. " I need to check on the pool. Make sure it's being cleaned properly."

"You were never one to miss pool cleaning day, were you?" Julia said. Her skepticism hung in the air between them.

Marcus let the question dissipate unanswered as he crossed the room and entered the closet that had long ago been divided into 'His' and 'Hers' territories. The space held the remnants of his past life—suits and dress shirts pushed to the back, artifacts of a career that had become a distant memory.

With socks in hand, he glanced one last time at the closet's contents, the muted colours and patterns of a life lived in lecture halls. Nostalgia still tugged at him, the ache for identity wrapped in the crisp folds of a well-worn suit, yet he turned away. What use were they now, he thought? They were relics of the man he was long ago, now left behind in the corridors of academia.

He exited the room, closing the door to both the closet and the chapters it represented, leaving behind Julia, still lost in the glow of her electronic escape.

Marcus retreated from Julia's vantage point on the bed, her gaze lingering on the door long after it clicked shut. How many years had it been since they'd shared more than a passing conversation? She couldn't remember, and perhaps that was a mercy. Jealousy still pricked at her heart—ridiculous, she scolded herself. But old habits die hard, and Marcus, despite his years, could not shake his.

She rose, her body the product of the discipline she now maintained. At 72, her reflection still bore the fruits of a dedicated fitness regimen. A soft sigh escaped her lips as she considered the crop tops and tight shorts of her youth—no, that wasn't her style anymore, yet she could still turn heads.

Her hair, salted with grey and brightened with blonde highlights, fell in gentle waves around her face. The water rower in the corner caught her eye; the machine had become her ally in the battle against the inevitable. It promised clarity, strength, and perhaps a momentary escape from the complexities of her inner world.

"Later," she said to herself. After breakfast, she would immerse herself in the rhythm of the rower, each pull against the water a stroke towards something resembling peace.

Julia stepped into the closet, her gaze drifting over the garments that had defined her life's various stages—today called for something sporty—a reminder of vitality in a house that was all too silent. She settled on a fitted jacket and leggings, the fabric forgiving yet still flattering. As she dressed, her eyes lingered on Marcus's side of the closet, where his suits stood as reminders of a life long past, untouched but for the dust settling on their shoulders.

"Retirement still doesn't suit you, Marcus," she said to herself, her tone edged with irony. "But when will you let go of all of this?" It was more than fabric and thread; it was about accepting change, something she and Marcus danced around like a pair of skilled yet tired partners. She decided then, as her hands brushed over the wool of his jackets, that she would start to ease them out of the closet, one by one. Would he notice? Or had they reached a point where the material possessions meant less than the memories they couldn't quite hold onto?

She turned away from the suits, pulling the door closed behind her. In the sanctuary of their bathroom—now hers—Julia studied her reflection with an analytic eye. Uncluttered by Marcus's shaving cream or cologne, the mirror held her image. Touching the skin beneath her eyes, she acknowledged every laugh line, every furrow earned through years of private battles and public smiles.

"Facelifts are for those who fear the past," she said, her fingers tracing her jawline with a tactile memory of youth. But she had never feared growing older, only growing apart. They navigated this journey with an emotional distance that stretched with each passing day. Her routine was a preservation ritual, creams applied methodically to mask the turmoil brewed inside.

She untangled the waves of her hair with a brush, examining the roots for signs of time's insistence. Not yet, she thought; she still claimed some semblance of the woman she once was, the woman who had once lived and loved but had locked away her dreams years ago.

A final glance at her reflection caught her attention. She lifted her shirt, cradling her breasts in her hands; the weight of years was kinder than they might have been. They still held their shape, defying gravity just enough to bring a smile to her lips. It wasn't vanity that made her look; it was a search for recognition, for the identity she clung to amidst the shifting sands of time.

"Still here," she affirmed before letting the fabric fall back into place. With one last look, sealing away the secrets and silent conversations within the room's walls, Julia turned off the light, shut the door, and stepped into the day, leaving the secrets of the past behind her, if only for a moment.

In the kitchen, Julia gripped the warm ceramic of the coffee mug. The kitchen was awash with morning light, spilling over the granite countertops and glinting off the stainless-steel appliances. She perused the fridge's contents, opting for a spartan breakfast— yogurt, granola, and berries, each spoonful a reflection of her disciplined life that had taken years to develop.

Settling at the kitchen island, she carved out a moment of peace with her meal. But then, laughter floated in, trespassing through the open window, its carefree cadence drawing her gaze toward the backyard.

Julia stood, abandoning her half-finished breakfast as laughter lured her in. She crossed into the living room and saw them through the window—Marcus and the pool girl.

The image struck Julia: the contrast between Marcus's seasoned frame and the girl's supple youthfulness. His hand rested almost proprietarily on the small of Kate's back while her hands mimicked the grace of a diver's poised entry. A pang of something sharp and acidic twisted in Julia's gut, jealousy mingling with a begrudging acknowledgment of the girl's vibrant glow.

"Hi, Mrs. Dempsey!" Kate said to Julia as she emerged from the home, her voice buoyant as the sunlight on the pool surface.

"Hello, Kate. How are you today?" Julia said, her words a careful veneer over the storm that brewed within.

"Great! Marcus was showing me how to improve my diving form. I'm on the college team this year."

"Marcus?" Julia echoed, the informality jarring. No Professor Dempsey here, only Marcus, a name that bridged years in a single breath.

"Hey, look, I did a bit of diving in my time," Marcus said, a hint of defensiveness creeping into his voice. He averted her eyes, retreating from the unspoken accusation between them.

"Marcus was nice enough to tell me that I could come over anytime and practice," Kate chimed in, oblivious to the undercurrents swirling beneath the surface of their exchange.

"Of course," Julia nodded, her lips curving into a practiced smile. "You're welcome to practice here." It was the expected response, the gracious one, but her heart rebelled against the generosity of her spirit.

"Are any boys on the team?" Julia asked, a subtle probe laced with implication.

"A few," Kate said, unaware of the scrutiny.

"Your coffee is getting cold," Julia said to Marcus, her words pointed like an arrow finding its mark. She didn't wait for his response, turning on her heel and retreating to the house. The laughter died away as Marcus, having completed his lesson, followed her back into the kitchen.

The microwave hummed a low, mundane tune as Marcus slipped his neglected mug inside. With the press of a button, the machine whirred to life, and the coffee spun in its artificial dawn. Julia sat at the kitchen table, her spoon poised mid-air, dripping yogurt back into the ceramic bowl, cradling her breakfast.

"Making a big deal about nothing, Julia," Marcus said, his voice carrying a nonchalance that was too rehearsed. "I was offering some friendly advice."

Julia rolled her eyes, a gesture she couldn't suppress, an involuntary admission of her skepticism. "Oh, I know all about your 'friendly advice,'" she said dryly. "Kate doesn't need an old man ogling her under the guise of kindness."

Marcus scoffed at the accusation, his laughter devoid of humour. "Ogling? Julia? I'm not some lecher." His tall frame slumped into the chair opposite her, the groan of the wood under his weight punctuating their strained silence.

Julia stared at Marcus as he poured a sugar-laced cereal into a bowl. "It's one of the few pleasures left to me," he quipped as he poured. He unfurled his newspaper, the snap like a flag of truce—or surrender—depending on the ear that heard it.

"Your pleasures are going to put you in an early grave," she said, her gaze dropping to her phone. Her thumb swiped through messages and emails, failing to find anything meaningful in the digital expanse.

Marcus peered over the edge of the paper, eyes scanning the headlines but seeing nothing of interest. There was a time when the world on those pages mattered, and he could lose himself in foreign affairs and political intrigue. Now, they were ink-stained relics, his interest in them as stale as the day-old bagel he'd resurrected for breakfast.

"Julia," he said, the word hanging between them like a plea, but the courage needed to bridge the gap failed him. He burrowed deeper into the article before him, a shield against the chill of their conversation. She waited for him to say anything, but the moment had passed, as they all do. The scrape of her chair against the tiles announced her retreat, leaving Marcus to his paper and the cold comfort of his resurrected coffee.

Chapter 2

The laughter of old friends punctuated the air as Marcus Dempsey settled into a high-backed chair overlooking the sprawling greenery of the golf course. Conversations from nearby tables provided a comfortable soundtrack to the friend's reunion. Daniel, James, and Trent were huddled around the mahogany table; their faces flushed with the satisfaction of a morning well spent.

"Marcus, that last swing—who knew you had it in you? I thought you were going to send the ball into orbit!" Daniel jested, nudging Marcus with his elbow.

"Maybe he's been cheating on us with a private instructor," James said, "two-timing us." He raised his glass, and laughter rippled through the group.

"Guess I'm just starting to pick this game up," Marcus said. On the inside, however, Marcus was ambivalent about the game, and the act wore thin even among these long-standing friends.

"Retirement is starting to suit you, my friend. It's only taken you ten years," James said, leaning back in his chair and stretching out his legs. "What about you, Daniel? Travelling the world and planning trips with the Mrs."

"Yup," Daniel said, his eyes lighting up. "We've got this little ritual of pinning destinations on the map. Our next stop is Barcelona."

"Adventurous," Marcus said, his voice even, hiding that he couldn't remember the last time he and Julia had ventured beyond their backyard together.

"It doesn't compare to your escapades in Thailand, James," Trent said, turning his attention to the group's single man. "It must be thrilling to roam about without any ties."

"Freedom has its perks, though that freedom cost me half my 401k," James smirked.

The conversation shifted to Marcus. "And then there's Marcus," Daniel said, tipping his glass toward him, "with a beautiful wife, a perfect home, and two kids."

"Got it made," Trent said, nodding.

Marcus nodded a hollow gesture. He knew it was easier than voicing the chasm between the life his friends imagined and the reality he lived—a life where regrets stacked like books on a shelf, and every shared silence with Julia built the wall between them higher.

"Here's to Marcus," James said, raising his glass higher.

"Cheers," they echoed, the word reverberating in Marcus's chest like a drumbeat out of sync with his heart.

"Cheers," Marcus said under his breath, his drink untouched. He envied their unencumbered lives. But amidst the idle chatter and the warmth of friendship, Marcus held tight to his part in the facade. He had become a masterful actor on a stage he had never wished to occupy.

"Anyway, I don't know how you guys did it at the University for so many years," Trent said, changing the subject. "Academic life isn't what it used to be. The students—they run the show now." He shook his head in disbelief. "I have to pepper my syllabus with trigger warnings to avoid bruising their delicate sensibilities. Can you imagine? Trigger warnings for discussing Genghis Khan's campaigns."

A collective murmur of dismay circled the table. Daniel offered a wry smile in Marcus's direction. "Remember how you'd charm your way through those lectures? You had the students hanging onto your every word."

Marcus relished the memory of the classroom, his domain and where he would hold a group of twenty-somethings under his rapture. A genuine smile appeared on his face, tinged with nostalgia.

"Ah, and the socials," James chimed in, a mischievous twinkle in his eye. "I can only recall half of what happened at those gatherings, but I'll never forget how the female students admired our Marcus here."

They laughed and revelled in a past that looked nothing like the present, and for a moment, Marcus allowed himself to bask in the glow of a past that was once filled with endless possibilities.

"Speaking of admirers," Daniel said, shifting gears. "The big anniversary with Julia is coming up. How many years is it again?"

"Fifty," Marcus said; the number felt monumental.

"Fifty years," Trent echoed, impressed. "You've got to tell us, what's the secret?"

Marcus hesitated, words failing him. His life with Julia, once brimming with love and promise, had become an act of endurance. "Communication," he said. It was a banal platitude.

"You must be doing something right," James nodded. "Whatever the secret is, we'll see it on full display at the party. Daniel, I assume you'll be there?"

"I wouldn't miss it for the world," Daniel said. "We'll all be there to celebrate with our Marcus."

"Appreciated," Marcus said, his voice steady despite the turmoil. As his friends stood to leave, they shook hands and patted each other on the back, unaware that Marcus's perfect life from outward appearance was fractured beyond repair within.

The group disbanded, leaving Marcus to his thoughts. They had seen only the sheen of his life, not the rust beneath. Marcus rose from the table and prepared to return to the home that became more like a cell than a sanctuary.

Outside the club, Marcus shifted the car into drive and searched his mind for any errands he needed to make on his way home—errands that had become distractions.

The road home was a familiar drive. He wound through the streets, each curve and hill rolling beneath him like waves. As he passed a section lined with tall trees, Marcus slowed. Their gnarled limbs reached overhead as if to pull secrets from him—truths he dared not voice even in the quiet of his car. He pressed on the accelerator, leaving them behind, just as he had left so many uncomfortable truths in the shadows of his mind.

Home came into view—the ranch-style bungalow at the end of a cul-de-sac. It had been a symbol of success but now stood as a silent witness to the chasm between appearance and reality. Marcus parked the car in the driveway, the gravel crunching under its weight as though protesting his return.

"Julia, I'm home," Marcus said as he entered, his hollow and expectant voice echoing off the walls. Silence greeted him, a silence that had become a constant companion in what should have been the most intimate spaces of their shared lives.

He tossed his keys into the bowl by the front door and entered the house. Each step took him past relics of a happier past: old photographs that smiled back at him and remnants of a time when two people shared more than a name and a house.

The family room opened before him, its large fireplace standing proud and solitary, marking the division between it and the kitchen. Marcus moved like a ghost through his home and entered the kitchen.

"Julia?" He said from the door that separated the Kitchen from the backyard.

He stepped through the back door and emerged into the backyard. It was a place that had once resonated with the sounds of children's laughter and the sizzle of barbecues. Now, it lay serene, almost unnervingly so, with only the distant hum of suburbia to fill the void.

"Out here," her voice said beyond his sight.

Marcus stepped into the glow of the afternoon sun, his eyes adjusting to the light as the backyard unfolded before him. Julia was on one of the sun-bleached couches adjacent to the pool. A plush robe hung over her swimwear; flip-flops discarded at her feet. As if she were trying to outrun thoughts that clung more stubbornly than shadows, she had likely gone for a dip after her workout. Marcus noted the book by her side, its spine creased from use: "Longevity," it read—a title promising secrets to everlasting vitality.

The phone was pressed to her ear. Julia's conversation was a silent pantomime to Marcus until her gaze lifted and met his. Her lips formed the word "Nicole" without sound. There was a familiar tightness in his chest—the involuntary response to his daughter's name, a knot of pride mixed with pain.

He gestured towards her, fingers twirling, signalling her to amplify Nicole's voice. At first, Julia resisted, shaking her head with a weariness that said she preferred the solitary world of her call. But Marcus persisted, a plea for inclusion in their daughter's life. Julia set the phone down and tapped the speaker button, surrendering privacy to shared participation.

"...And he won't stop talking about this new game he's playing," Nicole's voice filled the space between them, caught mid-sentence, unaware of the expanded audience. The mention of video games conjured images of Jamie as a boy, lost in digital worlds.

"Nicole," Julia said, her voice steady but softer now, a hint of apology woven through her words. "I've put you on speaker. Your father is here."

"Hi, Dad." The greeting was warm but cautious as if Nicole were navigating a minefield of past grievances. "Are you still meeting your old colleagues for golf?"

Marcus allowed himself a small smile. "Yes," he said, "And yes, they'll all be coming to the anniversary party."

"I can't imagine how long it's been since I have seen that lot," Nicole said, though Marcus heard the underlying question in her tone, the unspoken probing into the state of affairs. Beneath the veneer of pleasantries, Marcus knew the truth. Like the aging facade of their home, their lives required constant upkeep, a fresh coat of paint to cover the cracks that time had wrought. And as the sun dipped lower, casting long shadows across the lawn, the weight of years bore upon him, each anniversary adding another layer to the façade they maintained.

The afternoon sunlight danced on the water's surface. Julia's voice was a gentle hum in the background, and the whir of the pool filter accompanied her words. He shifted his gaze to Julia, noting how the sun caught the silver strands in her hair. His heart tightened for reasons he couldn't quite name.

"Have you spoken to Jamie?" Marcus asked, breaking into the conversation. His voice had an uncharacteristic hesitance, a subtle tremor that betrayed his concern.

The line went quiet for a moment. When Nicole spoke, it was with a weirdness that couldn't be disguised. "Dad, I wish I wasn't always stuck in the middle with you and Jamie," she said, her voice full of exasperation.

Marcus sighed, his gaze shifting from the pool to Julia. "I know, Nick... I don't understand why he keeps us at such a distance."

"It's nothing new, Dad," Nicole said, her voice tinged with resignation. "Anyway, I've been in touch with him, and it looks like he'll be coming over tomorrow night to stay before the anniversary."

At this, a spark akin to hope flickered in Marcus's chest. He exchanged a glance with Julia, whose eyes mirrored his cautious optimism. "That'll be wonderful," Julia said, the corners of her mouth lifting. "Having everyone together again."

Nicole's response carried a sarcastic undertone. "Yeah, just like old times," she said, though the sentiment hung heavy and hollow between them.

"Is he bringing... Sheila?" Marcus ventured.

"Jamie hasn't been with Sheila for years, Dad. Why would you even—" Nicole's reply was sharp, puncturing the bubble of nostalgia that had enveloped him.

"Well, we all know that Jamie is always full of surprises," Marcus said, shrugging off the tension though his shoulders remained rigid.

Turning the conversation to the party preparations, Nicole's practicality seeped through the phone line. "Mom, did you check with the caterer? Are there enough plates?"

Marcus winced at the mention of the gathering. The thought of it crowded his chest. "Why does it have to be such a big affair?" he said, more to himself than to the others.

"Because people expect it, Dad," Nicole said. "Remember how you used to throw those huge parties? Then you stopped. It never made any sense to me. I'm sure it confused your friends too".

"Times change," Marcus said, his gaze drifting to Julia. Their look was one of shared history, a silent acknowledgment of what they had weathered together and apart.

"Anyway, you can't exactly ignore a fiftieth anniversary," Nicole chided. "People would talk, think it strange—or worse, they'd think you were hiding something." Nicole laughed at the last part, "Maybe you can use your speech to reveal all your dirty secrets." Now Nicole was scolding him. Marcus looked at Julia, suddenly regretting being added to the call.

Chase's voice called for Nicole in the background, a reminder of life's ceaseless demands. "I have to go," she said, her tone softening. "Chase needs me."

"Of course, sweetheart. We'll see you tomorrow," Julia said, her voice steady yet distant as if she were already retreating into her thoughts.

Marcus squinted against the sun's glare reflecting off the pool's surface, the shimmering ripples casting fragmented light across Julia's posed features. Their conversation paused, filled only by the distant hum of a lawn mower.

"All right then," Nicole's voice cut through the silence over the speakerphone. "Oh, before I forget, I also invited Janice from next door to the party."

The reaction was immediate; Marcus's eyebrows knitted together while his chest tightened, and Julia straightened up, her lips parting in surprise.

"Nicole, why would you do that?" Marcus couldn't mask the edge of irritation in his voice.

"Because she's your neighbour, for god's sake," Nicole retorted with a hint of exasperation. "You've known her almost as long as you've been married. It'd be weird not to invite her."

"I don't know," Marcus said under his breath, earning Julia's sharp look. "She's so sad."

"Exactly," Nicole said, echoing Marcus's thoughts. "We can't ignore her."

"Everything will be fine," Julia said, raising a hand to hush Marcus. "She probably won't stay long, but Nicole, you'll need to ensure she's included."

"Fine," Nicole said, the finality of her tone signalling at the end of the discussion.

"See you tomorrow night," Julia said.

"Bye, Mom," Nicole said and disconnected the call.

Marcus turned to face Julia, frustrated. "Why would she do that? When was the last time you talked to Janice?"

"Nicole's right," Julia said, her voice measured. "It would look odd if we excluded her. We have to consider how things appear."

He shook his head. "I don't know why we're going to all this trouble for the party."

"Because it's what normal people do, Marcus," Julia said, folding her arms across her chest. "Normal couples celebrate anniversaries like these."

"Are we normal, then?" he challenged, searching her face for anything to bridge the growing gap between them.

"Maybe nobody is normal," Julia shrugged, her gaze drifting away from him, settling on the horizon where the sky bled into the evening. "Happy families are all alike; every unhappy family is unhappy in its way," she said.

Marcus looked up at Julia with a bemused look. "Since when were you a Tolstoy fan," he said.

"It's from my book club," Julia said, "I'm expanding my horizons."

"Well, it's easy for you," Marcus countered, his tone rising with perplexity and outrage. "But there are some things I can't forget."

"I'm not asking you to forget," she shot back, her voice firm yet tinged with exhaustion. "But you need to live in the present, not the past."

The words hung heavy between them, a chasm of unspoken history and buried pain. They stood on the edge of it, each lost in their myriad of regrets.

"Relax, Marcus," Julia said, her voice softer now. "You need to move on from things better."

"Move on?" His response was laced with disbelief. "How can you say that?"

"Because," Julia replied with a sigh, turning away from him, "it's either that or we let the past consume us. When will you finally forgive yourself? How long can you continue like this?"

Julia rose from the cushioned lounge with a weary sigh, her robe hanging around her, mirroring the fatigue that clung to her shoulders. She glanced at Marcus; his silhouette etched against the shimmering blue of the pool—a man adrift in his waters of contemplation.

"I'm going to shower," she said, "There's a lot to do before Jamie and Nicole arrive."

Marcus gave a faint nod, his gaze not leaving the undulating reflections on the water's surface. The distance between them stretched further with her every step toward the house, a tangible reminder that proximity was no measure of closeness.

She navigated the familiar path through their bedroom. The sound of running water filled the room as she turned on the shower, steam blossoming and settling on the mirror.

The robe slipped from her skin and fell to the floor. Julia stepped into the shower, and the door clicked shut with a finality louder than intended. Water cascaded over her, rivulets tracing the contours of her body, masquerading as the caresses that had grown sparse over the years.

Her fingers splayed against the cold tiles, anchoring her as she tilted her face upwards. The droplets mingled with tears. Here, she allowed herself the vulnerability she hid beyond these walls.

A sob caught in her throat and was muffled by the shower's roar. She cried for the loss of connection and the ever-present ache of what might have been. Her heart grieved not for her losses but for the chasm that had widened between her and Marcus.

Marcus remained motionless outside, fading light casting long shadows across the deck. He stared into the depths of a pool that mirrored back nothing but the ripples of his discontent.

Chapter 3

Nicole heard the train wheels grating against the tracks, signalling Jamie's impending arrival. As she peered through the glass of her car window, the station was abuzz with passengers coming and going. She watched a woman run to meet a man, jumping up and hugging him as he gripped and swung her around. Nicole wondered what life choices the woman had made to lead to that happiness. As the couple embraced, a pang of longing tugged at her chest, a yearning for a connection that was currently out of reach in her life.

"Chase," she said, tilting her head to catch a glimpse of her son in the rearview mirror. The boy's eyes were fixed on the luminous screen cradled in his palms, headphones wrapping him in a private auditory world. She said again, louder this time, "Chase!" But her voice was swallowed by the music pulsing through Chase's headphones.

She gave up, returning her attention to the platform where travellers waited for their connection. The anxiety in her stomach churned like a storm waiting to break when Jamie stepped off the train.

Her thumb traced the worn leather of the steering wheel. It had been almost ten years since Jamie had last been to their childhood home and five years since she'd seen her brother's face anywhere outside the confines of pixelated video chats, his life revealed through the stuttering connection of long-distance calls.

"Nic, I'm fine; you know how it is," Jamie echoed in her memory. His voice was always tinged with a restless energy that danced away from the truth. She remembered pressing the phone to her ear, straining to hear the untold stories lurking beneath his casual tone.

"Jamie, are you eating well? Are you... happy?" she had asked one evening.

"Happy is a relative term," he had said, and then laughter bubbled through the line before dissipating into silence.

Nicole sighed, resting her forehead against the glass. Jamie's evasiveness was a wall she could never scale. How often had she rehearsed this moment and found the perfect blend of words to break his defences? Yet now, as the piercing shrill of the arriving train's whistle cut through her thoughts, all the carefully constructed sentences crumbled before her.

The swell of passengers rose like a tide, a deluge of bodies spilling onto the platform. Jamie would be among them any minute now, carrying his life in a backpack slung over one shoulder.

"Jamie," she said to herself, the name a talisman against the unease that threatened to overwhelm her. They had a shared history, full of unspoken traumas that they carried like chains. Could today be the day they begin to let go? Or would they again dance around the edges of what remained unsaid, each step a delicate maneuver to avoid the cracks in their fragile bond?

As the crowd began to thin and faces became distinguishable, Nicole braced herself, ready to peel back the layers of time that had settled between herself and the brother she still hoped to know.

Jamie emerged from the train; a figure lost in the kinetic swirl of commuters. As he stepped free from the current, his eyes found Nicole, and for a heartbeat, time stuttered, the clamour of the station dulling to a murmur.

"Hey, Nic," Jamie said, his voice threading through the station's noise. His short hair looked like it had been crudely shaved. The beard hugging his jaw was scruffy, two or three days past needing a trim. Once bright with mischief, his eyes carried the muted sheen of fatigue. He looked leaner than she remembered, and the features of his face were more pronounced.

"Jamie." Nicole's smile bridged them as she stepped forward, her arms opening to wrap him in a tentative but tight embrace. "It's been too long. You look pretty good for forty-eight," she said with a smile. "Though that makes me forty-six, can you believe it?"

He pulled back, his gaze shifting to the backseat where Chase remained ensconced in his digital world. "Chase, look who's here," Nicole said, though her son's attention remained tethered to the glowing screen.

"Let him be," Jamie said with a shrug, a half-smile playing on his lips. "Remember us with our Atari?" It was a flicker of understanding, a silent acknowledgment of his disregard for family customs.

The drive began with an exchange of trivialities, comments on the weather, and the light hum of the car's engine, providing a steady backdrop to their conversation. As the miles unfurled, so did the veneer of small talk.

"So," Nicole ventured, "how's the walking business treating you?"

"Good days, bad days," Jamie said, tracing the seam of his backpack strap. "Dogs don't complain much, and they're good listeners." His laugh was a ghost of its former self. "I get to walk and think while getting paid. What more can a guy ask for? And you?" he asked, turning towards her. "How's freelance life?"

"The flexibility is a blessing," Nicole said, her hands steady on the wheel. "I get to pick Chase up from school, work from a coffee shop, whatever I want." Her smile didn't quite mask the undercurrent of weariness in her voice.

"It sounds ideal," Jamie said, his gaze drifting out the window. His fingers were tapping an absent rhythm against his knee.

"Is it ever really?" Nicole's question hung between them, an invitation to step beyond the boundaries of their usual discourse.

"Fair point," Jamie conceded, a sigh escaping him, unbidden. Their conversation moved with measured steps, each wary of the other's shadows.

"Look," Nicole said, "I know we've both got our shit. But I'm glad you're here. We can figure it out, you know?"

"Figure what out?" Jamie's tone was noncommittal, a deflection wrapped in a question.

"Whatever needs figuring," Nicole said, a soft insistence in her voice. "We're still family."

"Family," Jamie echoed, the word trailing off like smoke. They drove on, the silence not uncomfortable but heavy with the things left unsaid.

The road hummed beneath the car, a persistent drone filling the spaces between Nicole's thoughts and Jamie's silence. She glanced at her brother; his gaze still fixed on the passing landscape. His rolled-up sleeves revealed forearms marked by the sun and work.

"Jamie," Nicole started, her voice firmer than she intended, "I don't get it. You breeze in and out of our lives like—"

"Like what?" Jamie's voice was flat and disinterested as if he had heard this accusation before and had long since become numb to it.

"Like nothing ties you down," Nicole said, her grip tightening on the steering wheel. "I'm here, dealing with Mom and Dad's shit, and you're... what? Wandering the world?"

"Is that what you think? That I'm out there enjoying my life carefree?" Jamie scoffed, and the bitterness in his laugh caught Nicole off guard. "Nicole, I haven't enjoyed my life since—" He stopped, his eyes narrowing as if he'd revealed too much.

"Since when Jamie?" Nicole asked, but he turned away, shaking his head to end the conversation.

"Never mind," he said, looking back outside where the scenery blurred into streaks of green and brown.

"What about Mon and Dad?" Jamie said, switching tracks. "How's Dad with retirement?"

"It's been ten years, Jamie," Nicole said, an edge of reproach in her tone. "They've settled into their routines, for better or worse."

"I never understood why they stayed together." Jamie stared straight ahead, his voice contemplative. "They were never happy."

"People find happiness in different ways," Nicole said. "They seem to have manufactured some semblance of happiness, or maybe it's just contentment."

"Happiness," Jamie echoed, a distant look crossing his features. "There was a time when everything was okay, wasn't there?"

"I don't know, was there? I think I was too young." Nicole's question was soft, probing. But before Jamie answered, the familiar outline of their childhood home came into view.

"Look, we're here," Jamie said, cutting off whatever revelation might have come next. Nicole sighed, letting the moment pass, and focused on navigating the car into the driveway.

The car's engine fell silent; the only sound now was the peaceful drone of suburban life that had become so foreign to Jamie. He rested his head against the seat, eyes tracing the familiar lines of the ranch bungalow.

"It hasn't changed at all," he said, the words tinged with a reluctant affection.

Nicole glanced over at him, a wry smile tugging at her lips. "Built to last, like us," she said, nudging his shoulder with hers. The gesture, light as it was, forged a momentary alliance, a truce amid their shared battles.

Jamie exhaled, a smirk fleeting across his face as he stepped out of the car. A gust of wind stirred the leaves above, and he could hear the echoes of laughter and screeching bike tires from years gone. He squinted against the sunlight, allowing himself a moment to dwell on those carefree days.

"Come on," Nicole encouraged, her voice steady but soft, sensing the weight of his hesitation. "I've got your back, you know."

"Thanks," he said, quieter than intended, the word scarcely more than a breath.

Rising to his feet, Jamie's gaze wandered to the house next door. His eyes lingered on the window that once framed faces of friends, now reflecting only his solitary figure. He shook his head, casting off the cobwebs of memories and returned to his childhood home.

"It looks the same," he said, trailing his fingers along the weather-beaten siding as they approached the door, "but it's like someone stripped all the colour from the place."

"Time has a habit of doing that," Nicole said, reaching past him to push open the door.

The scent of aging wood and lemon polish greeted them, a smell that had somehow defied the passage of time. Jamie paused at the door, engulfed by the flood of memories—the good mingled indistinguishably with the bad. Each creak of the floor, every shadow cast by the afternoon sun through the curtains, brought stories of a past that clung to the walls like ivy.

"Mom? Dad?" Nicole asked into the quiet house, her voice disrupting the stillness as she ushered Chase inside. He slipped past them, still engrossed in his digital world and planted himself on the couch in the family room.

Jamie took a deep breath, stepping into the home that had shaped him. The familiarity of the space weighed on Jamie, memories both cherished and painful flooding back with each creak of the floorboards. His gaze travelled over the worn furniture, the walls adorned with faded photographs frozen in time, capturing moments of a family long fractured yet forever bound by blood.

Chapter 4

Nicole's feet brushed against the patio as she stepped into the backyard. The familiar scent of cedar mingled with the aroma of grilled meat. Marcus stood beside his barbeque, engrossed in turning skewers laden with peppers and onions that sizzled in protest. A few feet away, Julia lounged on the couch. Her fingers traced the lines of text in a book that now rested forgotten in her lap.

"Mom?" Nicole's voice sliced through the calm, tentative yet clear.

Julia's head lifted, and recognition flickered across her features. Her eyes immediately landed on Jamie. The sight of him stirred something within her—a tremor of times long past.

"Jamie…" she said, more to herself than anyone else, as if trying to conjure the child from the man before her. He was thinner than she remembered, his face etched by life's relentless demands.

Jamie stood at the entrance to the backyard, taking in the landscape of his childhood. The backyard was a canvas of memories for him. He took in the pool, which glimmered and reflected the sky above, but his eyes were drawn to the barren patch of earth where the playground once stood. He heard the laughter and saw the ghost of his younger self as he rushed through sprinklers or scaled the playground in search of refuge.

Marcus turned to face them. His eyes met Jamie's, seeking the boy in the face of the weary man standing before him. A strained silence enveloped them all, thick with the words left unsaid and the years unshared.

Julia rose, her movements slow, as though time had become viscous around her. The memory of Jamie as a vibrant child—chasing after his friends on two wheels or plunging into the forest's depths with unbridled zeal—clashed with reality. He was no longer the embodiment of youthful exuberance but a man marked by the passage of decades.

Still, to Julia, he remained the boy who had skinned his knees and dreamed impossible dreams under the watchful eyes of the towering pines. She had missed so much of his journey. The moments and milestones had slipped through her fingers like grains of sand. Only yesterday, he had been that hopeful child, not the middle-aged estranged man who now stood in her garden.

Julia approached Nicole and embraced her. She released Nicole, and her hands lingered before falling to her sides. Her eyes darted around Nicole as she appraised Chase's whereabouts. "Where's Chase?" she asked.

"Inside," Nicole said, a half-hearted chuckle escaping her lips. "He's probably glued to his phone by now. Found the Wi-Fi, probably."

Julia turned toward Jamie, taking slow steps that showed reluctance. How long had it been since she had held her son? She thought it shameful that she couldn't remember. With open palms exposed and vulnerable, Julia beckoned to the man who stood before her. To the child, she had cradled in her arms so many years before.

"Hello, Jamie," she said.

Jamie hesitated, his fingers trembling as they reached out to meet hers. He thought we would feel more, maybe a spark when they touched, but instead, it was just flesh on flesh. Julia enveloped his hands in hers, holding them with a tender firmness.

"Hello, Mom," he said back, the word heavy on his tongue.

Julia encircled him with her arms and drew him close. Jamie stood rigid, his arms held at his sides before they rose to return the embrace. His gentle taps on her back signalled a sense of unease.

Stepping back, Julia eyed Marcus as he approached from the grill. He was wiping his hands on a dishtowel, his expression unreadable. "Nicole," he said to his daughter.

"Hi, Dad," Nicole echoed. Her sturdy voice was tinged with a scent of warmth. She had told herself to try after all.

Marcus fixed his gaze on Jamie, sizing him up as if he were a puzzle to be solved—a collection of pieces scattered over the years. Though Jamie's features had matured, his recognition struck a chord within Marcus, echoing memories of bedtime tales and shared laughter.

"Jamie," Marcus said, extending his hand in a manner more befitting of a business meeting than a family reunion.

"Marcus," Jamie said, clasping the hand offered. The formality of the name hung between them.

"How are you, son?" Marcus asked, his voice friendly but with a hint of scrutiny.

"Good," Jamie said.

"Hope you brought your appetite," Marcus said, a hint of challenge colouring his words. "Looks like you could use a decent meal."

"Can we wait at least an hour before criticizing each other?" Nicole said, her tone a gentle rebuke.

"Guilty as charged." Marcus conceded with a sheepish shrug, his defences lowered. "Make yourselves at home. Your rooms are as you left them."

Jamie exchanged a glance with Nicole, his eyes seeking solace in hers. With a silent plea etched into his features, he mouthed, "Help."

"Come on," Nicole said, reading the unspoken need. "Let's go freshen up. Dinner can wait."

Jamie's steps faltered as he entered his boyhood room, long since stripped of the Van Halen and Christy Brinkley posters. His fingers traced where posters had been and where they had left their adhesive residue. The bed, a twin pushed into one corner, was the same, except it was missing the "Empire Strikes Back" sheets that had been his childhood shield against the dark.

He lowered himself onto the mattress, its springs creaking a familiar, if not comforting, protest under his weight. His gaze wandered to the desk. The space where his Vic 20 once relentlessly hummed, sucking the air from the room. Jamie breathed through his lips and turned his attention to the window. A quick inspection confirmed it was shut tight. Some habits die hard, Jamie thought to himself. He lay back with his arms folded across his chest and his eyes fixed on the ceiling. He traced the patterns of shadows as they danced in the waning light. He listened for the familiar sounds of his youth, his sister on the phone with a girlfriend in the next room or his parents arguing in their main bedroom. All he heard was silence. A silence that Jamie found to be deafening.

Down the hall, Nicole nudged Chase into the guest room, her voice soft but edged with authority. "Leave your bag here. We're only staying a few days, so you hardly need to unpack."

"Two whole days?" Chase's tone mixed teenage sarcasm and genuine curiosity as he tossed his bag onto the bed.

"Make yourself comfortable," she said, unfolding a towel and placing it at the foot of the bed. "And if you want, there's the pool." Nicole thought of the parties around that pool when she was a teen—or maybe a tween. Now, she struggled to get her son to engage with a natural person. She wasn't sure which one was better, so she decided to call it a draw.

Chase flopped down, sinking into the unfamiliar bedding, and turned his head to gaze up at Nicole. "Why don't you like them?" he asked, his eyes narrowing. "Grandma and Grandpa seem pretty cool."

Nicole paused. "I don't dislike them, Chase," she said, measuring her words. "It's just... there's a lot of history. It's complicated stuff I can't dive into right now. One day, I'll tell you the whole story, okay?"

"Sure," he said, reaching for his headphones and retreating into his cocoon of music.

She saw bits of her in his reflection. The wit and sarcasm came from her, for sure. Corinne had provided the retrospective character, if only through an environmental proxy. Nicole left the room, closing the door to the muffled sounds of a world only Chase could hear.

Down the hall, Nicole's hand hovered over Jamie's door. With a gentle tap, she announced her presence and found him sprawled on the small bed. His eyes were fixed on the ceiling as though deciphering some cryptic message only he could see.

"Remember when I took your Billy Idol Rebel Yell album to Jenny Stevenson's house, and her dad thought the words were so foul that he snapped it in half?" Nicole said as she entered the room and leaned against the desk. "It wasn't until years later that I listened to the words and understood where he came from; given we were only 11, he probably wasn't wrong."

"Yeah," Jamie said with a slight smile on their face. "And I made you deliver my papers for a month to work off the debt."

"I bet you could still fit through the window if you wanted to sneak out later," Nicole said with a sly smile.

Jamie looked at her with a surprised expression. "You knew I snuck out?" he said.

"Of course," Nicole said. "This comes from someone who has had her share of people sneak in."

"Jesus, Nicole," Jamie said with a feigned look of disgust. "Anyway, I suppose it's showtime?" Jamie said with a voice that was a blend of resignation and jest. He couldn't hide the apprehension beneath.

"Come on," Nicole said, smiling. "It won't be that bad."

He sat up, the bed creaking under his weight, his movements slow and deliberate. They walked together down the hallway through the kitchen and into the dining room.

Jamie stopped at the dining room's opening and took it in. It was like a stage set from another era. Chase slid into his seat beside Nicole, his attention already stolen by the screen of his phone. Jamie took the chair across from her, casting furtive glances through the large windows that framed the neighbour's house.

Marcus and Julia anchored either end of the table as if they were bookends to the family. The room itself hadn't changed from Nicole and Jamie's youth. Jamie recognized the metallic bulb light fixture, the dark wood on the wall's cut-out that overlooked the adjacent living room, and the geometric wallpaper, all remnants of a different time.

"Let's raise our glasses to..." Marcus's voice trailed off, searching for conviction. "...to family." His attempt to infuse warmth into the toast failed to mask the underlying tension. His words fell flat like stones in water. Nicole saw the ripple effect in Jamie's tight-lipped nod and Chase's indifferent shrug. They were a family of strangers bound by blood, she thought.

The dinner had been arranged to include an array of meat and vegetables that Marcus had tended to with almost cere-monial care. They ate silently except for the sound of utensils scraping across the porcelain. There was an undercurrent of reluctance to broach anything of substance. Nicole cleared her throat.

"Mom, Dad," she said, fingers tracing the rim of her wine glass. "The anniversary... Fifty is quite the milestone. How are you feeling about it?"

Julia's fork paused mid-air, a spear of asparagus dangling like a question mark. She exchanged a glance with Marcus, and their eyes conversed in a language neither Nicole nor Jamie could decipher.

"Fifty..." Julia's voice was a wisp, her smile a practiced curl at the edges of her lips. "Honestly, we're just glad everyone's healthy and here."

Jamie's gaze lingered on his mother, noting the slight tremor in her hand as she placed her fork down. The space between them was filled with the debris of years left unspoken. His parents' vibrancy had weathered, their composure contrasting the raw, vivid characters etched into his childhood memories.

Jamie was surprised at himself. He missed the vibrancy they once radiated, even if it manifested in a certain intensity that bordered on the unhealthy. Now, they were like faded photographs, the colours having been drained away, leaving behind only muted tones and forced smiles. This new version of his family was disconcerting. Like a scene from someone else's life, Jamie's hands folded in his lap as he sat at the table. He absorbed the atmosphere, taking stock of every strained smile and every careful bite. His eyes darted from Marcus's stoic profile to Julia's evasive gaze, from Nicole's hopeful expression to Chase's youthful indifference. Despite their familial ties, each was like a solitary figure, drifting further apart despite their proximity at the table.

Something was unnerving about how they all danced around the truth, skirting the perimeter of the past and being extra careful not to disturb sleeping ghosts. He knew what lay beneath was full of unexplored feelings and festering wounds. But tonight, the performance would go on, with each character at the table playing their part in a script long since memorized.

Nicole's voice pulled him back, a life raft thrown into the murky waters of his thoughts. She offered the faintest hope that this gathering might bridge the gaps that had widened over time. Yet Jamie remained adrift, playing the role of the silent spectator in this familial theatre. His thoughts shifted to his dogs. He imagined he was wandering the trail that had become his office. Dogs running around him in circles, waiting for him to throw their ball. His mind went blank in those moments, letting his thoughts wander wherever they wanted. In those moments, he was free of pain and free of guilt. He was so far from that space now, sitting in the same seat and at the same table where he had shared many meals and memories from his youth.

The clinking of silverware against china waned as Marcus leaned back in his chair, eyeing Jamie with a mix of curiosity and something that bordered on concern. "So, Jamie," he said, his voice carrying the weight of unspoken years between them, "tell us about your life. Do you still see that woman? How's the job?"

Jamie shifted in his seat, discomfort settling like an unwelcome guest at the table. Before he could muster a reply, Nicole interjected, her tone laced with protective defiance. "Her name is Sheila, Dad."

Marcus waved a dismissive hand, his gaze never leaving Jamie. "Yes, Sheila. Is she still in the picture?"

The room contracted, pressing in on Jamie as he cleared his throat. "No, it... it didn't work out. We still talk sometimes, but she has her own life now." His eyes flickered away, finding solace in the patterns of the tablecloth.

"And the job?" Marcus prodded, undeterred by the threadbare response.

With a sigh that spoke volumes, Jamie answered in hesitant fragments: "It's fine. I walk dogs for a living. I can't handle office spaces—they're claustrophobic, with too many people crammed together. I'm free and try to be outside with the dogs as much as possible."

Marcus's eyebrows rose fractionally. Jamie continued, but before he voiced the judgment teetering on his injured, a newfound resolve steadied his voice. "I'm planning to move out to the country. I've been researching off-grid living. Self-sufficiency—I think I can make a go of it."

A silence descended, rippling outwards to fill the space with tension. Julia finally broke it, her voice tinged with puzzled disbelief. "But why isolate yourself even further, Jamie? Isn't that a bit extreme?"

Jamie's fingers tightened around the stem of his water glass, the cool surface grounding him as he navigated the terrain of their skepticism. "It's not about isolation. It's about control over my own life," he said.

Marcus leaned forward, elbows on the table, his brow furrowed in thought. "You were always such an adventurous child, Jamie. Always exploring, always seeking. But this..." He trailed off, struggling to bridge the gap between past and present.

Nicole's heart ached for the brother who had wandered so far from the boy they once knew. She saw the longing in Jamie's eyes, a yearning for simplicity and clarity, for a life untangled from the disappointments that had shadowed their family.

The conversation meandered through practicality and idealism, Marcus and Julia volleying concerns across the table while Jamie deflected with quiet determination. Each argument, each counterpoint, was like a brick in the wall that had been built between them.

The tension knotted tighter with each exchange, like a rope pulled to its breaking point. The air was thick with unsaid things, and she could almost feel the old floorboards creaking under the weight of their collective history. She cleared her throat, an audible signal to turn the page on this uncomfortable chapter.

"Mom, Dad," she said, her voice steady but soft, "have you ever thought about what comes next for this house? Maybe finding somewhere smaller, easier to manage?"

Julia's eyes lifted from her plate, a faint crease forming between her brows. "Leave here?" she echoed; her tone laced with genuine surprise. "But why? This house... it has everything we need. It's our life."

Marcus nodded in agreement, his knife and fork pausing mid-air. "It's been our home for so many years. I can't imagine living anywhere else," he said, his words a touch respectful, as if the walls were sacred.

Jamie clenched his hands into fists beneath the table, knuckles whitening. He had listened, simmering as the conversation meandered around him. Nicole's interjection offered a momentary respite, but Jamie knew evasion when he heard it.

"Why did you stay?" he blurted out, his voice frayed at the edges, frustration seeping through. The others turned to look at him, startled by the rawness in his tone. "This place... Why do you cling to it? Everywhere you look is a reminder of how messed up things were here. This wasn't a good place. And we weren't a normal family. I know you have fought long and hard to perform a good act and did a pretty good job of fooling people, but things weren't great here. I don't know how you can't see that. I don't know how you can go on with this act."

Jamie's words hung in the air, heavy and unyielding. His gaze swept his family's, the familiar yet foreign family. Nicole bit her lip; her earlier attempt at redirection crumbled in the face of Jamie's pain.

Julia's eyes met Jamie's, a flicker of something—regret, perhaps—passing through their depths. She reached across the table; her hand trembled as it hovered over the tablecloth. But she didn't speak, and her hand withdrew, leaving Jamie's words to dwindle into nothingness. Silence swelled to fill the gaps between them.

Marcus's charm, usually adept at smoothing over life's rougher textures, faltered now. His mouth opened and closed, and for a moment, the charismatic professor was a man who was now uncertain and exposed.

Marcus clenched his jaw as he replaced the silverware on his plate, his eyes steady on Jamie. "We're just trying to have a nice dinner here," he said, his voice a rumble that betrayed a controlled irritation.

"Nice," Jamie echoed, an edge of bitterness in his tone. "That's one word for it."

"Jamie," Marcus said, a warning note in his voice, "you haven't been around. You don't see the day-to-day—"

"Exactly," Jamie said, his hands fidgeting with the napkin. "I haven't been around. And there's a reason for that, isn't there?"

Nicole could no longer bear the pretense of pleasantry. The weight of history pressed down on her. "Dad," she said, her voice soft but firm, "we all know this isn't just about having a nice dinner."

"Nicole," Marcus said, turning to her, his face a mask of attempted composure.

"Look," Nicole said, her gaze shifting from her father's stern expression to her mother's quiet sadness. "There's a lot of history in this house...and not all is happy." Her eyes pleaded for understanding. "Mom, you, of all people, should know that."

Julia, who had been silent, shrunk into herself, the lines of years etched onto her face deepening. "Nicole…"

"Memories are all around us here," Nicole said, "memories we've all tried to escape from in different ways." She paused, eyes scanning the room, her childhood home, where shadows clung to corners. "It's so hard to reconcile the good times with the bad. It's hard for us to feel like we belong to a place with so much pain."

"Nicole," Julia said. Her fingers reached out, then withdrew, as if touching her daughter might bring forth a flood of truths better left unsaid.

"Can't we just—" Marcus started, but his words faltered under Nicole's steadfast gaze.

"Can't we what, Dad?" Nicole asked, her voice rising. "Pretend? Ignore what's going on? We've done enough of that over the years. So much that you don't even see it anymore."

"Enough," Marcus said, standing, his chair scraping against the hardwood floor. "This is not the time or the place."

"Then when, Dad?" Nicole said, rising to meet his eyes. "When do we talk about it?"

"Talk about what, Nicole?" Marcus's voice was a booming echo, a defensive barrier against the siege of questions.

"About why we're all so distant, why Jamie can hardly stand being here," Nicole said. "About the secrets and the silence that's always hung over us like some fucked up shroud."

"Secrets?" Marcus scoffed, though his eyes darted away, unable to hold her stare.

"Secrets," Nicole affirmed, her own eyes never wavering. "The kind that keeps you awake at night, wondering what might have been if we had dealt with things head-on. I don't know what happened here, but we lost our way. Very early on. Maybe it was always like this, I don't know. But we weren't normal. Putting a roof over our heads and letting us have wild parties around the pool doesn't make us normal. I lost my way when I was a girl, and you two were too busy with your separate lives and arguments to see that. I needed—."

"Enough!" Marcus's shout was a crack of lightning, splitting the room's tense air. But the storm had only just begun, and in its wake, the possibility of reconciliation was as distant as the fading light beyond the dining room windows.

Tempers flared as Marcus and Nicole stood face to face. Jamie's fingers drummed on the tabletop; his lips pressed into a thin line.

"History isn't just on the pages you taught, Dad!" Nicole's accusation held an edge sharp enough to cut through years of silence. "It's what we lived, what you made us live through!"

"Nicole, I—" Marcus said, but she was relentless.

"Did you ever think how it was for us? Growing up here?" Her voice broke through decorum, shattering the glassy surface of a dinner that had been nothing more than a pretense.

Across the table, Chase dipped into the sanctuary of his earbuds. The world outside dimmed as he thumbed the screen of his handheld game; the digital beeps a welcome respite from the palpable tension that clung to the air like humidity before a storm.

"Your mother and I did everything for you kids," Marcus said, his hands outstretched in an appeal for reason amid the chaos. His once commanding voice now grasped at straws, trying to weave together a narrative that had long since unravelled.

"Everything? Or everything that was convenient for you?" Jamie's voice joined the fray.

"Jamie, please," Marcus implored, turning toward his son with eyes that sought understanding amid conflict. "Can't we focus on the now? The good we have in our lives?"

"The good?" Jamie echoed hollowly, the single word a testament to their chasm.

"Look at us, together, after all these years." Marcus's gesture encompassed the room, the family, the remnants of a shared past. "Chase is growing into a fine young man. Nicole, you enjoy your work. And Jamie, you've always had the strength to follow your path. You're figuring things out."

"Strength?" he said, a flicker of vulnerability showing through Jamie's guarded exterior. "Or was it just that I had no other choice?"

"Jamie..." Marcus's tone softened, "Let's talk about the future," Marcus said, striving to steer the sinking ship of their evening back to safer waters. "We can build something from this. There's still time for us to learn and grow. Isn't that worth focusing on?"

The question lingered unanswered as each family member grappled with their version of life in the Dempsey home.

Jamie's fork clinked against the plate, a solitary sound that echoed in the room's stillness. His eyes, darkened by thoughts that had clawed their way to the surface, finally met those of his parents.

"We're always hiding," he said, his voice steady but tinged with an edge that cut through Marcus's well-meaning platitudes like a knife through the smoke. "That's what we do. We hide things away and pretend they don't exist. But they do. Secrets, lies, mistakes—those are the foundations of this family."

Julia's hands paused mid-air, napkin half-folded in her lap, her expression crumbling. Marcus's mouth opened, then closed. "Jamie, that's not fair," Julia found her voice, though it wobbled, betraying her. "We've always tried to—"

"Try?" Jamie said, the word sharp and brittle. "To do what? To ignore the truth? We all know there's something wrong with this family, things you've never said. It's like there's a trail of breadcrumbs that lead nowhere. It's suffocating, living with ghosts all the time."

Nicole glanced between them, her pulse beating with the resonance of Jamie's words. Her silence was tangible, a shared breath held too long.

"Son," Marcus's voice was a low rumble, carrying undercurrents of something deeper yet restrained. "I think you are looking for ghosts where there are only shadows."

"Am I?" Jamie challenged, leaning forward, the metallic clink of his fork against the plate punctuating the tension. "Because every corner of this house seems to be full of secrets. Why does it feel like walking into a mausoleum every time I step through the door?"

Chase shifted; his game forgotten as the weight of Jamie's words sank like stones in still water. Nicole's gaze flitted across the table, seeking an ally or perhaps understanding in her brother's haunted stare.

"Jamie…" Julia's lips trembled, eyes searching her son's face for the little boy she once cared for. The strength to rebuke him faltered as she drowned in the sea of his accusation, her defences washed away by his release of allegations.

"Enough, Jamie." Marcus's attempt at authority now sounded brittle and hollow. His posture straightened, but he was smaller now, somehow diminished.

Jamie's chair scraped back, the sound echoing off the walls, a gunshot in the quiet. He stood, his face a mask of mixed emotions—anger, pain, and a desperate longing for resolution.

"Maybe it's better if we just…" But he didn't finish. Instead, he turned on his heel and left the room, his departure leaving a vacuum that none dared to fill.

Julia's hand fluttered to her mouth, stifling the sob that threatened to break her composure. Marcus, his face etched with lines of regret, remained silent, staring at the empty seat where his son had been moments before.

Nicole reached out her hand, hovering over the space between her and her mother, hesitating before letting it fall back onto her lap. When she spoke, her voice was a whisper.

"Secrets…" She let the word hang there, a reminder of the threads that bound their family together—and the very same ones that could unravel them all. Julia rose from her chair, "I'm going to check on Jamie." she said.

"Let him be, Julia," Marcus said. His words carried an intractable weight. "He's not a little boy anymore. He needs space to find his way back here, in his own time."

Nicole's heart was heavy with the burden of unspoken truths. She turned to her parents, her gaze steady. "It's not about giving Jamie space," she said. "It's about acknowledging why he needs it in the first place."

Marcus' eyes, windows to a soul troubled by memories and regrets, met Nicole's. "We all have our demons, Nicky," he said. "Jamie was such a joyful kid, always laughing, until...until he wasn't."

"Because something broke inside him," Nicole pressed on, her voice a crescendo of years of pent-up frustration. "Something we all saw but no one dared to face."

Julia's hands trembled where they lay folded on the tablecloth, her knuckles whitening. "Life throws us curveballs, darling," she countered, though her eyes revealed the storm behind her calm. "People try their best but don't always get everything right—"

"No, Mom," Nicole said, the dam of her resolve cracking, spilling forth a torrent of truth. "You don't get to brush this off as life's unpredictability. We know when everything changed for Jamie. And none of us—he needed us—weren't there for him. You were too lost in your issues, and you, Dad, were buried in your books and lectures."

The accusation hung between them, a ghost from the past that refused to be exorcised. Julia reached across the table, her fingers seeking her daughter's, a lifeline thrown across an ocean of sorrow. "If we turned back time, Nicole..."

"But we can't," Nicole said, her eyes awash with grief. "But we can be honest with each other. We can acknowledge what went on here. Maybe that will bring Jamie a sense of peace. Look how long it has taken Jamie and me to get to a place of stability in his life."

The tension at the table lingered like a stubborn fog. "Nicole," Julia said, changing the subject, "How is Corrine? Does she see much of Chase?"

Nicole's eyes flickered, frustration flitting across her features. She pressed her lips together, then released a breath she'd held captive. "Corrine's relocated for work—to another city," she said. She calls Chase and tries to stay involved. But it's me—he's with me most of the time."

"Are you seeing anyone?" Julia asked, tiptoeing into Nicole's personal life.

"There was someone," Nicole said, reluctant but resigned to the inquiry, "from my building. It didn't last. He... wasn't ready for a child in his life."

Marcus cleared his throat, a signal that served as an exclamation and command. "Let's not dredge up the past," he said, his voice a mixture of firmness and weariness. "We should look ahead. What matters is tomorrow—the celebration."

Nicole's eyes narrowed, the ghosts of old battles rising in the space between her brows. Still, she yielded, recognizing the futility of persisting at this point. The conversation turned—steered by Marcus' authoritative hand—to the logistics and schedules for the anniversary event, a topic sterile enough to cleanse the air.

Afterwards, plates were cleared in silence, and a temporary truce was established. Nicole stood, stretching the stiffness from her limbs, "I've got some work to catch up on," she said. "I'll be by the pool if anyone needs me." To Chase, now picking at the remnants of his meal, she said, "Grab your swimsuit. Go enjoy the water."

Chase nodded, his mind already adrift in his digital reveries.

At last, alone, Nicole stepped outside and let the warm evening air envelop her. She settled into a poolside chair, the glow from her laptop screen illuminating her face in gathering dusk. Across the yard, Chase's form cut through the water with youthful abandon, the ripples catching the last rays of sunlight.

Marcus and Julia were cleaning up the last remnants of the dinner in the kitchen. Marcus turned to Julia, his eyes mirroring the worried lines etching deeper into his forehead.

"Julia," he said, his voice betraying a vulnerability seldom heard, "the kids... they're carrying so much baggage from back then." His hands gestured as if trying to disperse the lingering tension that clung like cobwebs. Julia met his gaze. There was steel in her voice, honed by years of private battles, as she responded, "We did our best, Marcus. That's all we could do." Her lips pressed into a thin line, a dam holding back an ocean of regret. "I need to go check on Jamie."

The soft tread of her footsteps receded into the silence. Alone, he dragged his hands down his face, the stubble scratching at his palms. He reached for a bottle of wine, uncorking it with practiced ease. The glug of the liquid filling the oversized glass was a lonely sound in the quiet house.

He raised the glass to his lips, but his attention was drawn outside. Through the window, he saw Nicole, her silhouette framed by the glow of her computer screen. Beyond her, Chase moved through the water, the pool's surface breaking and reforming in a fluid dance of light and shadow.

Marcus set the wine down, untouched, as a torrent of memories washed over him. Laughter and cries, scraped knees and slammed doors, whispered promises and shouted regrets; each scene played out before him.

He remained deep in contemplation, watching the play of life outside the glass. The ghosts of the past were his only company, tugging at him to return to a place he had long tried to bury. Marcus stood up, his chair scraping against the tiled floor in a grating sound that echoed in the empty kitchen. He made his way to the back door.

As he stepped outside, he smelled the familiar scent of cut grass. Nicole glanced up from her laptop, her expression softening at the sight of her father's tired eyes.

"Hey, Dad," she said, a note of concern lacing her voice. "Are you okay?"

Marcus nodded with a small smile as he approached her by the poolside. "Just needed some fresh air," he said, sinking into a chair beside her.

Nicole closed her laptop,

Chapter 5

The home buzzed with the murmur of guests who had spread across the back of the house. Groups mingled on the pool deck, taking in the afternoon sun, while others sat or stood in the living room, drinking punch and snaking on finger sandwiches. The home lent itself to this type of gathering with its open concept. Years ago, in another life, the house had been a frequent place of get-togethers full of smoke and fondue. Now, the silver-haired guests, still spry in their tailored suits and flowing dresses, wandered the home as they exchanged stories from the past.

"Fifty years," said one woman, her voice tinged with awe as she peered at Julia, whose wavy gray hair cascaded over her shoulders, framing her eyes. "And this home! It's as beautiful as the day you moved in."

Julia's lips curled into a practiced smile, her glance flitting across the room to where Marcus stood amidst a group of well-wishers. His friends still seemed to hang on to his every word as he lectured them about academic politics and the university's future.

"Here's to fifty more!" David, the friend and colleague with whom Marcus had sparred over countless debates, raised his glass, his wife Rose nodding in agreement.

Jamie stood in the corner of the living room, next to the stereo system, which still housed a weathered but functioning turn table. His lean frame almost melded into the shadows. His shaved hair and distant gaze set him apart from the rest of the group. His eyes darted through the crowd, recognizing faces aged by time—friends of his parents who once frequented the home when he was a teenager.

A chuckle from an old man caught Jamie's attention, and he turned to see James, a colleague of Marcus's from years past. The sight triggered a memory, vivid and unwelcome—a girl that had been Nicole's age, she was James's daughter, with eager hands, drawing him into the lit cabana by the pool while her parents drank and played games in the sunken living room. The recollection made his stomach churn; he had not seen her since, and the thought that she might walk through that door filled him with a quiet dread.

"Jamie, my boy!" James approached, oblivious to the discomfort he stirred within the younger man. "You've grown up so much. Your father tells me you're walking dogs now. That's admirable work." He looked around the room and turned back to Jamie, "I'll tell you, we had some good times here, Jamie; I just wish your parents had kept that going."

"I guess all good things have to come to an end," Jamie said, tugging at the collar of his shirt. He offered a weak smile that failed to reach his guarded eyes. He excused himself quickly, retreating further into the recesses of his mind and away from the banal banter that was so alien to him. As laughter and clinking glasses filled the air, Jamie couldn't help but feel like an intruder in his own home.

Gentle applause rustled through the crowd like a breeze. Guests took turns at the front of Julia and Marcus's living room, each sharing anecdotes that had been polished by time. Jamie stood somewhat apart, watching his parents' stories summarized and exalted by friends and colleagues.

"Are you going to say anything?" Jamie asked as he saw Nicole sidling up next to him. Nicole shook her head. "No," she said, "being here is enough. A speech would be too much."

Jamie nodded, understanding. They lingered together in silence, spectators in their own home.

Then Janice, their neighbour with the kindly eyes that held a well of sadness, moved toward the center of the room. The chatter ebbed away as she introduced herself, though there was hardly a soul present who didn't recognize her from years gone by.

"Marcus and Julia moved in just weeks before I did," she said, her voice steady but warm. We've seen this neighbourhood change and children grow. We had some great times when we were young—endless summers, with barbecues and pool parties that stretched long into the night."

A collective nostalgia settled over the room, and many guests savoured the memories sweetened by time. Even Jamie found himself lost, recalling images and feelings from when he was a child.

"Life, though," Janice said, and her voice faltered, "has its share of challenges. Many years ago, I went through something quite difficult." She left the sentence hanging. "Through it all, Julia and Marcus were there for me. They became more than neighbours; they were my pillars. Their strength inspired me to keep going."

Julia's face was awash with emotion, every line etched with the history Janice evoked. Marcus stood beside her and awkwardly put his arm around her to provide comfort. In Julia, Jamie saw a woman who, like himself, had struggled with the demons of her mental health, and in his father, he saw a man who buried his turmoil beneath work and distractions. And in Janice, he saw a profound sadness that seeps into your bones and never leaves.

Nicole reached for his hand, squeezing it. They both grappled with the complexities of their lives, of trust and of what it meant to belong to a family like theirs—a family that had been fractured so long ago.

Julia's hand trembled against the stem of her wine glass, the liquid mirroring the flush spreading across her cheeks. Janice's voice, tinged with nostalgia and sorrow, washed over the room. Each word an echo in the hollows of her own heart, reminding her of her long-fought battles with shadows that only she saw.

"Julia, are you alright?" Marcus leaned in.

"I'm fine," she said, but her voice quivered, betraying her words. She drew a breath and aimed to steady herself.

The room blurred as tears welled up, distorting the faces of her friends. She heard her name, and her hands reached out, but they were distant, disjointed from the storm of emotions inside her. Her resolve crumbled, and tears broke free, streaking down her face, unbidden and unchecked.

"Julia," Marcus's tone was sharper now, edged with panic and the need for control. He guided her by the elbow, trying to shield her from the prying eyes. "Let's step outside for a moment."

A hush fell over the gathered guests as they witnessed Julia's breakdown. Whispers swirled around the room as concerned guests looked on.

"Is she okay?"

"I think that speech was too much..."

"Never seen her quite like this before."

"Marcus, what's going on?"

"Everyone, please," Marcus raised his other hand, commanding the room with an authoritative calm that belied his racing heart. "Give us a moment."

Nicole exchanged a look with Jamie, her eyes wide with fear and understanding. They knew the depth of their mother's private struggles; the public unravelling was as jarring for them as it was for the observers who had never glimpsed behind the curtain of Julia Dempsey's stoic demeanour.

And then, as if the world resumed its orbit, conversations restarted. But the atmosphere had shifted, stained by the spectacle of vulnerability laid bare by Julia's reaction. Some guests sipped their drinks with renewed pensiveness, while others cast furtive glances towards the door where Julia had made her quiet exit.

"Should we go see if she needs anything?" Nicole said to Jamie. Jamie nodded, setting his jaw. "In a minute," he said.

James, Marcus's old friend from work, stood with his glass raised high, his voice commanding the fragmented attention of the room. "To Julia and Marcus," he said, a practiced smile smoothing the creases of his age-worn face, "they have shown us that the dance of marriage is one of enduring grace and tireless partnership."

The guests lifted their glasses in unison, a chorus of crystals chiming under the room's lights. "To Julia and Marcus," they echoed.

"Cheers," Marcus managed to articulate, having re-entered the room moments before. His hand trembled as he touched his glass to James's, the clink devoid of its usual cheer.

As the toast concluded, groups began to disengage. The laughter and banter that had once filled the home were now more subdued, replaced by an air of solemn reflection—the party, still rich with the scent of wine and floral arrangements, carried on.

Marcus circulated among the clusters of friends and acquaintances, offering farewells. "Thank you for coming," he said, his handshake firm, his gaze drifting toward the hallway where Julia had retreated. "It means a lot to us."

One by one, the guests filed out, their goodbyes punctuated with lingering looks of puzzlement. Some reached out to touch Marcus's arm, their grip communicating unspoken support, while others nodded, their eyes searching his for answers they would not ask aloud.

"Are you alright, Marcus?" James asked with genuine concern.

"Of course," Marcus said, the word clipped, a shield against the onslaught of his brewing storm. "Just a long day, you understand."

"Sure," James said, although his skepticism hung unsaid between them like an unfinished sentence.

When the last guest had departed, Marcus stood in the foyer. He turned, looking back at the expanse of his home and the remnants of the celebration. He exhaled, the breath he'd been holding finally escaping as a surrender to the night's revelations.

Down the hall, beyond the reach of the fading echoes of the guests' departure, an old argument awaited. With it, the chance to again confront the distances they had allowed to grow between them awaited. Marcus steeled himself for the encounter, knowing that in the quiet aftermath of their anniversary party, the true reckoning of their marriage was poised to begin.

The laughter and chatter had long since drained away, leaving behind an oppressive stillness that pressed against the walls of the Dempsey home. In the living room, Nicole settled onto the couch with her son, their forms silhouetted by the flickering light of the television screen.

On the adjacent couch, Jamie lingered, an old photo album sprawled open on his lap. His fingers traced the edges of photographs, and memories flooded his mind. He paused at a picture of himself, six years old and carefree, a time when the weight of the world had not yet pressed the light from his eyes. The faces of friends long gone stared back at him, their youthful exuberance frozen in time—a stark reminder of all that had been lost.

He turned the page and saw Nicole, her hair wild and untamed, laughing with abandon, and beside her, himself, a shadow of uncertainty lurking behind his tentative smile.

"Jamie?" Nicole's voice pierced his reverie, gentle but tinged with concern.

"Hmm?" he said, not lifting his gaze from the album.

"Are you okay?"

"Yeah," he said, the word slipping out before he could tether it to the truth. "Just... remembering."

"Sometimes I wish we could go back," she confessed, her gaze returning to the screen.

"Back to when things were simple?" Jamie said more to himself than to her.

"Maybe," she said, "or maybe just back when we thought they were."

Jamie closed the album abruptly.

Down the hall, the door to a bedroom clicked shut, a soft decree of privacy as Marcus turned, his eyes finding Julia's. The festive air that had buoyed the guests earlier was now a shroud that clung around them.

"Julia," he said, his voice low to modulate the disappointment that teetered on the edge of his words. "What happened out there? You know how people talk. It's not like you lose your composure like that in public. Not after all these years."

Julia's hands trembled, and she clutched at the fabric of her dress—a futile effort to steady herself against the swell of emotions that threatened to break free once more.

"We don't deserve tonight," she said, her deep-set eyes brimming with sorrow that stretched back through the years. "All this celebration, all this... pageantry. It's a farce, Marcus. We're living a lie."

"Julia," Marcus's voice sharpened, a crack in his charismatic facade revealing the turmoil that churned beneath. "We've worked hard for what we have. We've earned our place." He paused, struggling with the resentment that clouded his judgment. "We deserve what we get," he retorted, the words tasting of both defiance and bitter guilt that he could never fully articulate.

Julia looked away, her gaze falling upon the mirrored vanity that reflected a couple that had grown into strangers. There was no hiding from the woman in the reflection, whose veneer had slipped just enough to reveal the cracks in her armour.

"Marcus," she said, her resolve softening as she reached for something beyond the hurt, "I just... I need you to understand."

"I do understand, I of all people understand," he said, his tone layered with complexity, a mix of compassion and frustration. "But understanding doesn't change perception. It doesn't change people's thoughts when they see us like that."

In their bedroom, the space between them was like a chasm filled with the debris of their shared history—a history that had become as much about the moments they had celebrated as it was about those they wished they had forgotten.

Marcus's voice rose, a crescendo of years of pent-up frustration, "You can't do this—remember whose idea it was, Julia. This is your doing, and you can't go around with your heart on your sleeve. Not now. It's too late for that."

"My idea?" Julia's voice cracked with intensity, her eyes ablaze with anger. "Do you think I chose this? That I want to continuously live with what we have buried?"

"Buried? No, Julia, nothing gets buried; it's all around us!"

"Which is why you chose never to be here!" She stood, her chair scraping back against the hardwood floor, a battle cry in its own right. "This isn't just about tonight. It's about the silence and every excuse for why you couldn't be there when..."

Her words trailed off, but the accusation hung in the air, palpable and as sharp as glass.

In the living room, Nicole and Jamie sat in the dim glow of the television. The light flickered across their faces, illuminating the weariness etched into their features. They could hear the muffled rise and fall of their parents' voices through the walls. Jamie glanced at Nicole, noticing how she pulled her cardigan tighter around herself—a shield against more than just the chill.

"Are they ever going to stop?" Jamie said. "We're full-grown adults, but being here and hearing them makes me feel like a teenager all over again."

"They'll tire out soon," Nicole said in a flat, resigned voice. "Sometimes, I wonder if they even know how to exist without the fighting."

"Like some twisted form of... affection," Jamie said.

"Or survival," Nicole said, returning to the TV screen.

The argument down the hall reached a fever pitch. Julia's grief-stricken sobs and Marcus's bitter retorts were portraits of a marriage that had come undone.

"Maybe it's all they have left," Jamie said, "the anger, the hurt. Without it, what are they to each other?"

"Strangers," Nicole said, the word slipping out like a confession. "Just like us, Jamie. Strangers playing at being a family."

The voices from the room fell into a tense silence, and for a moment, the only sound was from the TV. Nicole and Jamie sat together, united in their isolation, each lost in thoughts of what might have been—and what might still come to pass in the shadow of their parents' fractured love.

The album lay open on Jamie's lap, its pages frayed at the edges. His fingers hesitated over a photograph that had slipped loose from its moorings. There they were—Marcus and Julia Dempsey, younger and unburdened by the complexities that would strangle their lives. A wood-panelled station wagon sat behind them, a relic from an era that Jamie struggled to recall. Marcus's arm was slung around Julia's waist, and her head was tilted back in laughter as if she had been amused by something outside the frame. Jamie lingered on the photo. He wasn't sure why it gripped him, but he struggled to tear himself away.

"Seen enough old ghosts for tonight?" Nicole's voice cut through his reverie; her silhouette framed against the flicker of the TV screen.

"More like skeletons," Jamie said without looking up, thumb brushing the edge of the photograph.

"Sometimes I think they keep these albums around to remind us that there were good days... or maybe to convince us that the bad ones weren't all there was," Nicole said.

"Or maybe," Jamie said, as he took the photo and placed it atop the pile, "we hold onto them because letting go is too much like erasing who we really are."

"Even the parts that hurt?" she asked.

Jamie nodded, though Nicole wasn't sure he agreed. Nicole settled back on the couch with her son, grabbed her laptop, and opened the case. She began to type, letting work become a distraction against the silence that now enveloped the home. The photo rested on the album and stared back at Jamie. He traced the outline of the station wagon, his fingers moving across the faux wood panelling as his mind raced back to a time he thought he had forgotten.

"Who were you back then?" he asked the people in the photo, "And what have we become?"

Part 2

2003

Chapter 6

The morning sun was creeping through the blinds in Julia Dempsey's kitchen, illuminating an array of breakfast ingredients laid out with practiced precision. A small television in the corner of the kitchen had been turned to the national news. Julia was watching as Baghdad fell to the American forces. The program showed a group of Iraqis pulling down a giant statue of Saddam, tearing it to pieces.

Julia moved about the kitchen methodically as she arranged her breakfast. She placed slices of toasted wholegrain bread on a small plate, their surfaces buttered. Beside them, she put a series of avocado slices augmented with a splash of lemon juice to preserve their colour. A small cup held a serving of non-fat Greek yogurt and a sprinkle of chia seeds. Each item was positioned just so, but her gaze passed over them without interest or intent to indulge.

"Are you going to eat that today?" Marcus's voice cut through the early morning stillness as he entered the kitchen. His tall frame leaned against the doorframe; his gaze fixed on the untouched food before Julia.

"Of course," Julia said, stirring the yogurt to mix in the untouched honey at the bottom of the bowl. "I just like it well-blended."

Marcus approached; his skepticism written on his furrowed brow. "Every morning, the same thing. You make it, you stare at it, but I never see you eat it."

"You should worry more about yourself, Marcus," she said. "When was the last time you had your cholesterol checked."

Marcus wasn't paying attention to her anymore. His gaze had shifted to the television and the scenes in Bagdad. "This war. The invasion of Iraq. It's all so... misguided."

"Misguided? But isn't it supposed to be about stopping terrorism and liberation?" Julia said as she pushed her plate further into the middle of the table.

"Yes, well, that's the official line. But Iraq is a complex place with a long history. The region has been in a series of conflicts and alliances for centuries. Invading it... we're just stirring a hornet's nest," Marcus said as he eyed the television.

"So, you think it will just make things worse?" Julia said.

Marcus nodded, "I do. Look, Saddam is a tyrant, there's no doubt about that, but this will leave a power vacuum that could destabilize the entire Middle East. Repercussions could last for decades."

"Teaching night school again?" Julia said, changing the subject. Her tone was casual as she glanced up at him, gauging his reaction. This global event only propelled Marcus further into his work. He was a history professor, after all. This type of news was fodder for his lectures. She could see him at his pulpit droning on about geopolitical events and historical contexts as doe-eyed students, particularly females, hung on his every word.

"Yes. It's the never-ending cycle of eager minds and endless papers to grade." He shrugged off his jacket and hung it on the back of a chair.

"Maybe you should get a room at the university, then," Julia quipped, her words sharp, hinting at the chasm between them.

The comment stung, casting a shadow over his face. "Julia, I'm trying to—"

"Trying to avoid coming home?" she said. "You've always found every reason to bury yourself in work rather than face what's left here."

"Is this what we're doing now? Another argument on the same bloody subject?" Marcus exhaled; the weariness evident in his voice. "I don't have time for this; I'll be late."

With that, he grabbed an apple from the fruit bowl, took a hasty bite, and made his way out of the kitchen, leaving Julia alone with her uneaten breakfast.

She heard the front door click shut, leaving her in a heavy silence. Julia stood motionless, the remnants of her conversation with Marcus clinging to the air like cobwebs. Her eyes scanned the untouched breakfast on the counter; she slid the plate's contents into the trash and rinsed the dish.

"Wasting food again, Julia," she said to herself. The food disappeared beneath a crumpled newspaper, hiding it from view to conceal the shameful act. An outsider might have pondered the oddity, but to Julia, it was a simple act of control in a life beyond her grasp. She looked at her phone, a small Nokia device that could now receive text messages. There was a reminder for her upcoming therapy appointment that morning. Julia stacked the dishes in the dishwasher and prepared for her appointment.

Dr. Helen Andrews' office had an artificial calm about it, with its walls adorned with serene landscapes that Julia couldn't quite place. Julia had been coming to Dr. Andrews for the past five years. She had been recommended by her family physician, who had become concerned about her weight loss. Julia had protested but had eventually relented. She now found the sessions mildly therapeutic, even if she only grazed the surface of what was on her mind.

She sat across from the therapist, her hands clasped in her lap."Tell me about your mornings, Julia," Dr. Andrews said, her voice soft yet probing.

"Oh, I don't know. There's not much to say. They're as routine as ever," Julia said, a practiced smile gracing her lips. I make breakfast and watch a little TV, though I'm not usually too hungry in the morning."

"Is this about controlling your environment, perhaps?" the therapist leaned forward, eyeing Julia.

"Control? No, I wouldn't say that," Julia deflected, shifting uncomfortably in her chair. "It's just...a habit."

"Let's explore these habits a bit more." Dr. Andrews paused, allowing the words to linger between them. "Sometimes our daily routines can be a window into our deeper concerns."

Julia's gaze fell to the patterns in the carpet, tracing the lines as if they might lead her away from the impending intrusion. "Well, I suppose that could be true in some cases," she conceded.

"Marcus is occupying your thoughts a great deal." The therapist's change of direction was subtle but purposeful.

"He's absent as usual. He's Department Head and never really gave up any of his course load," Julia said.

"Absence can create space for personal reflection," Dr. Andrews said. "What do you think about when you are alone?"

"Personal reflection?" Julia echoed, with a laugh devoid of humour. "No, I've spent half my life reflecting, and it hasn't done me or my family any good. Now I just try to fill my time with gardening, reading, and other things." She trailed off, knowing full well the hollow echo of avoidance.

"Other things," Dr. Andrews said, allowing the silence to invite confession.

"Yes, simple things, things that don't hurt my head," Julia said after a moment. "What's the point of reflecting on pain? It hasn't done me any good over the years."

"Simple things are OK," the therapist said, nodding slowly. "But beneath the surface, that's where the truth often lies, right?"

The walls closed in on Julia, the depth of her secrets pressed against her head. Her heart raced, and she shifted in the chair. "Maybe so," she conceded, her words clipped. "But my experience tells me that some truths are best left buried."

Dr. Andrews leaned back in her chair; her gaze unwavering. "Buried truths have a way of resurfacing, Julia. They weigh on us, shape us, control us without our even realizing it."

Julia's eyes flickered with a mix of defiance and fear. "Do you think it's easy to drudge things up that have been buried for so long, doctor?"

"It's never easy, Julia," Dr. Andrews said. "But it is necessary. To heal, we must first acknowledge and embrace all facets of ourselves, even those we'd rather keep hidden."

Julia's hands trembled in her lap as she grappled with the swirling emotions inside her. "What if facing those truths means destroying everything I've built?

The therapist's voice was a steady presence in the room. "Sometimes, Julia, we have to break down to rebuild." Dr. Andrews studied Julia for a moment and saw that this path of discussion would not progress much further, not right now. "So, tell me more about Marcus," she said, pivoting the conversation.

"Marcus is... preoccupied," Julia said, her fingers tracing the armrest of the plush chair. Dr. Andrews sat across from her, pen poised above a notepad, her expression open and expectant.

"Preoccupied with work?" Dr. Andrews asked, her tone gentle yet probing.

"Always work," Julia said, tucking a stray wisp of gray hair behind her ear. It's his everything. It's always been how he defined himself: professor, Department Head, rarely Husband or Father. There was a time when he was those things, but that's now long in the past."

"What do you think he is avoiding?" The therapist leaned forward, signalling her full attention.

"Regrets, I suppose," Julia said, the word coming out like a puff of smoke, dissipating quickly. "He has many. We all do, I suppose?"

"Is that why he teaches night classes so much?"

"Yes, I think so." Julia let out a dry chuckle. "At least now it's just teaching. There was a time when his extracurricular activities involved more than books and lectures." She raised an eyebrow as if to punctuate the innuendo.

"And what about you, Julia? Did you have many extracurricular activities?" Dr Andrews asked, probing Julia.

Julia sat forward in her chair as a look of surprise crossed her face. "Whatever I did, it was nothing like Marcus. I was home for my family, regardless of what happened."

Dr. Andrews nodded, jotting down a note begging back an attack on Julia. "And what about your son and daughter? How are they faring?"

"Nicole has found some stability," Julia said, her voice softening. "She still lives with her partner, Corinne, and they are raising Chase together. It's not the traditional picture I had imagined for her, but she's content—safer than before."

"Safer is better," Dr. Andrews echoed. "You have spoken before about her youth. It sounded like she was avoiding something, too, which often manifests in young people in risky behaviour.

Julia waved her hand dismissively. "Oh, you know, youthful rebellions, wrong crowds. But she's come a long way."

"And Jamie?" the therapist pressed.

Julia hesitated, her eyes clouding over. "Jamie is... still lost. He still lives on and off with Sheila, the older woman he met years ago. I don't want to pretend to be the therapist, but it's as if he's trying to find a mother in every other woman he meets. I must have failed him pretty badly. His sobriety is a rollercoaster—it goes up and down. I help when I can through Nicole. At least there's still a thread connecting him to us."

"We spoke about this before, but was there an event that led him to this path?" Dr. Andrews asked, her voice steady.

"An event..." Julia said, trailing off. A shadow passed over her face. "No, no specific event. It's just who he is. Or maybe it's who we made him." Her words were tight, guarded.

"Who 'we' made him?" the therapist asked, sensing the significance of Julia's words.

"Never mind," Julia said as her defences rose. "It doesn't make sense that Marcus or I caused such a spiral. There's something broken inside him, but he would never speak about it."

"Is it related to what's causing the strain between you and Marcus?" Dr. Andrews ventured.

Julia paused, eyeing Dr. Andrews, searching for some ploy or trick in her question. "No," she said. "The issues in our marriage... they're our issues."

"Sometimes, Julia, the lines intersect more than we realize," Dr. Andrews said.

Julia looked back at the therapist, her eyes brimming with unshed tears, then stood. "I think that's enough for today."

"Of course," Dr. Andrews said, setting aside her notepad. "We'll pick up from here next time."

Julia offered a terse nod, gathered her things, and left, eyeing the banal landscapes in the waiting area again as she went.

Julia left the Therapist and proceeded to a section of town lined with restaurants and cafes. Her friend had coaxed her to meet for lunch. She had known Helen since they were young adults. They would double-date often, Julia with Marcus and Helen with James. James works with Marcus at the College, though he has always taken a more balanced perspective on work, saving time for family and friends. She met Helen at a place that served overpriced croissant sandwiches and artisanal coffee.

Julia entered the restaurant and saw Helen sitting in the corner, sipping a foam-topped coffee. They exchanged their usual greetings, with Helen hugging Julia for an extended period. The lunch crowd buzzed around them. The waiter came right away, and Julia ordered a tomato salad. Helen's face gave away a frown as she took Julia's order. "Are you sure you don't want the ham and cheese croissant? They're to die for," she said. "I'm good," Julia said. "I had a large breakfast, and I'm not that hungry."

The food arrived quickly, and Julia began to push the tomatoes around her plate. "Julia," Helen said, her voice laced with concern, "you haven't touched your food."

"I'm fine," Julia said. "My stomach has been off this morning."

Helen wasn't convinced. "It's not just this morning, though. You've been looking... frail for a while now."

"Frail?" Julia echoed, a defensive edge creeping into her tone. "I think you're overreacting."

"Am I?" Helen pressed, her brows knitting together. "I care about you. I can't pretend I haven't noticed how thin you've become."

"Enough, Helen." Julia's voice was sharp. "I don't need another person monitoring my eating habits."

"Someone has to," Helen retorted, her frustration mounting. "You're isolating yourself, Julia. We're worried."

"Who's 'we'?" Julia challenged, her fingers tightening around her napkin until her knuckles turned white. "Has Marcus been talking to you?"

"Me and James," Helen said, reaching across the table to bridge the gap. But Julia recoiled as if the touch burned, pushing back her chair and standing. "I'm sorry Helen, I'm not very well. I have to go," she said. She laid down enough cash to cover her uneaten salad. Helen looked up at her with a concerned look on her face. "Please don't go, Julia. How about next time I come by your place? We haven't sat out by your pool forever." Julia's face softened at her friend's request. "OK, let's set something up for next week; I'm sure I'll feel better then." She then turned and walked out of the restaurant, resisting the urge to look back to see if Helen was scrutinizing her as she left. She got in her car and gripped the steering wheel, cursing herself, the restaurant and Helen in one breath.

The drive home was a blur, Julia's mind replaying the confrontation with Helen on an agonizing loop. The quiet streets of her neighbourhood contrasted with the turmoil inside her, and as she passed by one house with a "For Sale" sign staked in the yard, something compelled her to pull over.

Maybe it was the "Open House" sign that beckoned her. The home reminded her of her home, which looked like the perfect suburban setting. She pulled up alongside the curb and got out. She looked at the sign with a photo of a beautiful young woman holding a number one sign. Julia stepped through the front door as if an invisible thread drew her. Inside, the home smelled of fresh paint, a scent that once had invigorated her, but now it only stirred memories.

She passed by the kitchen, avoided signing in at the table, and decided not to pick up one of the floor plans. She was familiar with the home already. She followed the hallway down to the main bedroom. Inside, she caught her reflection in the large mirror that leaned against one wall. Her gaze drifted to the bed, and for a moment, she was transported back to a memory mixed with excitement and regret.

She proceeded into the main bathroom. She opened the mirrored medicine cabinet and studied the containers that lined the shelves. Her eyes fell on the bottle labelled Prozac. It was ironic, as Julia's therapist was happy to prescribe her medication, which Julia had always refused. Now, she was drawn to the bottle in someone else's home. She lifted it out and opened the bottle. It was half full. She shook out two pills and popped them into her mouth. She ran to the sink, cupped some water in her hands, and drank, forcing the pills down her throat. She closed the cabinet and looked at herself in the mirror. Now you've done it, she thought to herself. Now, you've crossed a line. She was alive, though, the most alive she had been in weeks.

"Julia Dempsey?" A young woman's voice was pulling her back to the present.

Julia turned to see the bright-eyed real estate agent regarding her with recognition. "Yes, that's me," she said.

"I thought so! You once sold this house, didn't you? About ten years ago?"

"That's right," Julia said, a faint smile touching her lips. She exited the bathroom and quickly shut the door behind her. "Walking down memory lane, I suppose."

"Are you in the market again?" the agent asked, hopeful.

"No, I'm just reminiscing, I suppose," Julia said. "But I must say, the market does seem to be recovering."

"Your name was everywhere when I was a teenager. You must have been an incredible agent," the young woman said. "I wish you'd held on after the crisis. Things are picking up again."

"Thank you, that's nice of you to say," Julia said, touched despite herself. "I'll give you a tip. Always remove everything from the bathroom. You don't want some kid overdosing on some drug while his parents tour the kitchen."

"Oh my god, thank you, Mrs. Dempsey!" The agent beamed as she entered the bathroom and rifled through the cabinets. I guess you've seen it all in your time."

"Call me Julia," she said. "I'll let you get back to your work. Good luck with the sale. It's a lovely home.".

"Thanks, Julia. Let me know if you ever want to get back into the game. I'm sure you'd still be great," the agent said. Before Julia responded, the agent was intercepted by a young couple with a child no more than eight. Julia let herself out of the home and walked back to her car.

Julia returned home and headed straight for her closet. Her fingers trembled as they grazed the fabric of a silk blouse, its hue a soft lavender. Her closet, a cavernous space filled with relics of her past self, echoed her growing unease. She pulled at the hangers, wrenching them from where they hung neatly in rows.

"Useless," she said, her voice brittle. The word hung in the air, a verdict on more than just the clothes before her. With each garment wrenched from its place, the anger that seethed beneath her controlled exterior surged. Years of repressed emotions tangled with the linen that piled on the floor.

She bundled the clothes into a chaotic sphere and stormed through the house. Her footsteps were heavy against the polished wood floor, each step a drumbeat to her rage. She flung open the side door, the sunlight blinding her. With a force that came from a place deep within, she hurled the clothes into the bin, the clatter of hangers an exclamation point to her act of defiance. The lid slammed shut, and she stood, breathing heavily, staring at the receptacle.

Then, as her strength deserted her, she slid down against the cool metal, sobs erupting from her in waves. Her shoulders shook as she wept, the salt of her tears mingling with the bitter taste of regret.

When the sobs subsided to shuddering breaths, Julia pushed herself up and went to the backyard. She stepped onto the overgrown grass; her gaze drawn to the pool. It lay dormant under its cover, contrasting with the vibrant hub of activity it once was. Memories cascaded through her mind: sun-soaked laughter, the splash of water, her children's voices calling to each other.

A wave of dizziness swept over her. The edges of her vision blurred, and the world tilted. Her body swayed, and then darkness crept in. Julia crumpled to the ground, the grass a soft cushion against her cheek.

Time passed—was it a minute or an hour? She could not tell. When consciousness returned, her sight refocused on the sky peeking through the branches above. A sigh escaped her lips, releasing the fear that had gripped her.

"Get up, Julia," she said to herself. "You've been through worse." Her hand pressed into the earth, steadying her rise. She straightened her back, willing the weakness to go away.

"Just a spell," she rationalized, brushing the grass remnants from her clothing. "Nothing you can't handle." Yet the tremor in her hands had revealed a vulnerability she dared not acknowledge.

Julia Dempsey stood, gathered herself, and retreated to the office.

The room was dim, the pale glow of the computer screen casting ghostly shadows across Julia's face as her fingers moved across the keyboard. She poured over article after article, each a breadcrumb trail leading further into the myriad of medical jargon and potential diagnoses. Dizziness, fainting spells, loss of appetite – each symptom typed into the search bar was an admission, a tangible acknowledgment of her frailty.

Julia clicked on links, absorbing information about blood pressure drops, dehydration, stress responses, and neurological conditions. The words blurred together, paragraphs merging into a myriad of possibilities that wove tighter around her chest.

"Nothing I can't handle," she said again, the mantra less convincing in the silence of the study. Her eyes darted to the clock at the corner of the screen; hours had passed in what felt like moments. With a final glance at a forum discussing fainting spells, she cleared the browser history, erasing the digital footprints of her fear.

The house was silent as she made her way to the living room. She drew a shawl tighter around her shoulders, suddenly aware of the night's creeping chill, and approached the bookshelf where dusty albums stood in solemn rows, sentinels of the past.

With hands that trembled, Julia selected an album, its cover worn from the passage of time. The leather creaked as she opened it, the sound a prelude to the flood of memories contained within. There they were, smiling faces frozen in time: Marcus with his arm around her, both young and unaware of the fissures that would form in the bedrock of their marriage; Nicole, her eyes bright and rebellious, before life taught her hard lessons in love; Jamie, a boy with a mischievous grin, not yet shadowed by the spectres of his choices.

Each photo was a window into a world that no longer existed, of moments that Julia could never reclaim. Julia traced her finger over a picture of them all at the pool, the water, a mirror reflecting the sky, the laughter echoing across years of distance.

"What did we do?" she said, the question hanging in the air, unanswered. The images before her were cruel in their static happiness, betraying nothing of the undercurrents that had swept them all along divergent paths.

A tear escaped, slipping down her cheek, as Julia closed the album with a soft thud. She leaned back against the couch, swallowed by the enormity of the room. The weight of unresolved issues pressed upon her, an invisible burden borne alone in the quiet of the night.

Julia's eyelids fluttered, giving way to the realm of sleep where her consciousness began to wear strange and familiar. She found herself walking through an endless corridor, the walls lined with doors, each marked with a plaque indicating years past. She reached for one that read '1973', but as she touched the knob, it disintegrated into dust, slipping through her fingers like the years themselves.

"Julia," said a soft yet insistent voice from down the hall. She looked at Marcus, not as he was now, but as the young man she had fallen in love with, his eyes still holding the spark of unspent potential.

"Can't you see what you're doing?" he asked, his figure blurring at the edges as if threatening to fade away.

"Doing? I'm trying to hold everything together," she said, but her voice echoed back at her, hollow and unconvincing.

"Are you?" Marcus's image began to recede, and in his place stood Nicole and Jamie, children again, playing by a pool that shimmered with an unnatural brilliance. They laughed, carefree, unaware of the shadow that loomed over them—a giant wave suspended in the air, threatening to crash down.

"Mommy, help us!" they said in unison, their hands reaching for her. But Julia's feet were rooted, her body paralyzed by an unseen force.

"Darling, you have to let go," said a voice from within her, the words weaving around her.

"Let go of what? I can't..." her plea trailed off as she stared, helpless, the impending deluge about to engulf her children.

"Your fears, your control, your past," the voice said, more persistent now. "They're drowning in the life you couldn't live."

Julia's heart clenched, a raw ache spreading across her chest. The wave hung motionless, a spectre of her deepest anxieties—the impermanence of happiness, the inevitability of loss, the guilt of choices made and unmade.

"Save us, Mommy!" The children's voices rose to a crescendo, a piercing alarm that jolted Julia awake.

Her breath came in ragged gasps, her nightgown clinging to her sweat-drenched skin. The room's darkness pressed in on her, a physical manifestation of the isolation that had crept into her waking hours. The remnants of the dream lingered, its symbolism clear—her struggle with relinquishing control, her fear of confronting the chasms in her family. "Forgive me," she said into the silence as she wrestled with the ghosts of her subconscious.

Chapter 7

Marcus Dempsey stepped out into the dawn, his hand cradling a steaming mug of coffee. The quiet backyard lay still, save for the leaves rustling in the morning breeze. He was 54, and though his reflection bore the marks of a life lived, it was a life that looked better from the outside than it was on the inside.

His gaze wandered to the closed-up pool, its once vibrant blue now hidden beneath a gray tarp, its waters stilled, and its purpose forgotten. Much like his own life, the pool had been neglected for years. Shifting his thoughts, he turned back toward the house. The kitchen light was still on, glowing against the creeping daylight. Julia was still there, her slim figure framed by the window, her face drawn with the familiar look of concern that Marcus had become so used to seeing.

"Julia, you need to eat something," Marcus had said, trying to shift the topic from the Middle East to something more immediate and manageable.

"I'm not hungry," she said, her tone deflecting further discussion. Her eyes met his before darting away.

He knew of her struggle, of the therapist's appointments scribbled in her neat handwriting on the kitchen calendar. It was a battle fought mostly in silence, with small victories and setbacks that left no lasting mark. Yet Marcus hoped that this time, healing would come.

"Take care of yourself, Julia," he said as he had left.

Stepping off the porch, Marcus set his empty cup on the railing, the last droplets clinging to the ceramic edge. Pulling his jacket closer against the morning air, he took a long breath, watching it turn to mist before disappearing into the day.

"Time to face the world," he said to himself, a mantra for the march into the unyielding rhythm of life. With one last glance back at the quiet house, he slid behind the wheel of his car and started the engine.

Marcus Dempsey pulled into the University parking lot and found the space reserved for the history department head. He stepped out of the car, locking it behind him as his gaze swept across the familiar campus grounds. Marcus began his short walk towards the history building, a path he had traversed hundreds of times over the years.

"Hi, Mr. Dempsey," said a voice, pulling him from his thoughts. He glanced up to see a pair of students lounging on a nearby bench, their youthful faces alight with the easy camaraderie of college life. They were two girls who might have once prompted him to linger and engage in a charming exchange showcasing his wit and wisdom.

"Good morning, ladies," Marcus said, his tone warm yet tinged with a restraint born of self-awareness. For a fleeting moment, he considered walking over, but the image of Julia flashed through his mind. With a polite nod, he continued, leaving their laughter to fade into the background.

The corridors of the history department were quiet, the bustle of the day not yet begun. Marcus moved with a sense of belonging from years of navigating its halls, his footsteps echoing against the polished floor. He approached his office, the gold lettering on the Department Head door gleaming under the fluorescent lights.

"Mr. Dempsey," said Linda, his assistant, as he entered the main office, "the President asked to see you."

"Did he now?" Marcus said, arching an eyebrow. There was no tremor in his voice, no hint of apprehension. His tenure at the University had seen its share of summons to higher offices—some routine, others less so—but whatever the reason, there was an odd detachment, as though the stakes had somehow lowered with time.

"Do you know what it's about?" he asked, knowing that Linda's connections often provided her with insights few others possessed.

She shook her head, her expression neutral. "No, but he said as soon as you can."

"Alright, thank you, Linda." Marcus nodded. He turned away, the weight of her curious gaze on his back as he made his way to the President's office. Marcus's hand rested on the polished brass knob of the President's office door, a pause in motion before he turned it and stepped inside. The room was awash with the morning light filtering through half-open blinds, casting long, thin shadows that lay like bars across the carpet. President Hargrove sat behind his expansive mahogany desk, his fingers steepled, eyes expectant.

"Marcus, please, have a seat," he said, gesturing to the leather chair across from him.

"Thank you, Richard," Marcus said, easing into the chair. His gaze found the framed degrees on the wall—reminders of their shared history at the institution.

"Marcus." Hargrove's voice was even yet carried an under-current of concern. "I've been reviewing the departmental workload reports, and well, your name seems to be attached to an inordinate number of classes and committees."

"Occupational hazard of caring about the institution," Marcus quipped, but his smile faltered beneath Hargrove's unyielding scrutiny.

"Your dedication has never been in question. It's your health I'm worried about," the President said, leaning forward. "The balance between work and life isn't just some trendy mantra; it's essential, especially at our stage in life."

Marcus shifted in his seat, the leather creaking. "I appreciate the concern, Richard, but I assure you, I'm doing just fine."

"Are you?" Hargrove asked. "Because there's more to life than work, Marcus. And we both know how easy it is to get lost in its trappings."

There it was—the veiled reference to years past, to choices made in the heady mix of ambition and academia—the tension coiled within the room, a tangible thing that threatened to resurrect ghosts best left undisturbed.

"Richard, if memory serves, we were both young professors once and navigated the same temptations. Extracurricular activities weren't foreign to either of us, might I remind you."

"Touché," Hargrove conceded with a resigned tilt of his head. The briefest flicker of a shared, rueful grin passed between them—a silent acknowledgment of youthful recklessness turned wiser caution.

"Look, just consider what I'm saying, Marcus. Lighten the load a bit," Hargrove said, his tone softening. "Focus on your personal life, too. There's no point burning out when you should enjoy the fruits of your labour."

Marcus nodded slowly, a non-committal gesture that hid the churn of thoughts beneath his composed exterior. He rose from his seat, the conversation etching itself into the folds of his mind, where it would be dissected and debated in the quiet hours to come.

"Thank you for the advice, Richard. I'll give it some thought," Marcus said as he approached the door.

"Think about it, Marcus. Think about it carefully," Hargrove said after him, the genuine concern in his voice trailing Marcus as he exited the room.

Marcus returned to his office and closed the door behind him, the click of the latch a definitive sound in the otherwise peaceful corridor. The walls were lined with bookshelves, each spine part of the cycle of knowledge acquired and lessons imparted. He leaned against the door wood, the grain pattern pressing against his blazer—its texture a familiar, grounding pressure.

His eyes drifted to the framed photo on his desk, one of Julia in her younger days, a frozen smile that now looked more like a question than an expression of happiness. Could he consider retirement? Would the silence at home be his solace or suffocate him?

The President's words lingered; unspoken implications heavy in the air. Marcus walked to his chair and sank into it, the leather creaking under his weight. The unfinished manuscript on his desk called to him; its pages were filled with years of research, an endeavour meant to be his magnum opus, yet incomplete as so many other aspects of his life.

"Ten more years," he said to the quiet, "at least ten." But the echo of his voice sounded hollow, even to him. Ten years to do what? To avoid the widening gap between him and Julia, to pour himself into work that didn't fulfil him as it once did.

The office was a capsule of his history at the University. Diplomas, awards, and commendations adorned the walls—a visual chronicle of a rise to prestige that demanded sacrifices at every turn. It had cost him time with Jamie and Nicole, strained smiles over dinner with Julia, and countless weekends buried in papers.

As department head, he'd seen bright-eyed students become colleagues, witnessed their potential unfold—or sometimes crumple beneath the weight of academia's relentless grind. His ambition had fueled him, propelling him through ranks and roles with the voracity of a man who needed to prove his worth to the world and himself.

"Personal costs," he said to himself, the phrase catching like a thorn.

He swivelled his chair to face the window, where the campus lay, still vibrant with youthful aspiration. How much of his vigour remained? How much had been sapped by the years and the quiet desperation that now gnawed at his resolve?

"Richard is right," Marcus said. Was there a point to all this—the late nights, the missed anniversaries, the ever-present disquiet—blurring before his eyes, growing dimmer with each reflection?

With a sigh, Marcus Dempsey pushed back from the desk and rose. The questions wouldn't end there; they would follow him into the classroom and then home. But for now, they would remain unanswered, hovering like spectres over a life half-lived, demanding attention he wasn't sure he was ready to give. For now, he had classes to teach.

As the day ended, Marcus slid his lecture notes into a worn leather pouch, the corners of countless papers peeking out like eager students themselves. His fingers traced the spines of books lining his office; they were more like mile markers on the road, and he wasn't sure he still wanted to travel. The fluorescent light hummed overhead, contrasting with the dwindling twilight outside that signalled the approach of his night class.

He paused, pressing a palm against the mahogany desk that had been both anchor and albatross through his years at the University. The lines on his face were more profound in the reflection of his computer screen, which displayed a slideshow not yet finalized for tonight's lecture. Marcus's eyes, shadowed with concern, flicked to the clock—it counted down the minutes until he was due to stand before an auditorium of expectant faces.

"Another night," he said.

His hand found its way to the desk's bottom drawer, quickly pulling it open. A discreet flask lay inside, between stacks of ungraded essays and spare pens. "Small measure," Marcus said to himself as he unscrewed the cap, "just to take the edge off."

The amber liquid caught the light as he poured it, a delicate stream that belied the strength of its contents. With a practiced tilt of the flask, he measured out the few ounces that experience told him would dull the sharpness of his anxiety without clouding his mind beyond function.

He raised the flask to his lips and took a sip, the familiar burn sliding down his throat, spreading a false sense of calm through his tense muscles. The minor concession to his nerves had become a ritual.

"Steady now, Dempsey," he said, taking another controlled swallow.

The drink settled in; its effects subtle but insistent. He closed the drawer, the metal flask hidden again amongst the papers. Turning back to his computer, Marcus clicked through the remaining slides, each advancing with a mechanical certainty.

"Let's see if we can't make history come alive," he said, a half-hearted attempt at rallying his spirits.

With one last glance around the office—a mausoleum of aspirations and achievements—Marcus hefted the satchel over his shoulder and stepped out into the corridor. The empty halls echoed with the click of his shoes, a solitary march toward a classroom where rows of young minds waited.

Each step was heavier than the last, challenging his resolve. Yet onward, he proceeded, hoping that under the guise of the exchange of ideas and pursuit of understanding, he might rediscover a glimmer of why he chose this path so many years ago.

Marcus stood at the front of the room, the projector casting a pale glow on his face as he navigated through the intricacies of the historical period on display. His voice was steady, the lecture practiced and polished after years of refinement. Students sat in various states of attention, some scribbling notes, others staring out the window.

"Remember," Marcus said, pausing for emphasis, "the context of these events is crucial to understanding the motivations of the figures involved."

A hand shot up from the back row; it was a young and earnest student, eyes filled with curiosity and a challenge.

"Mr. Dempsey," the student said, their tone respectful but probing. "How can you reconcile the glorification of these historical figures with the atrocities they committed? Aren't we responsible for acknowledging the full scope of their actions rather than perpetuating a one-sided narrative?"

The classroom fell silent, the question's weight hanging in the air—a familiar tightness coiled within him, the kind that comes when long-held beliefs are questioned.

"History isn't about glorification," Marcus said, his response more terse than intended. "It's about understanding the complexities of human behaviour within the context of their time."

"But doesn't that context change with new perspectives?" the student asked. "Shouldn't history be a living thing that grows and adapts to contemporary values?"

Marcus clenched his jaw, and his patience frayed. The warm buzz from the drink earlier did little to dull the edge of his irritation.

"Contemporary values do not alter historical facts," he said, rising voice. "They lived in their time, not ours. It is presumptuous to judge them through a modern lens. I'm sure you've said over ten things today that, in fifty years, you will be considered arrogant, ignorant, or both. The people we study have risen to the upper echelons of power in some of the darkest times in history. You live in the most affluent and peaceful time the world has ever seen, and you think you have the right to judge the peoples of the past."

There was a collective shift in the room. Students exchange glances, sensing the undercurrents of tension. Marcus saw the generational divide in their faces, like a chasm too vast to bridge.

"History does evolve," he conceded, his tone softening as he sought to regain composure. "But let's not mistake evolution for revisionism. We have to tread carefully so we don't distort the past to fit present narratives."

The student nodded, though the look in their eyes suggested the conversation was far from over. The momentary flare of conflict receded, leaving behind a residue of unease. He cleared his throat and returned to the slides, resuming the lecture with a renewed focus, eager to leave the disquiet behind.

Marcus concluded the lecture and disbursed the students. He remained at his podium; papers strewn about like casualties of the evening's intellectual skirmish. He moved to his office. The soft hum of his computer was the only sound greeting him as he sank into his chair. He leaned back, eyes closed, massaging his temples where the tension knotted, seeking solace in the darkness behind his eyelids. "Revisionism," he said. That was his bastion against the tide of change, a fortress of scholarship that seemed besieged by the youthful vigour of new ideas.

Yet, as he sat there in contemplation, the armour of his justification began to break. What if his rigidity had stifled the essence of historical inquiry? Was he guarding history or simply entombing it?

He glanced at the stack of evaluations on the corner of his desk. "A brilliant mind," they said, "but often unyielding." Marcus winced as he conjured the words. Each semester, he promised himself he would be more open and adaptable. And each semester, he found himself retreating to the safety of his long-held beliefs.

"Damn," he said into the quiet room. Regret gnawed at him, an insidious worm that feasted on the certainty he once held dear. Had his sharpness cut too deep this time? Had he crossed the line from educator to tyrant?

He rose and paced before the book-lined walls, the spines staring back at him. They whispered of a younger man, hungry for knowledge, eager for discussion and debate. Where had that man gone?

"Marcus Dempsey, defender of the old guard," he scoffed, running a hand through his hair. His reflection in the window pane was ghostly pale, and he wondered if his youth's vibrancy had faded so much.

"Is this who I've become?" His question hung in the air, unanswered. Shadows crept across the room as the night aged. He could almost hear the soft echo of his lectures, admonishing students to consider context and understand complexity.

"Complexity," he said, the irony not lost on him. Here he was, wrestling with the complex threads of his own identity, his trust in his life's work fraying at the edges.

He poured a measure of whiskey, the amber liquid catching the light. He stared at it, seeing in its depths the cyclical nature of his internal battles—the pull between the allure of traditional scholarship and the pressing need to adapt and grow.

"Here's to you, Professor Dempsey," he said to no one, raising the glass to toast his reflection. He drank; the warmth spread through him, a temporary balm for the sting of self-reproach.

Setting down the empty glass, Marcus knew the night would offer no rest. He would sit there, haunted by the echoes of confrontation, by the spectre of change, until dawn crept through the slats of his blinds, offering a new day—a new chance, perhaps, to reconcile the professor he now was with the person he hoped to be.

Marcus slumped in the leather chair that had moulded to his form over years of late nights. His fingers found the grooves in the armrests. The classroom confrontation replayed in his head—sharp words like darts, striking targets that were as much a part of himself as the student who posed the question.

"Have I become an artifact?" he said, the words settling in the silence of his office. A sense of dissonance gnawed at him; the historian—a chronicler of change, resistant to the very evolution he taught.

A soft knock on the door jolted him from his reverie. "Rooms locked up for the night, Professor Dempsey," the janitor said. Are you headin' out soon?"

"Shortly, thanks," Marcus said, but his voice lacked conviction. He was stalling, avoiding the empty house that awaited him.

Once alone again, the walls of his office closed in, lined with books mocking his current strife. "What impact am I having?" he said to the spines. Were his lectures just echoes that faded before they reached the minds of those he sought to inspire?

The unease twisted tighter within him, and a visceral response propelled him to his feet. He needed a destination, something tangible to anchor the storm inside. With a restless energy, he grabbed his keys and jacket, locking the door behind him. The campus was shrouded in darkness, save for the scattered lampposts standing guard along the paths.

His car, a dependable sedan that mirrored his practicality, received him without judgment. As he drove, the familiar streets blurred, and his thoughts turned to Jamie, his son—the boy who once looked up to him with wide-eyed admiration, now a man estranged by the chasms of regret and missed opportunities.

Without conscious thought, Marcus found himself steering toward Sheila's house. The impulse was a surge from deep within, a father's instinct to mend what was broken, to salvage some piece of the past before it slipped entirely through his fingers. He gripped the wheel, knuckles whitening, each mile bringing him closer to the reality of his son's life—a life from which he was excluded.

Sheila's house loomed ahead, a place that Marcus had never really known. Parking across the street, he cut the engine. Marcus sat idle in the shadow of his sedan, the chill of the leather seat seeping through his blazer. His hands rested on the steering wheel, not intending to drive but as a futile attempt to tether himself to the moment. Outside, Sheila's house stood bathed in the soft glow of the porch light.

He exhaled, fogging the window beside him. Each breath was a battle, a rhythmic struggle between courage and the creeping tendrils of fear. He thought of Jamie, the son who had become a question mark in his life's narrative.

The time for reflection had passed; action demanded its due. With a resolve that was more fragile than he cared to admit, he opened the car door and stepped out into the night.

The walk to Sheila's doorstep was short, but each step was heavy. He raised his hand, the knuckles pale and unsteady, and knocked.

The door swung open, revealing Sheila. Her features were familiar yet lined with the passage of years and trials, much like his own. "Marcus," she said, her voice tinged with surprise.

"Hello, Sheila," he said, the words sounding foreign, as though they belonged to someone less fractured.

"Is it about Jamie?" She cut straight to the core, her gaze holding his.

"Yes." His throat tightened around the name. "I... how is he?"

"Getting by," Sheila said, her tone even, protective. "He's working hard at staying clean, but it's a daily fight, Marcus."

"Does he... is he..." The queries died on his lips, choked by the realization of how little he knew of his own son's struggles.

"Jamie needs support," she said, measured against the chasm of their shared failures. "Real support, not just... this." She glanced at the wallet he hadn't realized he'd been clutching since exiting the car.

He nodded, the gesture hollow. "I want to help, truly."

She looked at him then, and in her eyes, he saw the reflection of a man who had let too many moments slip through his grasp. "You should tell him that yourself, Marcus. He needs to hear it from you, not me."

The silence that followed was laden with the weight of all that remained unsaid. They stood on the porch, two custodians of a broken history, bound by a love for someone beyond their reach.

Marcus stood, the crisp night air brushing against his skin as he clutched a wad of cash in his shaking hand. The street was quiet, save for the rustling of leaves in the gentle breeze. He extended his arm toward Sheila; the banknotes were like a meagre bandage over a gaping wound.

"Please, give this to Jamie," he said. "It's all I can—"

Sheila cut him off with a firm shake of her head. "You need to give it to him, Marcus. Not me." Her gaze held a mixture of concern and resolve, a silent urging for him to bridge the gap that had grown between father and son.

He tried to meet her eyes, but shame fastened his stare to the ground. "I don't think he wants to see me," Marcus said, the truth tasting bitter on his tongue.

"Maybe not," Sheila conceded, taking the money with reluctant fingers. "But he deserves to hear you say sorry. To face you."

"I didn't want to bother you; I'm sorry. Goodnight, Sheila," Marcus said, stepping back.

"Goodnight," she echoed. She stepped back, the door closing with an air of finality that sealed away any hope of reconciliation. Marcus lingered before turning away, his heart heavy with missed opportunities and unspoken apologies.

Retreating to the silent street, he looked up at the darkening sky, the stars obscured by the ambient light, distant and indifferent. The void above mirrored the yawning deep within—a man torn between the world he had built and the one he had neglected.

Marcus got into his car and drove away from Sheila's house, the weight of his failures pressing down on him. He tried to push aside the thoughts of Jamie, but they lingered in his mind like a stubborn stain.

The road home led him to a familiar yet secluded area with tall trees. Marcus pulled over and turned off the engine, the cool night air seeping through the cracks in the windows. He rested his head against the steering wheel and sighed. A tidal wave of emotions he had dammed up for years breached its confines. He grasped the steering wheel with trembling hands as if it were the lifeline tethering him to sanity.

"Dammit," Marcus said under his breath. He'd been outmaneuvered by life itself, boxed in by decisions made and opportunities forever lost. A career spent cultivating history's narratives, yet he failed to author his own with any semblance of grace.

He leaned back against the seat, releasing a long, shaky breath. The leather creaked, a reminder of how everything around him seemed to age, to change, except for the gnawing sense of incompleteness within. His thoughts wandered back through the decades—ambitions pursued with relentless ardour, but at what cost? Friendships were neglected, and family was relegated to the margins of his priorities. Julia's quiet despair, Nicole's veiled disappointment, and Jamie's growing chasm of estrangement painted a portrait of a man more spectator than a participant in his life.

"Where did I go wrong?" he asked, his voice piercing the stillness of the night. It wasn't a question of one mistake, though that certainly existed. It was a series of subtle failings, a gradual erosion of the foundations upon which he built his identity.

Once a source of pride, the weight of his professional mantle now pressed down on him with suffocating force. Was each lecture delivered and paper published just desperate bids for validation? And for what? The admiration of students who would soon forget his name, colleagues who knew little of the man behind the accolades.

A bitter laugh escaped him, humourless and self-deprecating. "Some legacy," he scoffed, the words cutting through the air like a knife through the fabric. The irony of it all—a man entrusted to teach history, only to be left behind by its relentless march forward.

Marcus closed his eyes, the darkness behind his lids mirroring the void inside. This moment, this solitary confrontation with his demons, was a crossroads. He could continue down the well-worn path of denial or face the painful truth:

he had become a relic in his own time, a cautionary tale about the cost of unchecked ambition.

"Is this it?" he asked aloud, the query hanging unanswered amidst the towering trees. "Is this all there is?"

But the trees offered no solace, no wisdom to ease the ache of regret. There was only the wind's gentle murmur.

In the silence that followed, Marcus realized that his greatest fear had been realized—not failure itself, but the recognition of failure too late to amend. How many more nights would he spend in fruitless contemplation, wrestling with ghosts of what might have been?

"Enough," he said, declaring to himself and the night. Marcus opened his eyes and started the car. He looked around at the tall pine trees and the deserted road and shifted the car into drive.

Marcus turned the key in the lock, the click of the deadbolt disengaging sounding loud in the quiet of the late hour. He stepped into the darkened house, the familiar scent of aging wood and Julia's lavender air freshener welcoming him—or perhaps accusing, he couldn't be sure anymore. His eyes adjusted to the dimness, noting the silence that blanketed their home. This silence, a companion growing ever more comfortable with its residency, greeted him most nights since his evenings stretched longer at the University.

He removed his coat and hung it at the entrance. Marcus stilled as a soft glow emanated from the study, a sliver of light beneath the door. Curious and without sound, he approached and nudged the door open with the slightest pressure of his fingertips.

There sat Julia, her back to him, her silver hair reflecting the computer screen's pale luminescence. She was hunched over, her posture betraying a concentration so deep that it was as if she was trying to absorb the words through osmosis. On the monitor, a web page lay bare with bold headings: "Understanding Your Eating Disorder" and "Paths to Recovery."

Marcus's throat constricted. A battle was being fought in silence; a private war waged in the still hours of the night, where he was just a spectator, perhaps even an unwitting adversary. The urge to bridge the gap between them, to envelop her in assurances and support, swelled within him.

"Julia," he said, yet she didn't startle—not even a flinch. As though she expected him, or maybe she was too absorbed in her quest for answers to be disturbed.

"Marcus," she said, her voice steady, not turning around. There was a strength there, a resolve he had missed—or chosen not to see—in the daylight hours.

"Is there anything I—" he started, but the sentence hung incomplete, suspended in the shared space.

"No," she said, "I need to do this alone." Her fingers resumed their dance across the keyboard, searching, seeking.

He lingered, watching the woman he knew yet didn't know grappling with secrets that were hers to keep or share. In her silent determination, he saw a reflection of his struggles—his reluctance to face the realities of a life built on shifting sands.

Retreating from the doorway, Marcus left her to the solitude of her research, respecting the boundary she had drawn around herself. He understood boundaries; he lived within them, erected them, and sometimes hid behind them. And in that moment, he respected hers as much as he did his own.

His steps were soft as he withdrew, leaving behind the screen's glow, the soft tap of keys, and a part of himself that yearned to connect, to mend what had frayed between them. In the stillness of their search for meaning, Marcus realized they were both navigating the uncharted territories of their vulnerabilities, each alone, yet somehow together in their isolation.

Marcus stood once more in the shadowy expanse of his backyard, the twilight sky stretching above him. In his hand, a glass of whiskey glinted under the muted glow of the porch light, its amber contents swirling with each subtle shift of his wrist. His eyes lingered on the dormant silhouette of the pool, its surface a mirror to the darkening heavens, concealing what lay below.

He sipped the liquid heat, letting it burn a trail down his throat—a familiar sensation that failed to comfort as it once had. The quiet was punctuated only by the distant hum of the city and the occasional rustle of leaves in the evening breeze. Marcus took a deep breath, tasting the cool air.

Each sip echoed the cyclical nature of his failings. He pondered the repetitive motions of his life—how he circled issues, never addressing them, much like how he now traced the rim of his glass with his index finger. It was a protective dance, a well-rehearsed routine that kept him at arm's length from the raw edges of his emotions.

"Round and round we go," he said into the quiet night. The phrase was a mantra for his life, a summary of his actions—or lack thereof.

The stark reality of his visit to Sheila's house returned to him like an uninvited memory that resonated with the sting of whiskey. He thought of the cash he had handed over, a paltry substitute for presence and guidance. A token gesture when Jamie needed a father who reached across the chasm of years and misunderstandings.

"Is this it?" he asked the empty yard, the stars, and the universe. "Is this all I leave behind?"

No response came save for the slow, steady rhythm of his heart—a reminder that life marched on, indifferent to the minor crises of men. The silence returned to claim him, wrapping around his frame like a cloak.

He took another drink, the whiskey now bitter on his tongue. He wondered if there was redemption in the endless loop of his mistakes. Could he break free and redefine the legacy he would leave, or was he doomed to repeat the same patterns until the end of his days?

As the night grew heavier around him, Marcus remained motionless, a solitary figure wrestling with the ghosts of his past and the uncertainties of his future. There were no easy answers, no magic solutions to untangle the complexities of identity and trust that threaded through his life.

"Tomorrow," he said, the promise hanging in the air, thick with possibility and doubt. "Tomorrow is another day."

Chapter 8

Nicole Dempsey filled two mugs with the dark, aromatic coffee she had just brewed. The steam danced into the air, carrying a rich scent throughout the kitchen. Her partner Corinne sat at the breakfast table, watching Nicole prepare the breakfast while she lightly tapped on the laptop computer that lay open before her.

"French toast okay for you?" Nicole asked as she turned to face Corinne.

"Perfect," Corinne said. "Especially if it comes with your homemade berry compote."

"Coming right up," Nicole said, reaching for the loaf of bread she'd baked the previous afternoon. The knife made a satisfying crunch through the crisp crust as she sliced it into it, revealing the fluffy interior. It was rhythmic work, therapeutic almost, a reminder of the stability she now fostered in every aspect of her life.

"Remember that mess of an apartment I had when we first met?" Nicole said, dipping the bread slices into an egg and cinnamon mixture.

Corinne smiled, the memories flooding back. "How could I forget? You've come so far since then, and you've lived a long life already for someone who's just twenty-six."

"I never thought I'd be someone who finds joy in making breakfast, of all things," Nicole confessed, placing the soaked bread onto the sizzling skillet. It began to brown and fill the room with its sweet scent. "I used to live off of the worst cereals when I was a kid.

"Life's funny like that," Corinne said, sipping her coffee. "You find happiness in the smallest of rituals."

"Small rituals... but big changes," Nicole said, flipping the French toast. She placed the golden-brown pieces, drizzling them with the vibrant red compote she had prepared from the season's berries. Every action was precise, reflecting the order she now held dear.

"Here you go," Nicole said, setting down the plate in front of Corinne, who looked up with warmth in her eyes. They shared a smile, a silent acknowledgement of the tranquillity surrounding them.

"Thank you," Corinne said, cutting into the French toast, the fork sinking through the layers. "This is delicious enough to be served in a fancy café."

"Who needs a café when you have a private chef?". She was grounded, rooted in something real and tangible, far removed from the turbulence of her earlier years.

They ate in silence, the kind only found between two people at ease with one another. The occasional scrape of cutlery against plates, the soft hum of the refrigerator, and the distant chirping of morning birds created a symphony of normalcy.

"Days like these," Corinne said after a moment, pausing to meet Nicole's gaze, "they're what life's about, aren't they?"

Nicole nodded, "yeah, they are," she said, a profound sense of gratitude washing over her. This was her present, her future—a life founded on trust and identity, no longer over-shadowed by anger and loss.

Nicole rested her elbows on the cool marble of the kitchen counter, cradling the mug between her hands. The gentle warmth seeped into her palms as Corinne entered the bedroom to dress for the day. Sunlight filtered through the sheer curtains, casting a soft glow over the room, and Nicole found herself lost in the stillness that stretched before her.

She turned her attention back inside to the empty plates that bore the remnants of their breakfast, the delicate scent of coffee still lingering in the air. It struck her how these mundane details stitched together the fabric of her newfound stability.

"Nic?" Corinne's voice floated from the other room, light and questioning.

"Right here," Nicole said, her voice steady, betraying none of the introspection that churned within her.

The thought of motherhood had been a distant whisper, quickly silenced by the clamour of her past. But here, in the sanctuary they'd built, the whisper had grown insistent, demanding to be heard. Nicole sipped her coffee, considering the prospect with reverence and trepidation.

She knew that nurturing a life would challenge the essence of who she had become. Her independence was hard-won; could it coexist with the vulnerability of motherhood? Yet, there was Corinne—her support structure and love- an unwavering constant.

"Everything okay?" Corinne emerged her presence a reas-suring balm to Nicole's spiralling thoughts.

"Yup," Nicole said, allowing a smile to touch her lips. Yet, within the confines of her mind, she grappled with the intricacies of adding another layer to her identity, one that per-haps would redefine her existence altogether.

Motherhood wasn't just about bringing forth life; it was a surrender, a reshaping of oneself. Would a child be able to drown out the ghosts of her past? Could she offer guidance when she was navigating through the fog?

"It's a beautiful day, isn't it?" Corinne joined Nicole at the counter, following her gaze out the window.

"Beautiful," Nicole echoed, her eyes fixed on the horizon where the sky met the cityscape. She saw the years stretching out like an endless canvas, possibilities painted in strokes of uncertainty and hope. Motherhood? The word hung in her heart, a pendulum swinging between fear and longing.

"Hey," Corinne said, reaching for Nicole's hand, "Wher-ever you are, I'm with you." Nicole's grip tightened around Corinne's hand, anchoring her to the moment. "I know," she said, acknowledging that they would face it together what-ever the future held.

In a room at the other end of the city, Jamie's eyelids flut-tered against the pale light seeping through the cracks of the blinds, casting a lattice shadow over the bedroom's disarray. The air was heavy, tinged with the scent of muskiness of unwashed linen. He groaned, his mind churning through the fog that clung to his consciousness.

"Here, take this," Sheila said, her voice grounded in the haze. She held a glass of water in one hand and two small pills in the other, her palm steady.

His fingers brushed against hers as he took the offering, the contact steadying the spinning room. The medication went down with a gulp. "Better?" she asked, tucking a stray lock of hair behind her ear as she watched him.

"Mmm," Jamie said noncommittally. His gaze drifted across the room: clothes strewn about, stacks of unpaid bills teetering on the brink. This was his life, and in the center of it all, Sheila—his anchor or perhaps his albatross.

"Jamie," she said, her hand resting on his shoulder, kneading the knots of tension with a tenderness that disguised her frustration. "You can't keep doing this to yourself."

"I know," he said. A knot formed in his throat, guilt mingling with the dregs of last night's poison still coursing through his veins.

"Then why—" Sheila asked, but the question hung incomplete, suspended in the space between them. It was an old dance they had performed too many times.

"Because it's not so easy," Jamie said, a flash of anger cutting through the lethargy. "You think I don't want to change?"

Sheila recoiled, a wounded look flashing across her features. "I'm here for you," she said, her voice softer now, "but you have to want to help yourself."

He looked at her, seeing beyond the caretaker to the woman who had seen him at his worst and yet stayed. Her presence was both a salvation and a reminder of how far he had fallen. Dependency had woven itself into the fabric of their relationship. The thread pulled tight whenever he tried to move away from her or towards something resembling a better version of himself.

"Thank you," he said, reaching out to trace the back of her hand with a fingertip. It was an apology, an admission, a plea—all wrapped into a small gesture that might have been lost.

"Let's just get through today," she said, her tone implying a challenge—a challenge to break the cycle, even if they could only manage to bend it.

"I'll try," Jamie said, knowing tomorrow was a word too fraught with hope to speak aloud. Instead, he focused on the now, the simple act of sitting up in bed, Sheila's hand supporting his back, guiding him into the day—one precarious step at a time.

Jamie sat on the edge of the bed, his fingers fumbling with the buttons on his shirt, a remnant of an ironed past now wrinkled by nights of uneasy sleep. Sheila stood behind him, her hands reaching over to correct his misaligned efforts. Her tender touch sent a shiver down his spine.

"Here, let me," she said, her voice a blend of exasperation and warmth. As she fastened each button, her presence enveloped him in a comforting and intoxicating fragrance. It was a routine filled with unspoken dialogues and the heavy breath of their interdependence.

"Thanks," Jamie said, though the word hung between them. It was a token of gratitude and a subtle acknowledgment of his shortcomings.

"Look at you," Sheila said with a half-smile, smoothing the creases on his shoulders. "Almost presentable." But her eyes betrayed the jest—there was concern there and something more, a fiery undercurrent that masked the maternal facade.

"Almost," he echoed, standing to face her. Their gazes locked, and they had a silent conversation where lines blurred—caregiver, lover, enabler, confidant. They shared a bond soldered by years of navigating Jamie's psyche, each turn revealing shadows and light in unpredictable measures.

With a final adjustment to his collar, Sheila stepped back. He took a deep breath, bracing himself against the day's uncertainties. The weight of his dependence on her was tangible pressure against his chest.

"Ready?" she asked, though they both knew readiness was a state Jamie hadn't felt in years.

"As ready as I'll ever be," he said, feigning a confidence that he hoped might one day materialize into existence.

Across town, Nicole sat among a circle of her peers, the hum of intellectual exchange filling the seminar room. She leaned forward, elbows on the table, her expression focused on engagement as she listened to the discussion. When her turn came, her voice did not waver; she spoke with clarity, weaving her thoughts into the academic discourse.

"Consider the protagonist's journey not just as a physical one but as an allegory for the internal struggle toward self-acceptance," she posited, her words flowing easily despite carrying the weight of her introspections.

The group nodded, some jotting notes, others arguing or preparing their counterpoints. Nicole had found a semblance of purpose here, away from the turmoil of her familial discord. Each class and interaction was a brick on the path to reconstructing a life derailed by years of emotional turbulence.

"Very insightful, Nicole," praised the professor, bringing her a sense of achievement that eclipsed her inner grief. Within these walls, she could pretend to be whole, untouched by the scar's life had etched on her soul.

Nicole glanced around the classroom as the students clustered in small groups, their youthful energy palpable in their eager discussions. Despite the engaging nature of the debate, a subtle dissonance hummed in her ears, a reminder that she was out of sync with this world, a visitor reclaiming lost time.

"Hey, Nicole, what's your take on this?" asked a bright-eyed student, snapping her back from her musings. She offered her perspective, her voice steady, but her fingers entwined and twisted with a nervous energy beneath the table.

"Thanks, Nicole. You always bring such a... mature approach," the student said with a smile that bordered on reverence, or maybe it was pity. The word 'mature' clung to Nicole like a scarlet letter.

Her gaze drifted to the corner of the room where a couple of male students lingered, casting occasional glances her way. Their looks carried an unspoken invitation that stirred within her a turmoil of conflicted desires and the stark remembrance of a past riddled with missteps in love.

"Are you joining us for drinks later?" one of them asked, his question laced with an interest that strayed beyond academic bounds.

"Maybe another time," Nicole deflected with a practiced ease, though part of her yearned for the simplicity of flirtation without consequence, a luxury her complex identity could seldom afford.

On the industrial side of town, Jamie's silhouette cut a lonely figure against the city's backdrop, his steps aimless as he sidestepped the morning bustle that swirled around him. Work had been a sliver of purpose, but today, it was like a noose tightening around a neck brimming with silent screams.

The bar he stumbled upon was an oasis of solitude amidst the chaos, its darkened interior offering a haven for the restless souls seeking refuge from the relentless glare of daylight realities. As he pushed open the door, the familiar scent enveloped him, an embrace that promised forgetfulness, however fleeting.

He settled onto a bar stool and waved away the menu offer. A glass of something substantial, something to dull the edges of consciousness—that was all he needed. The bartender obliged with an understanding nod, pouring a drink with the solemnity of a priest administering communion.

Jamie wrapped his fingers around the glass, the cool surface anchoring him to the present. But even as the liquid fire trickled down his throat, he couldn't shake the pervasive restlessness that had become his constant companion. It gnawed at him, a hunger for something undefined and perhaps unattainable—a longing for clarity in a life blurred by dependency and doubt.

Jamie's hand trembled as it ventured into the worn leather folds of his wallet, bypassing crumpled bills and expired cards to extract a photograph so frequently handled that its edges had softened to the texture of the fabric. His gaze lingered on the faces frozen in time—smiles that belied the fractures that would later splinter their family tree. He traced a finger over the image, pausing at his youthful face, unaware of the shadows that would claim his adulthood.

"Hey, man, you all right?" The voice cut through Jamie's reverie, its tone not unkind.

"Fine," he said, tucking the relic back into its hiding place, away from prying eyes he could never understand.

The door swung open, admitting a slant of light slicing through the bar's dimness. Nicole stepped inside, her eyes adjusting to the darkness. She scanned the room. She found him in the far corner: Jamie—a lone figure stranded on an island of solitude.

"Jamie..." Her voice was both a question and a lifeline as she approached.

He didn't look up, but the tightening of his shoulders betrayed his recognition of her presence. Nicole pulled out the chair opposite him, the metal legs scraping in reluctant protest. She waited for him to lift his eyes, to find in hers the same concern that had interrupted her class and had driven her here after Sheila's worried call.

"Nic," he said. It was enough to bridge the chasm of silence between them. They were siblings, bound by blood and their shared pasts—a past that clung to them like the residue of dreams upon waking.

Nicole reached out, her fingers brushing against the cold glass of Jamie's drink. His hand was a barrier, arresting her advance with a simple gesture.

"Jamie," she started, her tone a careful balance of concern and respect for his autonomy, "you can't keep doing this to yourself."

He met her gaze, his eyes weathered like driftwood, carrying the marks of storms weathered alone. "This is nothing new, Nic. You know that."

"Maybe," she conceded, pulling back her hand to fold it in her lap, "but it doesn't mean it's good for you." Her words were soft but laced with an iron resolve born from years of navigating the minefield of their family's love and turmoil.

Jamie snorted, a wry smile twisting his lips as he looked away. "What's good for us, huh? Did we ever really know?"

She sighed, the sound heavy with echoes of past arguments. "It's not about knowing, Jamie. It's about trying to understand it together." She leaned in, emphasizing the last word as if it could ward off the demons they both fought.

"Like Marcus?" Jamie's voice was suddenly sharp, and the mention of their father was a splinter under the skin. "Is he 'understanding it,' too? Buried under his books and papers, pretending we don't exist?"

"Actually," Nicole hesitated, weighing the impact of her next words, "it's mom I'm more worried about." Her voice dropped, carrying the weight of a secret shared. "She's not eating right, Jamie. I think it's getting serious."

His reaction was like a shuttered window, closing off at the mention of their mother's struggle. "She's always been good at hiding things, even from herself."

"Isn't that our family's legacy?" Nicole countered, her heart aching at the thought of their mother's pain. "We're experts at pretending everything's fine, even when it's breaking us apart."

Jamie's mouth twisted into a grimace, and he reached for the glass only to let his fingers dance around it again. "Can we not do this, Nic? Can we not dig up all this old shit today?"

Nicole wanted to press, open the facade, and reach the brother drowning beneath the surface. But she recognized the plea in his eyes.

"Okay, Jamie," she nodded, though her promise was based on the understanding that this conversation was postponed. "But we're going to have to face it. All of it."

"Eventually," he echoed, the word lingering between them like the last note of a song long since played.

Nicole paid the bill and managed to get Jamie out of the bar. She asked him to get in the car, but he insisted on walking. As Nicole drove away, she watched Jamie in the rearview mirror, hoping, as she always did, that this wouldn't be the last time she saw her brother.

Nicole turned the key in the lock and stepped into her home. It was late, and the conversation with Jamie had left a residue of unease that clung to her. She shrugged off her coat and tossed it over the back of a kitchen chair before making her way through the soft glow of the living room.

Corinne sat curled on the couch, an open book resting against her knees. Her eyes were not on the page; they were watching the doorway, waiting. Corinne gazed at Nicole, unravelling the knotted thoughts within her.

"Hey," Nicole said, her voice softer than she intended.

"Hey yourself," Corinne said, closing the book and marking the page with her finger. "How'd it go?"

"Same dance, different day." Nicole sighed, sinking onto the cushion beside her. "Jamie... he's just so locked up inside himself."

Corinne reached out, her hand warm as it enveloped Nicole's. "You can't force him, Nic. You've always been the one trying to fix things."

"Maybe that's my problem," Nicole said, turning her hand to lace her fingers through Corinne's. "I'm always trying to mend what's broken—my family, myself... even thinking about being a mother again, it's like I'm reaching for some kind of redemption."

"Is that what you think motherhood is? Redemption?" Corinne asked, her thumb stroking the back of Nicole's hand.

"Isn't it? A chance to do it right this time, to give someone the life I never had?" Nicole's eyes met Corinne's, searching, pleading for understanding.

"Motherhood isn't about righting past wrongs, Nicole. It's about love, pure and imperfect. And you have that in spades." Corinne's voice was steady, a lighthouse in Nicole's fog of doubt.

"Love wasn't enough for my mother. What if it's not enough for me?" The words tumbled from Nicole's lips, raw and unguarded.

"Your mother's choices aren't yours. You know that." Corinne shifted, leaning closer, her presence a tangible comfort. "You're not your past, honey. You're the woman who survived and found her way through it. That strength, that's what will make you an incredible mother—if that's what you want."

"I do want it," Nicole confessed, her resolve solidifying with the confession. "But I'm terrified. Terrified I'll fail, terrified I'll lose myself, terrified I'll..."

"Shh." Corinne pressed a gentle kiss to Nicole's forehead. "Fear is part of it, part of anything worth doing. But you won't face it alone. I'm here with you for every step, the good and the bad."

"Even when I'm a mess?" Nicole asked, though the tremor in her voice betrayed her vulnerability.

"Especially then." Corinne smiled, radiant and reassuring. "We're a team, remember? Your mess is my mess."

"I'm not sure you know what you're getting into," Nicole said, leaning into the embrace that followed. In Corinne's arms, she found the courage to hope, to dream, and perhaps to trust in the love that promised a future unfettered by the shadows of yesterday.

Jamie's hand trembled on the brass doorknob, a chill from the metal seeping into his bones. The door creaked open, announcing his return more loudly than he would have liked. He stepped over the threshold, his heart thrumming like a trapped bird eager to escape.

"Jamie?" Sheila's voice sliced through the silence of the hallway.

He found her in the living room, perched on the edge of their worn-out couch, lamplight casting shadows across her face that danced with the flicker of her emotions—relief at his return warring with the lines of frustration etching her brow.

"Where were you?" she said.

"I needed some air," Jamie said, avoiding the question in her eyes as he shuffled past. His gaze was fixed on a loose thread in the carpet.

"Air," she said, echoing his excuse. "You missed your appointment, Jamie."

"I know." He stopped, the admission hanging between them like a thick fog. The concern in Sheila's eyes was familiar, a constant reminder of the intricate web they had woven together—their dependency, a shared shroud enveloping them both.

"Sit down," she said, patting the space beside her. Her maternal tone made Jamie bristle, even as he obeyed.

As he sank into the cushions, Sheila reached out, her fingers tracing the contours of his tired face. "You can't keep doing this to yourself or me."

"Sorry," he said, but the word was empty, a placeholder for the myriad of things he wished he could articulate.

"Are you?" she asked, probing deeper than the surface-level apologies they traded like currency in moments of weakness.

"Nicole came to see me," he confessed, unaware that it had been at Sheila's insistence. "She thinks I'm losing it."

"Are you?" Sheila pressed, her palm now resting on his knee.

"Maybe," Jamie said.

"Jamie, look at me." Sheila's command was soft but insistent. He lifted his eyes to meet hers, pools of earnest worry reflecting at him. "I love you, but I can't keep doing this if you are determined to fail."

"Why do you keep helping me then?" His question hung suspended in the air, a note of despair threading through the honesty.

"Because I Love you, Jamie, but I can't keep doing this alone," she said, her voice cracking with the burden of their truth.

"I know," he said, "I know what I'm doing isn't fair to you. And i know your working on your own shit. I want to be a good person for you."

"Let's try, Jamie. For us," she implored, her hand squeezing his.

"Okay," he said. It wasn't the first time they'd made such pacts, but as Sheila leaned into him, her head finding a familiar rest on his shoulder, Jamie felt the faint stirrings of something akin to hope—or perhaps just the courage to confront the tide together.

Nicole's fingertips traced the edges of an old family photo; the colours faded to a soft palette with time's relentless passage. It was tucked away in her study—a room lined with books that told stories of other lives, other dreams. She sat at her desk alone, the silence punctuating the end of a day that had stretched and twisted with familial tension.

"Look at us," she said, studying the faces frozen in feigned happiness. Her younger self smiled back, a smile that didn't quite reach her eyes. The innocence she once carried was like a garment long outgrown, shed alongside the chaos of her past.

A sigh escaped her, not of regret but of recognition—the acknowledgment of each scar and triumph that mapped her journey from that snapshot to now. In the stillness, Nicole could almost hear the echoes of the laughter and cries that had filled the spaces of her life. She leaned back in her chair, eyes never leaving the photograph as she let the weight of her reflection settle around her.

The study was her sanctuary. Here, Nicole surveyed the distance she had covered. It was more than just years or miles; it was the expanse between who she was and who she had become. Nicole turned the photo over in her hands, her gaze settling on the words scribbled on the back—a date, a location, a memory's title. It was a chapter closed; its lessons etched into the marrow of her bones.

"Here's to new chapters," she said, her resolve thickening. She returned the photo to the drawer and closed it with a soft click that seemed to echo through the room.

She rose from the desk, the movement fluid and certain. In the mirror across the room, Nicole caught a glimpse of herself—the contours of her face illuminated by determination, the set of her shoulders squared against a world that had tried to break her.

"Here's to hope," she said, a true and steadfast smile playing on her lips.

This moment, quiet and potent, solidified her resolve. Once trapped by the tumult of her lineage, Nicole Dempsey stood clear-eyed and steadfast, ready to weave the dreams of tomorrow with the threads of a hard-won today.

Jamie's fingers traced the grain of the wooden porch railing, a tactile reminder of the solidity he sought within himself. The night air was cool against his skin, whispering through the messy strands of his hair as he leaned back into the creaking embrace of an old rocking chair. Above, the indifferent sprawl of stars gazed down upon him—silent witnesses to the quiet turmoil churning inside.

He drew a deep breath, holding it for a moment before releasing it slowly as if trying to expel the doubt that had settled in his chest alongside the evening chill. Sheila slept inside, her gentle snoring audible through the open door. Her rest was fitful—her brow would furrow, lips parting on silent words—but it was more peace than Jamie knew for himself.

"Dependency," he said. Dependency on pills that promised equilibrium but delivered fog. Dependency on Sheila, whose hands were both cradle and cage. Dependency on a past that clung to him with the tenacity of shadows at dusk.

The possibility of change was as distant as the constellations above. Yet, nestled within that expanse of darkness, a flicker of desire burned—the willingness to stand on his own, to break free from the ropes that bound him. How often had he envisioned a life unmarred by the need for chemical solace? A life where trust wasn't a commodity between wary souls but something as natural as breathing?

"Can I?" he said to the night, a sad echo that begged for an answer.

"Can I be different?"

"I have to change," he said louder this time, testing the words, rolling them around on his tongue like a new flavour, one that could wash away the years of bitterness. "I want... I need to change."

His gaze drifted to his hands. They were hands that could still shape a future if only he believed in their power. Jamie clenched them into fists, his resolve hardening amidst the fear.

"Tomorrow," he said, a vow cast into the void. "Tomorrow, I start over."

In the silence that followed, Jamie allowed himself the luxury of dreaming—of a life reclaimed, a self-restored. There was no grand epiphany, no sudden shedding of all that weighed him down. Instead, there was a slow, dawning recognition that the path to redemption was paved with small, deliberate steps.

Part 3

1993

Chapter 9

Marcus blinked open his eyes, the morning light piercing through the curtains with an almost accusatory glare. It took him a few seconds to gather himself, his mind piecing together the remnants of last night's faculty gathering. He rolled onto his side with effort, noting Julia's chest's rhythmic rise and fall as she lay beside him. Her sleep was undisturbed, peaceful in a way that was alien to him.

The bathroom tiles were cold against his feet, contrasting the warmth of the bed he had left behind. The shower sputtered to life, spilling over him in a cascade that did little to wash away the grogginess or the latent guilt that clung to him like a second skin. He dressed, choosing a tie without seeing it, his thoughts already on the day ahead.

"Julia," Marcus said as he stepped back into their bedroom. She stirred, and her eyes opened to regard him with a detachment that had become all too familiar.

"Morning," she said, the corners of her lips twitching upwards in an effort at warmth. "What are your plans today?" Marcus asked.

"Three showings," she said, pushing herself into a sitting position. Her hair fell around her face in waves, framing a face that, at the age of forty-two, still held a striking beauty. "I'll be busy. What about you?"

" I'm meeting Richard for a drink after work," Marcus said, the words sticking in his throat. "I want to bounce some ideas off him... about the book."

At the mention of the book, Julia's expression shifted, her facade slipping to reveal a flicker of impatience. "That thing," she scoffed, though there was an edge to her voice that couldn't be mistaken. "When will you ever make any progress on it?"

Her question hung in the air, with years of unfulfilled promises and expectations. It stung Marcus, the subtle accusation that she didn't have to voice for him to hear loud and clear. But he turned away, leaving the room without a word, the silence between them speaking volumes more than any conversation could.

He closed the door behind him, the dull thud signifying the physical barrier and the emotional distance that had crept into their marriage. The space where trust and identity once blossomed was now a breeding ground for doubt and regret. As Marcus walked down the hallway, he understood that loss was not just an event but a process unfolding quietly within the walls of what once was a home.

Marcus stepped out onto the pool deck; his hands wrapped around the warm ceramic of his coffee mug. The morning sun cast a soft glow over the water, dotted with reflections that danced across the surface. But the tranquillity of the scene was marred by the litter of beer cans strewn about—evidence of Jamie or Nicole's late-night exploits. With a furrowed brow, Marcus muttered a curse under his breath. As much as he wanted to attribute the mess to youthful indiscretion, it reminded him of the widening gap between him and his children.

He set his coffee down on the wrought-iron table and unfolded the newspaper, the black-and-white print stark against the bright colours of the morning. The headlines screamed of tension and conflict: "Day 40: Waco Siege Continues" and "Rodney King Assault: Civil Trial for Police." He scanned the articles, his eyes tracing over each word, but the stories were distant, disconnected from the quiet chaos of his own life. Eventually, he placed the paper aside, taking a moment to savour his coffee.

With a deep exhalation, he stood up, resigned to the day ahead. He crossed the deck, leaving behind the remnants of adolescent rebellion and national turmoil, and went to work. He grabbed his briefcase and headed for the door, not bothering to check on Nicole or Jamie, who would no doubt be late for school again.

He had a full day of lectures, only broken up by office hours, during which he tried to calm the nerves of students who were stressed out about assignments and exams. Later, seated in the orderly chaos of his office, surrounded by stacks of papers and books, Marcus was the image of academic dedication. The door swung open without warning, and Richard strode in, the picture of casual confidence.

"Finished with your lectures for the day?" Richard asked, leaning against the doorframe.

"Yes," Marcus said, setting down his red pen. A slight relief washed over him at the prospect of escape.

"Let's head to the pub then," Richard said with an ease that Marcus envied. His colleague was untouched by the burdens that weighed on Marcus's shoulders.

"Alright," he said, rising from his chair. It wasn't the thought of the drink that enticed him, but rather the opportunity to step outside the boundaries of his strained silences at home and the expectations of his professional life. The pub would be where he could pretend that the fragments of his existence fit together seamlessly.

The two men walked side by side through the university hallways, their footsteps echoing off the walls like the ticking of a clock marking time—time spent, time wasted, and time running out.

Marcus settled into the worn leather booth and took in the pub, constantly abuzz with youth and aspiration. "Are you still nursing that book of yours?" Richard's voice broke through the hum, tinged with a friendly yet pointed curiosity. He leaned back, one arm draped over the top of the booth, his eyes fixed on Marcus, and his brow tilted.

"Ah, the book," Marcus said, the corners of his mouth twitching into a semblance of a smile. There was no escaping this topic with Richard. "It's like Sisyphus and his boulder; I make some progress, then life rolls it back down."

"Ten years, Marcus." Richard's tone softened, but the undercurrent of challenge remained. "What's getting in the way?"

"Family," Marcus said, his gaze drifting past Richard to a group of students laughing over pints. Their worries were brief, their joys simple—a stark contrast to the complex web of responsibilities and expectations that ensnared him.

"Family can be... demanding," Richard conceded, sipping from his glass, the rich amber liquid capturing the dim light. "How are they, by the way? I always thought you were the picture of the perfect American family."

"Perfect?" Marcus let out a short laugh. It was easy to believe in perfection when peering from the outside. "Nicole and Jamie, they're..." He paused, searching for words that could encompass the tumultuous tides of teenage angst, "giving me the usual teenage grief."

"Teenagers, eh?" Richard nodded, though his life's choices had steered him clear of such familial complexities.

"Perfect is a myth, my friend." Marcus cut in.

Richard regarded him for a moment, his expression unreadable. Then, nodding, he raised his glass in a silent toast to unseen struggles and unspoken truths. They drank, each lost in contemplation, as the pub continued its lively dance around them.

The door of the pub swung open, admitting a cool draft that cut through the warm fug of conversation and laughter. Marcus glanced up—a reflex honed from years of watching bustling lecture halls—and found himself locking gazes with two familiar faces. They were young and carefree; their presence seemed to pull the light towards them, casting the rest of the room in a comparative pallor.

"Professor Dempsey!" Courtney's voice rose above the bar's hum as she waved, her smile bright and expectant.

Beside her, Kate mirrored the gesture, a hint of practiced coyness in her demeanour. They navigated the maze of tables and chairs, a fluid dance of youthful grace contrasting Marcus's sure movements.

"Mind if we join you?" Kate asked, her tone suggesting it was less of a question and more of a pleasant formality. Richard shot Marcus a look of weariness and a touch of sardonic amusement before nodding assent.

"Please," Marcus gestured to the empty chairs, the veneer of his professorial charm in place despite the internal disquiet their presence stirred.

They settled into the seats across from the men, all long limbs and eager energy. Marcus noted how students around them gave the girls a wide berth of admiration or envy. At the same time, his reputation as a distinguished professor afforded him a similar, though more respectful, space.

"Have you been watching the Waco siege on TV?" Courtney leaned forward, her eyes alight with curiosity, seeking out his thoughts as if they were the keynotes for an impending exam.

"Only the news reports," Marcus said, flicking back to the grainy footage of the grim standoffs broadcast for the world to see. "But television can't capture the full complexity of a situation like that."

"Kate thinks Koresh is cute" Courtney said, glancing at Kate for affirmation.

"Koresh is a dangerous man," Marcus said, the historian in him refusing to allow the quip to pass unchallenged. "Cute" was not a term used to describe zealots with messianic delusions. "And the government's response... it could fuel the fire rather than extinguish it."

"Really?" Kate's brow furrowed, her expression a mixture of confusion and intrigue. "But he has so many followers. They seem so devoted."

"Devotion is a double-edged sword," Marcus said, the weight of his words hanging heavy between them. "Especially when it's wielded by those who know how to exploit it."

Courtney nodded; her lips pursed as she processed this new perspective. Emotions played across her face, the earnest desire to understand, to dissect the world just as they dissected the events and figures of European history within his classroom walls.

"History is made by those who seize upon unrest," he said, sensing the pull of his pulpit. "It's a lesson worth remembering, far more than any transient media spectacle."

As they talked, their laughter mingled with the ambient sounds of the pub—a reminder that despite the gravity of the world beyond these walls, life persisted in its myriad, undulating rhythms.

The murmur of conversation ebbed as Richard leaned forward, the earnestness in his voice cutting through the din. "So, what do you think about this World Wide Web thing they're launching? It's meant to be quite the revolution."

Courtney and Kate exchanged a glance that spoke volumes of their indifference. "Seems complicated," Kate said with a nonchalant shrug, her attention flickering to a passing waiter.

"Complicated, maybe," Richard countered, his eyes alight with the enthusiasm of someone who has glimpsed the future. "But it will change everything—how we learn and connect. It's history unfolding before us."

"Speaking of history," he said, seizing the lull, "Marcus here is writing a book. Aren't you, Marcus?"

Both girls perked up at that, their youthful faces turning toward him like sunflowers to the sun. "Really?" Kate's interest was piqued, her previous apathy forgotten. "What's it about?"

Marcus cleared his throat, suddenly self-conscious. "It's an analysis of European history, tracing the threads of societal collapse and resurgence," he said. "Much like what we discuss in class."

"Can we read it?" Courtney asked, leaning in, her eyes bright with curiosity.

"It's not finished yet," he said. But Kate pressed on.

"Even so, I'd love to see what you've got."

The night had worn on, the edges of reality softened by the warm glow of alcohol. Laughter had come quickly, and time had slipped away unnoticed. Marcus bid farewell to Richard and the girls and was about to slip away when Kate's voice caught him.

"Professor Dempsey?" Her figure materialized under the campus streetlights. "Could I... could I see your office? Where do you write?"

The request hung between them, and for a moment, Marcus hesitated. The quiet around them seemed to pulse with potential, with the threat of decisions made and consequences yet unseen.

"Please," she said, her voice soft but insistent, her eyes searching his.

Marcus surveyed the empty campus paths, each a silent witness to what might pass. "Alright," he conceded, betraying the turmoil beneath his composed exterior.

As they walked, Marcus felt the gravity of his choices and the loss of alignment between the man he was in public and the one behind closed doors. In the distance, the university clock tower tolled, marking the hour and the fragility of trust, the erosion of identity, and the ever-present spectre of loss.

Marcus unlocked the door to his office. The room was a sanctuary cluttered with books that chronicled thoughts of bygone eras—his silent, constant companions. He flicked on the light, and Kate stepped in behind him, her eyes wide with reverence and curiosity.

"Wow, it's like a library in here," she said, running her fingers along the spines of the books before bouncing onto the worn couch. Her gaze settled on the cluttered desk, an island amidst a sea of academic chaos.

"Is that where the magic happens?" she asked, pointing at the papers across the mahogany surface.

"Magic," Marcus echoed dryly. "Something like that." He retrieved the stack of pages that formed the skeleton of his book, the weight of each unfinished chapter, and handed it to her.

Kate perched herself on the edge of his desk, flipping through the manuscript with an eagerness that reminded Marcus of his younger self. She cleared her throat and began miming one of his lectures, her voice an exaggerated version of his own.

"History is not only a series of events but a tapestry woven from the threads of human experience," she intoned, and Marcus couldn't help but laugh, a genuine sound he hadn't heard from himself in some time.

"Professor Dempsey, tell me," she said, setting the pages down and peering at him with a teasing glint in her eye. "Do people your age—married couples—do they still...you know?"

The air thickened, and the question hung between them like a dare. "Priorities change," he said, knowing the evasion for what it was—a shield against truths he wasn't prepared to face.

"Change," she said, sliding off the desk and closing the distance between them. Her movements were fluid and purposeful as she stood before him, her hands finding the hem of her skirt. With a playful flick, she reached down and removed her panties. She twirled them around her finger and flung them towards him.

"Kate—" Marcus felt discomfort and something else—a dangerous thrill—warring within him.

"Tell me you've never thought about it," she said. "I've never been with a published author."

"I'm not a published author," he countered weakly, the protest hollow even to his ears.

"Yet," she said, stepping closer, her belief shining in her eyes. "But you will be, Marcus. I believe in you."

Her confidence, so stark against his doubts, left him rooted to the couch, caught in the gravity of a moment that had spiraled beyond his control.

Kate's advance was deliberate, a dance of temptation that played out in the dim light of Marcus's office. She stepped forward, her eyes locked onto his. The air between them crackled with an electric tension as she straddled his lap, her hands finding the buckle of his belt with an ease that spoke of unspoken fantasies.

"Marcus," she said, her voice a velvet touch against his ear, "you look so tired; what's wrong." Her fingers worked at releasing his constraints, her movements both invasive and intimate. As she slid down onto him, he was lost in the paradox of desire and despair.

"Everyone deserves some happiness," she said, her hips finding a rhythm that drew a sharp breath from him.

He closed his eyes, shaking his head slowly. "No... some people don't deserve that," he said, his voice ragged, a confession to himself more than to her. It was the mantra of his guilt, the creed of his self-imposed penance.

But her hands cradled his head now, pulling him against her chest as if she could absorb his pain and offer absolution with the sinuous movements of her body. Marcus's hands gripped her back, his touch desperate, seeking solace in the warmth of her skin.

"You're sadness... where does it come from," she said, her lips brushing his temple. "Let me be your escape, just for tonight."

His protest died in his throat, replaced by a raw, primal need to feel something other than the void that had become his life. He buried his face against her, inhaling the scent of youth and recklessness, a stark contrast to the stagnant air of regret that had filled his lungs for too long.

Time slipped away, reduced to the rise and fall of breaths and bodies, until Kate finally disentangled herself from him, leaving behind a silence that pressed against his ears like a warning. She got up and looked around the room again. "Maybe that will inspire you to finish your book. See you in class tomorrow, Marcus."

The office door clicked shut, and Marcus sat alone on the couch, his hands trembling as he fumbled with his clothes. He reached for the bottle, its contents sloshing a familiar cadence as he poured the amber liquid into a glass as fragile as his composure.

He surveyed his life—a realm of leather-bound books and papers marked with red, a once proud bastion of academia now a witness to his unravelling. Memories of a time when his professional accolades mirrored a harmonious personal life taunted him, the reflections of a man he hardly recognized anymore.

With a sudden fury, he hurled the glass across the room, its shattering a sharp exclamation point to his inner turmoil. It was a breaking, not only of crystal against the wall but of the dam within him that had held back a torrent of anguish.

As the shards settled, Marcus dropped his head into his hands, the sobs that wracked him echoing off the walls. They were the sounds of a man confronting the chasm between the identity he presented to the world and the truth he harboured within—a dichotomy of existence that had become his prison.

Chapter 10

Julia's eyes opened to the digital glow of the bedside clock; its sharp and insistent numbers pierced the room's darkness: 4:00 AM. She turned towards Marcus's side of the bed, her hand reaching out across the cool, empty sheets. He wasn't there. A sigh escaped her lips as she curled back into herself, her gaze fixed on the ceiling. Sleep had become an elusive companion.

The kitchen was silent as Julia cradled the warmth of her coffee mug. Each sip was a small comfort against the morning's chill, but it did little to soothe the gnawing unease within her. The door opened with a creak, and Marcus stumbled in, his broad-shouldered frame casting a slumped shadow across the floor.

"Marcus," she said, her voice steady despite the tremor inside. His bloodshot eyes met hers, ringed with the telltale signs of a night drowned in alcohol.

"Hello, Julia." His words were thick, struggling against the hangover that held them down.

Julia drew in a breath as he neared, the air mingling with a scent that clawed at her senses—sweet and youthful perfume clung to him like a second skin. Her heart tightened, a knot of suspicion rooting itself within her chest.

"Rough night?" she asked, hoping her words would cut through the haze that enveloped him, revealing the truth that lay beneath.

He nodded, running a hand through his hair, futilely attempting to bring order to the disarray. "Yeah, a rough one," he said, though his tone skirted the edges of confession and deflection.

She longed for a glimmer of the man she once knew, a man whose charm had masked the turmoil that now seemed to spill from him in waves. Silence stretched between them, laden with questions unasked and answers ungiven.

Julia returned to her coffee, the bitterness on her tongue reflecting the growing void within her. The scent of strange perfume returned as a ghostly reminder of all that had been lost.

Julia's voice struck a dissonant chord as she faced him, her posture rigid with resolve. "Where have you been, Marcus?" The question's simplicity belied the complexity of suspicion that clouded her eyes.

"Out with Richard," Marcus said, his voice an unsteady hum. "I didn't make it home; I slept at the office." There was an attempt at casual dismissal in his tone, but it faltered under Julia's unwavering gaze.

"Sleeping? Or something else?" The accusation hung in the air between them, a tangible presence. Her nostrils flared as she inhaled, confirming the lingering scent that betrayed more than words could hide. "You reek of perfume. It's a young woman's scent. Don't think I can't tell."

"Your imagination is dangerous, Julia." He flashed a worn smile, an old defence mechanism that now failed to charm.

"Imagination has nothing to do with this." She crossed her arms as if bracing herself against the chill of his evasion.

"Look how we've grown apart, Marcus. Over the last decade, you've pushed me away, year by year."

He leaned against the door frame, "It's been harder than I thought," he said, almost to himself. "The past ten years... harder than I ever imagined they could be."

"Then let's leave it behind us." The urgency in her voice cracked through the morning stillness. "We made our decision; we committed to this life. We have to live with it and move forward."

"It was your decision, Julia." His rebuttal was soft yet cut deep, leaving a new wound upon the old scars of their shared history.

"How dare you," she said, the words a broken whisper that hardly reached his ears before he turned away from her.

"I'm going to shower," he said, leaving the kitchen. "Make sure you scrub real hard. It will take a lot of soap to clean off what you've done," she called after him. She got up and followed him into the bedroom. She could hear the shower already rinsing away his guilt. Julia's fingers trembled as they grazed the cotton fabric of Marcus's discarded shirt, crumpled upon their bed. She drew it to her nose, the scent sharp and unmistakable—a sweet, floral perfume that did not belong to her. Her breath hitched in her throat, a silent curse slipping through clenched teeth. She flung the garment aside as if expelling the lie it carried.

Stepping across the hall, Julia peered into Nicole's room, moonlight-painted silver streaks over her daughter's splayed form. She was only sixteen but already a woman in so many ways. The sight of Nicole caught between the throes of adolescence and the precipice of womanhood tugged at something primal within Julia, a protective fervour mingled with sorrow for the innocence that clung to her still.

The door to Jamie's room creaked open, revealing a scene of adolescent rebellion. His slight frame was sprawled beneath a thin sheet, his chest rising and falling in the deep rhythm of slumber. Julia's gaze fell upon the beer cans standing by his bedside.

"Jamie," she said, not loud enough to wake him but enough for the word to hang heavy in the air. Worry gnawed at her heart; the edges frayed with uncertainty about the paths he might wander.

Julia retreated from Jamie's world, closing the door on the disquiet. She dressed for the day in silence. She had work to do, which she hoped would distract her again from her domestic life.

Her heels clicked against the pavement as she approached the property set for today's showing. The sign declaring "Open House" plunged into the manicured lawn. She stood beside the sign and scanned the street. It was a street not unlike her own, with manicured lawns and wide lots. She thought of the families sleeping in their rooms and wondered if any of the inhabitants were lying awake, strategizing on ways to repair fractures in their families that had been left untreated. She thought not.

"Good morning," said Amanda, Julia's assistant, her eager voice cutting through the stillness of the morning.

Julia turned, pulled from her contemplation, and faced Amanda. "Morning," she said, her tone measured, betraying nothing of the storm she harboured. Why don't you take this one today? I'll handle the other one across town."

"Are you sure?" Amanda's brow furrowed, concern glinting in her eyes, but Julia dismissed it with a practiced smile.

"Absolutely," she said, her words relaxed. "You'll be great. Call if you need anything."

As Julia drove away, the rearview mirror reflected a snapshot of the life she had built—a facade as polished and as fragile as the image she presented to the world. Julia's fingers, tinged with the beginnings of age's claim, trembled as she positioned the sign on the lawn. Her image, captured in gloss and colour, smiled back at her, a relic of a younger self. The morning breeze toyed with strands of hair that had escaped her careful styling, and she brushed them away with a practiced hand.

She retrieved the boxes from her car and carried them across the driveway and into the home. Inside, the kitchen was awash with sunlight, its marble island a barren stage awaiting her touch. Unloading the platters, she scattered an array of snacks with deliberate casualness. She knew that hungry buyers didn't stick around, but a buyer with a full stomach may linger just long enough for her to work her charm.

The booklet for guest signatures lay open, its pages stark and expectant. Julia aligned it with the edge of the countertop. Nearby, she arranged the brochures, their glossy surfaces proclaiming the virtues of the home, promises of happiness and fulfillment.

With the scene set, Julia retreated into herself, appraising her work with a critic's eye. She straightened her hair, taming the rebellious waves that refused to conform, much like the thoughts she struggled to suppress. Her hands smoothed the fabric of her dress, skimming over it as if to iron out the wrinkles in her life. Buyers like attractive agents, she thought as she scanned her reflection in the window.

"Mommy, I love this room!" The voice broke through her contemplation, pulling her from the depths of introspection. A young family stood in the living area, their collective gaze touching upon each feature with the wonder reserved for new beginnings.

"It's quite spacious," Julia said, "and the natural light is perfect for your children to play."

"We'll have to think about it," the father said, eyes roaming the space with hope and calculation. "It's a big decision."

"Of course," Julia nodded, her smile never wavering. "Take all the time you need. Just call my office once you've decided. This house was made for a family like yours."

They exchanged pleasantries and contact information, and then the family departed, leaving Julia alone with echoes of laughter that were not her own. In the quiet aftermath, she lingered at the window, watching them pile into their car, the embodiment of unity and unspoiled dreams.

"Perfect for them," she said to no one, her reflection in the glass a ghostly companion, nodding in silent agreement.

The silence in the air was thick, a tangible presence Julia could almost touch as she sat at the kitchen bar. The appliances gleamed, and the marble countertop felt cold under her fingers. She looked around the perfectly staged kitchen, its engineered beauty contrasting the organic laughter that had just left the room.

A pang of something—longing and sorrow—seized Julia's chest. She thought of the family with their children, their lives stretching like an unmarked canvas. Remnants of their presence clung to the air, and for a moment, Julia allowed herself the luxury of envy. How untainted they were by life's relentless march, how untouched by the compromises and disappointments that had come to define her existence.

She leaned forward, resting her forehead against the coolness of the granite. A single tear betrayed her, slipping quietly down her cheek, mapping the contours of her weariness. It was a silent concession to the ache within her soul—a private acknowledgement of the dreams she'd once held dear.

"Hello?"

The voice startled her. Julia lifted her head and quickly wiped her eyes with the back of her hand; she didn't have the luxury of tears now. Composure was her ally, her armour.

"Hello," she echoed. Julia straightened up and forced a practiced smile onto her lips as she turned to greet the newcomer.

He stood in the doorway, his frame filling the space. He was perhaps a few years older than Julia—his presence a mirror reflecting her stages of life. Marcus's age, she thought to herself. He had on a loose-fitting polo shirt and jeans. His hair was darker and longer than Marcus's. He was athletic, she thought, probably a runner. Those people she saw out early on a Saturday morning pounding the pavement.

"Sorry to startle you," he said, entering the kitchen. His eyes scanned her face, perhaps searching for signs of the distress she had so quickly tried to conceal.

Julia was quick to regain her professional poise. "Not at all," she said, smoothing her dress and patting down her hair as she could manage. "Please, come in."

Her hands moved to her face, dabbing at the corners of her eyes to ensure her makeup hadn't smeared—the mask of normalcy must remain intact. She studied him, this man who had witnessed a rare crack in her facade.

"Are you interested in the house?" she asked, moving seamlessly back into the role she knew so well. Her heart still ached, but it was tucked away now, hidden behind a curtain of professionalism.

He extended his hand, a confident and warm gesture. "I'm David," he said with a voice carrying a note of sincerity that pierced through the veneer of the open house setting.

"Julia Dempsey," she said, accepting his handshake with a firmness that disguised her inner turmoil. "Should we wait for your wife to join us for the tour?"

A shadow crossed David's features, an almost imperceptible jaw tightening. "No, I'm recently divorced," he said, allowing the weight of those words to settle between them. "I'm looking for a place where my kids can stay with me on weekends."

The response prompted Julia to look at him anew, seeing not just another prospective buyer but a kindred spirit navigating the choppy waters of life changes. She nodded in understanding, though she found herself lost for words.

David's gaze lingered on her face, concern etching his brow as he took in her appearance. "Everything okay?" he asked. "You seem... a bit upset."

"Life," she said, a half-hearted smile on her lips. "It has its moments, doesn't it?" She brushed away the last traces of tears, invisible yet palpable.

"It sure does," David said, offering her a sympathetic head tilt. "But we've got to stay positive. Look, it can't be that bad. You've done a good job, and—" He paused, his eyes softening. "You're beautiful."

The comment startled a laugh from her—a short, sharp burst of disbelief. "That's very kind of you to say," she managed, shaking her head as if to dispel the absurdity of the compliment.

David looked puzzled; his earnestness unfeigned. "I'm serious." Then, after a moment's hesitation, he ventured further. "Are you married? Do you have a family?"

Her heart clenched, caught off guard by the intimacy of the question. "Yes, I have two children," she said, but something strange happened—a compulsion to reveal more than she intended. "And I do have a husband..." Her voice trailed off, and she added, with a surprising sense of relief, "But we're separated."

David absorbed this new information with a nod, his expression unreadable. "Why don't we have that tour now?"

"Of course," Julia said, grateful for the return to routine. She motioned toward the hallway. "Shall we start with the living room?" As they walked, the layers of her carefully constructed identity shifted, and she wondered how much more would unravel before the tour was over.

As they moved through it, the living room felt spacious and well-lit. The sunlight filtering through the sheer curtains cast a soft glow on the hardwood floors. Julia pointed out the crown moulding and the built-in bookshelves that flanked the marble fireplace.

"Very cozy," David said, fingers over the mantel's smooth surface. "Do you like to entertain, Julia?"

They stepped through the sliding glass doors onto the large deck, where the scent of blooming flowers mingled with the fresh morning air. She leaned against the railing, her eyes scanning the expanse designed for gatherings and laughter, now silent but for birds chirping in the distance.

"I used to entertain when my kids were young and before we had them," she said. "Now I'm usually buried in work or with the kids." She hesitated before adding, "Mostly just the kids these days."

David nodded, taking in the space. "It's a great space. I think my kids would love it," he said, almost to himself. Then, turning to face her with a curious tilt of his head, he asked, "Are you seeing anyone?"

The question, though innocent, sent an unexpected blush to her cheeks. "No, I—" She stopped, caught off guard by the sudden rush of adolescent shyness. "Work and children are my world." But beneath her words, an unfamiliar current stirred, a recognition of the attention being paid to her, the interest in her beyond her professional mask.

He looked at her as if he could interrogate her life. For a moment, she was seen in a way that she hadn't felt in a year, and it both alarmed and thrilled her.

"Let's... let's go back inside," she said, eager to escape the moment's intensity.

As they returned indoors, navigating the plush carpet of the hallway, Julia's mind wandered to the ghost of the morning's confrontation. The empty spot beside her in bed that Marcus had left cold, the bitter taste of betrayal that no amount of coffee could wash away. Each step toward the master bedroom was further into the tumultuous sea of her thoughts.

The bedroom door swung open, revealing an inviting space in neutral tones and soft lighting. A perfectly made king-sized bed lay spread out before them.

"Plenty of room here," David said, stepping into the room and surveying the surroundings with an appraiser's eye.

Julia stood frozen in the doorway; her gaze locked on the bed. The empty sheets were a mirror reflecting the hollow space beside her slumbering form, the void where Marcus should have been, his absence more palpable than his presence.

"Julia?" David's voice brought her back; his brow furrowed with concern as he noticed the sheen of tears threatening to spill from her deep-set eyes.

"Sorry, I..." She stumbled over the words, struggling to compose herself. "It's just been a long day already."

"Of course," he said, though his eyes lingered on hers with a knowing that suggested he understood there was something more. Something hidden behind the practiced smile of a woman well-versed in the art of concealment.

Tears welled up, breaking the dam of Julia's composure as she stood in the bedroom's doorway. David's question hung in the air, a gentle prodding that cracked the veneer of her professional façade.

"Julia?" David asked again, his voice tinged with genuine concern.

She shook her head, a futile attempt to dismiss the turmoil within. "It's nothing," she said, betraying the emotion she tried to conceal.

But David wasn't convinced. He closed the space between them, his movements careful and measured. "What's wrong? Is it your ex?" His inquiry was delicate but direct, piercing her defences like sunlight through clouds.

The mention of 'ex'—a term not yet materialized into reality but suddenly feeling imminent—unleashed a floodgate of sorrow. Julia's shoulders shook as sobs wracked her body, her pride dissolving into the ether. She was exposed, vulnerable under the scrutiny of this near stranger who seemed to see straight through her.

David reached out, placing his hands on her shoulders, drawing her toward him with an empathy she could neither reject nor comprehend. His embrace enveloped her, a warmth spreading through her chilled bones. She allowed herself to be pulled close, her face nestling into the fabric of his shirt. His scent—a mix of cologne and something intrinsically him—filled her senses, grounding her amidst the chaos of her emotions.

"Shh... it's alright," he said, his voice a soothing balm. Patting her back, David held her, his touch a comfort she'd long forgotten.

Julia's hands, trembling at first, found their way to the small of his back. The solidity of his frame against hers sparked a connection, tenuous yet palpable. It stretched between them, a silent understanding that transcended words.

Her fingers curled, gripping the fabric of his shirt as she pressed closer. She could feel the steady rhythm of his heart against her cheek, a counterpoint to her erratic pulse. His hands slid downward, tracing the contour of her spine until they settled just where her hips began to flare—a touch both innocent and intimate.

For a fleeting second, time ceased its relentless march forward. Julia experienced a forgotten sensation in David's arms—a sense of being cherished and seen. It was a poignant reminder of what had been lost to the years, what might have been eroded by the slow drip of neglect.

As they stood there, two souls entwined in the quiet solace of shared vulnerability, Julia realized that perhaps she had been missing the embrace and the permission to acknowledge the depth of her longing.

Julia's breath, a shallow tremor, hitched as she withdrew just enough to seek his gaze. "I'm sorry," she said, eyes shimmering with unshed tears and the vestiges of long-held sorrow.

"Nothing to be sorry for," David said, his voice firm yet tender, an anchor in the storm of her emotions. "You're a beautiful woman, Julia." His affirmation wasn't merely polite; it was weighted with sincerity, speaking to the core of her being that had been invisible for far too long.

She looked up at him, her eyes meeting his, and in that exchange—a silent conversation only they could comprehend—years of suppressed yearning rose to the surface. She leaned in and closed the distance between them with an almost imperceptible nod to herself as if granting permission to break free from her self-imposed shackles.

Their lips met, and something dormant within Julia sparked to life. The kiss wasn't a question; it was an answer she'd been searching for in the dark corners of her heart. David responded, his grip tightening around her, sealing the space between them with an urgency that mirrored her awakening desire.

As they parted for air, their breaths mingling, Julia's hands moved with newfound boldness to the front of his pants. Her fingers worked, unbuckling the belt with a resolve fueled by the anger she harboured towards Marcus—a flame now repurposed into a passion. The fabric pooled at David's feet, his vulnerability laid bare before her.

Her touch was tentative at first as she reached for him, but the pulse of his manhood against her palm galvanized her actions. She felt him harden, an acknowledgement of their mutual need, and a visceral thrill coursed through her. This connection, raw and undeniable, was the antithesis of the cold, disjointed encounters that had come to define her marriage.

Their world reduced to shared secrets and the intertwining of souls, Julia reacquainted herself with the woman she once knew: the woman who desired touch and lived with enthusiasm.

With an assertiveness that surprised even herself, Julia's hands pressed against David's chest, urging him down onto the untouched bed. A murmur escaped her as she peeled away the constrictive layer of her inhibitions along with her panties, discarding them like the remnants of a life too long spent in shadows. The cool air kissed her skin, contrasting with the heat from the man beneath her.

Her skirt bunched at her waist as she straddled him, their breaths synchronizing in the silent communion of the room. She leaned forward, capturing his lips again in a kiss that spoke volumes of unvoiced yearnings and muted dreams. His hands explored her body with an urgency that reignited the embers of her femininity. They gripped her breasts, each touch undoing years of emotional armour until they reached around, pulling her closer by the curves of her buttocks.

As she guided him inside her, a gasp punctured the calm, and she sat up, riding him with an enthusiasm that eclipsed the passage of time. Each movement was a reclamation of her identity, a shedding of the weight that had bowed her shoulders and dimmed the light in her eyes.

Then the dynamic shifted—he rolled her over, and she found herself looking up into his eyes, which held a depth akin to her own. His hips drove into her with a cadence that matched the quickening pulse of her heart. Her back arched, and a release spasm overtook her, drawing him deeper into the vortex of her awakening.

As they reached their peak, Julia squeezed her eyes shut, savouring the sensation of David's skin against her own, the rhythmic pounding of their bodies resonating through her very being. She was alive, whole, and genuinely connected for the first time in years.

Afterward, they lay side by side, two silhouettes bathed in the soft afternoon light filtering through the blinds. He turned his head, a smile playing on his lips that recognized the paradox of their situation, the absurdity of finding such a connection amid the staged perfection of a house meant for others.

Unbidden, laughter bubbled up from within her—a pure sound, untainted by the layers of sorrow and regret that had silenced her spirit. It was infectious, and he joined in, their joy a temporary balm for wounds old and new.

"I'll take the place," David quipped between chuckles, and Julia couldn't help but laugh harder. A laugh echoed off the walls, filling the room's corners with a sense of life and possibility.

The sun began its descent as Julia Dempsey's car pulled into the driveway, gravel crunching under the tires. She killed the engine and sat, collecting herself in the rearview mirror. Fingers trembling, she ran them through her wavy hair, attempting to restore some semblance of order. Her eyes, repositories of secret sorrows, peered back at her, searching for any residual signs of transgression.

She exited the vehicle, smoothing out the lines of her skirt, when the door to her home burst open. Nicole, her daughter, was on the porch, her features knotted with urgency.

"Mom!" Nicole's voice was sharp with reproach. "I'm having the pool party tonight, and you were supposed to help me get ready. Where have you been?"

"Nicole, darling," Julia's voice, a practiced calm, belied the storm that had raged within her just hours ago. "I've been at work, as usual."

Nicole stared at her mother with an intensity that cut through pretense. "Just make sure your blouse is tucked in, then," she said dryly, eyes flickering down.

Julia reached back, her fingers correcting the oversight. The fabric slipped smoothly beneath the waistband of her skirt, hiding away the disruption like a concealed truth.

"Is your father home yet?" Julia asked, a note of apprehension threading through her words.

"No," Nicole said, her gaze still lingering with a hint of suspicion.

"Alright. I'm going to go have a shower," Julia said, the exhaustion of the day bearing down upon her shoulders as she made her way to the sanctity of her bedroom.

Inside, she paused, hands resting on the bed's footboard they had shared for many years. The room was different now, as if the very air held the whispers of her infidelity. She lowered herself onto the mattress, the familiar softness offering no comfort. A laugh threatened to escape her lips—a residue of joy so foreign it scared her—but it died quickly, leaving only the urge to weep behind.

Lying back, she stared at the ceiling, the day's events replaying behind her closed lids. The breathless rush, the forbidden embrace, and the laughter that had sprung from depths long forgotten all swirled together in a maelstrom of emotion.

"Get your shit together, Julia. You're not 19 years old," she said, a bitter reprimand. Her movements were automatic as she entered the bathroom and closed the door with a soft click, sealing herself away from the world outside.

Chapter 11

Julia sat, her fingers tracing the rim of her wine glass. Her blue eyes flitted across the faces in the room: Marcus, still looking youthful and full of energy; James and Laurie; and Roger and Denise, who were speaking animatedly, their gestures expansive as they extolled the virtues of parenting with an open hand. James and Laurie's daughter Katie was somewhere in the backyard. She had been friends with Nicole since they were young, although they had grown apart in recent years. Roger and Denise's daughter, Rebecca, was Nicole's best friend. Thick as thieves, they would say.

The living room was aglow with soft, ambient lighting, casting warm shadows on the group. On the coffee table, an assortment of appetizers lay before them. The men sipped from lowball glasses, the amber whiskey catching the light, while the women held stems of white wine.

"Kids these days," Roger said, his voice laced with progressive pride, "need the freedom to explore and make their own mistakes." He gestured towards Denise, who nodded in agreement, her straight blonde hair swaying with the movement.

"Even if it means she gets pregnant?" James said with a chortle, half-jesting, half-serious, leaning back into the plush cushions.

"James!" Laurie's admonishment came swift, her palm connecting with his shoulder in a smack softened by affection. "Settle down."

"Of course, that's not what we want," Roger said, undeterred, his eyes reflecting a history of different times and choices. "But when I think about our youth, the things we got up to... well, a few boys sneaking in isn't the worst thing."

Julia looked at Marcus to see his reaction, finding none as he remained silent, his charm dormant in this private setting where no audience needed winning over. She knew him too well—how he could deflect and avoid when it suited him, how his charisma was often a convenient veil. And yet, there was comfort in the familiar rhythms of their social dance, a choreography learned over the decade.

"Freedom's important," Julia finally chimed in. "But so are boundaries. It's a delicate balance." She didn't say more, letting the statement linger.

The outside air pulsed with the sounds of adolescent revelry, punctuated by the occasional splash from the pool. Seated on the edge of an overstuffed couch, Julia felt the vibrations of laughter and chatter through the soles of her feet. Her eyes met Marcus's across the room, a silent conversation passing between them that only years of marriage could decode.

"Julia, you've been quiet," Denise said, tucking a loose strand of hair behind her ear. "Has Nicole given you much trouble lately?"

"Trouble?" Julia echoed, allowing herself a small smile as she glanced at Marcus again. "Just the usual teenage drama." She folded her hands together, her knuckles whitening. "Underage drinking, passionate flings with boyfriends—"

"Ah, the rites of passage," Denise said with a knowing nod. She gestured towards the windows that looked out onto the backyard where their teens mingled. "With so many boys and girls out tonight, we'd better keep a watchful eye." Her voice lowered conspiratorially. "One thing could easily lead to another."

Laughter emerged amongst the adults, a collective acknowledgment of their shared predicament. Glasses were refilled, the wine's golden hue contrasting with the amber of whiskey as they toasted to the complexities of parenthood.

Outside, Nicole perched on the pool's edge, legs dangling into the water as she surveyed the scene with Rebecca beside her. The night had wrapped the backyard in its embrace, the pool's surface reflecting the stars above like a mirror to the cosmos. A sense of boldness surged within her as she watched two figures entwined on the playground, their silhouettes blurred by shadows and desire.

"Check out Kevin Ramsay," Nicole said, her gaze fixed on the boy lounging on the opposite side of the pool. His movements had a predatory grace, an unspoken challenge in his posture. "I'm going to get it on with him tonight."

"Right in front of your parents?" Rebecca's eyebrows arched in amusement as she followed Nicole's stare.

"Please," Nicole scoffed, a reckless grin spreading across her face. "They're too caught up in their world—drinks, drama, you name it." She gestured toward the house, where her parents sat, oblivious to the teenage theatre unfolding outside.

"Besides," she said, "they wouldn't even know. They never do."

From her vantage point, Julia looked at her daughter—a flicker of concern etched into the creases of her forehead. The distance between them seemed to stretch far beyond the physical space of their yard, reaching into the emotional terrain that Julia had navigated with trepidation all these years. She knew the last ten years had been hard on Nicole. The constant tension in the home had driven her to find comfort, or attention, with her peers.

"Another round?" Marcus said, breaking into Julia's reverie with a raised bottle.

"Yes," Julia said, her voice steady despite the turmoil. "To our children and their untamed spirits." Her glass clinked against the others', a fragile sound that mirrored the delicate balance they all sought to maintain.

Outside, Rebecca's slender fingers delved into the depths of her purse, rummaging for a moment before emerging with a small, clear bottle. The liquid inside sloshed with a promise of stolen courage. She held it out to Nicole with a smirk playing at the corner of her lips.

"Need a bit of nerve?" she quipped, her voice tinged with mischief.

Nicole's gaze flickered between Rebecca's expectant eyes and the bottle of vodka. There was an allure in her casual defiance. "Sure," she said, her response calm, but her heart thumped with trepidation and excitement. Her fingers wrapped around the bottle, cool to the touch, as she tilted it back for a generous swallow. The vodka burned a path down her throat, a fiery trail of liquid audacity.

"Smooth," Nicole coughed, passing the bottle back with a grimace that belied the bravado in her words.

Across the lawn, a figure emerged from the side of the house. Jamie—jeans hanging loose around his hips, flip flops slapping against the concrete with each step—his presence disconnected from the revelry around him. He cradled a beer can, its aluminum surface catching the occasional glint from the pool lights. With a practiced head tilt, he drained the contents in a single, prolonged draw.

"Christ, look at him," Nicole said, watching as Jamie discarded the empty can onto a table cluttered with others of its kind. It clattered against the glass top, a hollow sound lost amidst splashing water and teenage laughter.

"Your brother's got that lone wolf vibe tonight," Rebecca said, her eyes tracking Jamie's languid movements.

"More like a stray dog," Nicole retorted, the edge in her voice sharper than intended. A pang of guilt twisted in her gut as Jamie navigated the periphery of their world—a solitary shadow skirting the edges.

Rebecca's gaze lingered on Jamie, her expression a blend of curiosity and something more—a hunger that belied the innocence of their poolside confessions. She leaned in, her voice lowering to a conspiratorial whisper, "Nicole, I need to tell you something."

"Spill," Nicole encouraged, her eyes still on her brother as he discarded his beer can with a carelessness that marked all his actions.

"I...I think I want to fuck your brother." The words hung between them like a rogue spark threatening to ignite.

Nicole's laugh erupted, incredulous and tinged with disgust. "Jamie? Please. He's just a weirdo who drowns himself in beer and video games. Plus, he's too old."

"He's only eighteen. That's only two years older than me. But there's something about him." Rebecca's eyes didn't waver from Jamie's isolated form. "He's mysterious."

"Or just messed up," Nicole countered. "Trust me, there are at least ten better guys here tonight than him."

Rebecca shrugged, a silent acknowledgment, but her fascination remained as Jamie settled into a chair set apart from the laughter and splashing—a solitary observer of the revelry he seemed to have no part in.

Nicole stood abruptly. Her movements were fluid and deliberate as she stripped off her shirt and shorts, revealing a swimsuit that barely contained the curves of adolescence newly etched into her frame. She was aware of the glances following her, and muted conversations paused, if only for the briefest moments, as she crossed the deck.

With an air of defiance, she dove into the pool, the cool water enveloping her in a world where muffled sounds and refracted light played tricks on the senses. She emerged on the other side, near Kevin and his friends, her hair slicked back, a sheen on her skin.

"Coming in?" she asked, her tone playful yet loaded with an invitation.

Kevin appraised her for a second, a silent communication passing between his friends before he acquiesced with a casual shrug. His shirt came off, muscles flexing in the dim glow from the house. Nicole watched the intensity of her gaze betraying an interest far beyond mere camaraderie.

Her breath caught as Kevin entered the water, his presence a new charge in the electric atmosphere of teenage anticipation.

Water lapped at the pool's edges as Nicole's gaze darted about, searching for Kevin beneath the surface. Her heart thumped against her ribs—a staccato rhythm at odds with the languid waves. She floated, suspended in uncertainty, until a sudden surge of water beside her announced his return.

"Boo!" His voice was muffled and bubbly as he broke through, grinning.

Nicole let out a startled yelp, followed by laughter; it sounded more genuine than she'd expected to produce tonight. She splashed him in the face with a playful glare, sending droplets scattering like tiny diamonds in the dim light.

"Hey!" he protested, wiping his eyes, feigning indignation before breaking into an easy smile.

Together, they swam to the secluded corner of the pool, where shadows draped over them like curtains, shielding them from prying eyes.

"Careful," she said, fingers catching the loose ties of his swim trunks. "Or you might lose these."

"Wouldn't you like that?" Kevin shot back, the corner of his mouth quirking up.

"Maybe," she said, her voice a flirtatious lilt that belied the surge of adrenaline in her veins.

His response was a slow, deliberate movement—hands finding the curves of her hips under the cool water. She leaned in, drawn by the current of a desire she hadn't fully acknowledged until now. His fingertips traced the edges of her bikini, tugging ever so, eliciting a shiver that wasn't from the chill of the pool.

"Careful yourself," he said, his breath a warm contrast to the night air.

Her hand moved of its own accord, grazing against him. A giddy laugh escaped her, and she looked up at him through dark lashes.

"You're not going to be able to get out of the pool now," she joked, the words a mix of challenge and invitation.

He chuckled a low sound that reverberated between them. "You're such a tease, Nicole."

Their gazes locked, and for a moment, the world beyond the pool, with its mix of teenage revelry and the murmur of adult conversation inside, ceased to exist. It was just the two of them—the promise of secrets yet to be shared, of boundaries to be tested.

The laughter and music from the party were distant now, drowned out by the intimate symphony of their intertwined breaths and the soft splash of water against their skin.

"Tease," he said, but there was no accusation in his voice. Only a note of something else—something like wonder.

Nicole's fingers traced a daring line along the waistband of Kevin's shorts, her eyes alight with mischief. The dimpled smile that had played on her lips moments before deepened into something more playful. "Why don't you take these off?" she said, a playful challenge in her voice.

Kevin's eyebrows arched in surprise, his grin fading into bemusement. He glanced around at the poolside spectators, the flicker of torches casting shadows over the water where their peers floated and flirted with abandon.

"Right here? With everyone watching?" he scoffed, though his tone held an edge of intrigue. He was torn between the desire coursing through him and the reality of their public display.

"Please..." Nicole purred, affecting a pout that seemed to wobble his resolve. But he shook his head, firm yet still enchanted by her audacity.

"Can't do it, Nicole. You know I can't." His words were a reprimand laced with affection, calling her out for the dance they both knew so well. She was the flare that drew looks, the flame that dared to be touched, but never without consequence.

"Fine," she said with mock resignation, but her eyes glinted with a fresh scheme. "Then come back later, when the party's done. My window will be open." Her suggestion hung between them, a whispered promise that sent a shiver up his spine despite the warm night air.

"Seriously?" he asked, a mix of disbelief and anticipation colouring his tone. He was caught, snagged on the hook of her invitation just as she'd intended.

"Seriously," she said, her gaze locked onto his. "My parents will be too busy with their friends or too wrapped in their drama. They won't notice. They never do."

In the shadows beyond the pool's light, Jamie leaned against the wall, another beer in hand. His messy hair framed a face marked by the cynicism that brewed within him. As his sister wove her web, his thoughts soured. Nicole always played the part, the center of attention, the party's pulse. Yet he saw the strain behind her performance—the relentless pursuit of something to fill the void.

A soft glow from the house next door cut through his brooding. A woman stepped onto her deck, her silhouette contrasting against the indoor lights. She peered toward the commotion of the Dempsey household, her posture rigid with discomfort or perhaps disapproval.

Jamie's eyes met hers across the divide of manicured lawns and unspoken judgments. For a moment, their gazes held—a silent conversation of weariness and recognition. Then, with a solemn wave, she acknowledged the chaos that spilled from his home like light from an open door.

He hesitated, the gesture unexpected, then lifted his hand in a return wave. As quickly as she had appeared, she retreated, and darkness reclaimed her space in the world.

Rubbing at his eyes, tired from more than just the alcohol, Jamie cracked open another beer. The sound of the can giving way was a crisp punctuation to the evening's ongoing narrative. He drank, the liquid cold and bitter as it washed down the staleness of his thoughts.

The world wobbled under Jamie's feet as he rose from his chair, the joy of the party fading into a dull echo with each step toward the cabana. The night air clung to him like a damp shroud, heavy with the scent of chlorine and the tang of sizzling barbecue that had long since ceased. He maneuvered through the darkness, guided by the soft glow of scattered fairy lights, until he opened the door to the cabana's sanctuary.

Inside, the familiar smell of cedar and charcoal filled his nostrils. He stumbled to the bathroom and relieved himself with his forehead pressed against the cool tile that spun beneath him. Shuffling into the adjacent room, Jamie reached into the mini fridge with a grunt, his fingers closing around the cold aluminum of another beer.

"Can you get one for me?" A voice sliced through the haze of his intoxication.

He turned toward the corner where the couch sat in shadow. Katie lounged there, her slender figure half-shrouded in darkness, a bottle dangling from her fingertips.

"What are you doing here?" Jamie's tone was stern, protective instincts poorly masked by irritation.

Katie shifted, her eyes catching the light as she looked up at him. "Boys out there are just kids," she said dismissively, "I prefer someone who's lived a little." Her smile was a mix of mischief and something older, something that didn't quite fit the youthful tilt of her chin.

Jamie found himself moving closer, drawn in despite himself. He sank onto the couch beside her, the worn cushions accepting his weight with a muted sigh. He kept his gaze fixed on the fridge's dim interior light, avoiding the intensity of her stare.

"Come on, sit closer," she said, patting the space beside her. Reluctantly, he complied, feeling the warmth of her presence as an unspoken question hung between them.

"Remember when we were kids? You used to be so happy, Jamie. What happened to you?" Her hand rested on his knee, stirring memories of sunlit afternoons and laughter free of burdens.

"Katie, don't," Jamie said. "You've had too much to drink. You're being stupid."

"Stupid or not," she countered, leaning forward, "something changed you. And I want to know what it was."

"Life isn't a fairytale," Jamie said, taking a swig of his beer, "not everyone gets a happily ever after." His eyes drifted over the room, avoiding hers, focusing on anything that would grant him reprieve from this conversation.

"Maybe not," Katie said, "but most people don't just give up so quickly. I won't leave until you tell me."

"Your dad will come looking for you, Katie. If he finds you here with me, you'll be grounded for eternity," he tried to deflect, but his words betrayed a weariness that betrayed his concern for her more than any intent to intimidate.

"Let him find me," she said with reckless bravado, but her eyes held a tenderness that reached out to him, asking for the truth behind the anger he wore like armour.

Jamie sighed, his defences crumbling like the ash of a long-extinguished fire. "There's nothing to say, really," he said, "it just is what it is."

"Fine," she said, withdrawing her hand but leaving a trace of her warmth on his skin.

The cabana was silent and broken only by the muffled sounds of revelry seeping through the wooden slats. Katie leaned closer, her breath warm against his ear, tinged with the scent of alcohol and youthful audacity. "Was it Trevor? What happened to Trevor?" she probed, her words sharp enough to puncture the bubble of isolation Jamie had crafted around himself.

He lurched upright like an electric current had jolted him from his stupor. His eyes, clouded with memories and drink, fixed on Katie's face—a mixture of concern and naivety staring back at him. "You don't know anything about Trevor," Jamie said, the raw edge in his voice betraying a tangle of emotions he couldn't disguise. "And you shouldn't talk about things you don't understand." He reached for another beer, the cold aluminum a temporary anchor in the turbulent sea of his thoughts. Popping the cap, he drank deeply, trying to drown the past that refused to be silent.

A single tear betrayed his stoic facade, carving a path down his weathered cheek. Her hand moved to wipe it away, but Jamie's hand shot up, pushing hers aside with a force that surprised even himself. The rejection stung, yet she persisted, her touch softer now, tracing the line of his jaw before settling back onto his knee, inching higher this time.

"Katie, what are you doing?" he asked, the undercurrent of panic rising in his chest.

"I'm helping you," she said, unphased by his guarded exterior. Her fingers worked at the button of his jeans and the zipper as if unlocking him might reveal the truths hidden within. When her hands ventured further, slipping beneath the fabric barrier, Jamie's body tensed, a mix of desire and confusion warring within him.

"You shouldn't," he managed to choke out, but the protest died on his lips as she leaned forward, her actions bolder than her years. Jamie closed his eyes, surrendering to the sensation, his hand finding the back of her head as he reclined on the couch.

Minutes later, when they emerged from the cabana, Nicole, Rebecca, and Kevin were sprawled on the lounge chairs, their inhibitions dissolving in the vodka's embrace. As Jamie and Katie walked past, Rebecca's voice cut through the night, venomous and steeped in jealousy. "Whore," she said under her breath.

Kevin chuckled, a hollow sound that echoed off the pool's surface. "You need to get laid, Becca. Forget Jamie." His gaze flitted between the two girls, a predator's grin spreading across his face.

"Who can I fuck then?" Rebecca's challenge was slurred but defiant, her eyes flickering with hurt and something darker.

Nicole laughed, her tone devoid of humour. "How about Kev?" A knowing glint in her eye spoke of secrets and shared misdeeds.

Kevin's surprised laugh held a note of intrigue; his attention caught between the two girls. But Nicole wasn't watching them; her gaze was locked on the living room window, where her father whispered sweet nothings—or perhaps bitter somethings—into Denise's ear. Everyone was drunk, Nicole thought, the realization sinking in like a stone. They were all bodies moving through the haze, seeking connection or oblivion, whichever came first.

Nicole's gaze lingered on the undulating shadows cast by the pool lights, her voice low but decisive. "You can have Kevin," she said to Rebecca, a wry smile playing at the corner of her lips, "but you're not having him all to yourself."

Kevin's eyebrows arched; his surprise palpable in the dimness. "Are you serious?" There was a hesitant eagerness in his tone, an uncertainty that bordered on hope.

With a nod, Nicole affirmed the unspoken pact between them. It was a game they played, each challenge raising the stakes in their reckless pursuit of thrills.

"Okay, why not?" Rebecca's voice held a note of resignation laced with the sharp tang of vodka-soaked bravado. She pointed towards the cabana, its silhouette a darker patch against the night sky. "Let's do it in there."

"That's fine," Nicole said, "but I'm coming with you." Rebecca looked at Kevin and then back to Nicole. She nodded and said, "Shall we?" Rising from the lounge chairs, their forms swayed as they traversed the deck. They paused only to survey the yard—a kingdom of adolescent chaos—before the trio slipped into the cabana with a conspiracy that needed no words.

From his vantage point, Jamie watched the scene unfold, his beer can cold against his palm. His sister's laughter reached him, a discordant melody twirling through the evening air, mocking the sanctity of family bonds. He shook his head in a gesture mingled with disgust and sorrow, the sight before him a mix of ignorance and indulgence.

His eyes drifted to the neighbour's house, where darkness enshrouded only one window. The drapes were drawn, hiding whatever life lay beyond. For a moment, he imagined another world of solitude and silence and felt the sting of envy.

Cracking open another beer, the aluminum yielding easily under his grip, he chugged it down, the liquid fire burning a path of numbness. The world around him seemed to blur and fade, leaving only the bitterness on his tongue and the weight of unspoken grievances heavy in his chest.

"Fuck this," Jamie said, the words lost amidst the din of splashing water and muffled giggles emanating from the cabana. He tossed the empty can onto the lawn, a metallic clatter swallowed by the night.

Pushing himself up from the chair, he stumbled, the alcohol lending an unsteady rhythm to his steps. With each movement away from the revelry, the noise of the party receded, replaced by the quiet hum of his thoughts. As he stepped into the house, he left behind the warmth of the summer night, stepping into the cool indifference of a home that had never truly been a sanctuary.

Part 4

1973

Chapter 12

Marcus slouched against the mahogany bar, his flared jeans hugging his legs as he shifted his weight. The fabric of his button-up shirt stretched across his broad shoulders, a testament to hours spent buried in dusty archives rather than the gym. The liquid swirled in his glass, the ice clinking like distant bells. His gaze was steady, but his mind was elsewhere, lost in the throes of history that seemed more tangible than the raucous present.

"Man, look at you," James said with a chuckle, leaning back in his chair and smoothing down the front of his turtleneck. The corduroy jacket he wore added bulk to his lean frame, making him look scholarly and out of place amid the laughter and clinking glasses. "That shirt is a dead giveaway that you are part of the establishment, man."

The jukebox crooned a classic rock ballad, its soulful guitar riffs weaving through the hum of conversation. Marcus tapped his foot to the rhythm, finding solace in the familiar tunes that were the soundtrack to their tumultuous times. Posters of The Rolling Stones and Led Zeppelin adorned the walls, interspersed with flyers announcing anti-war rallies and poetry readings, capturing the essence of their generation's unrest and hope.

"Maybe I am," Marcus said, his voice nearly drowned by the music. "But at least I don't look like I just stepped out of Easy Rider."

"Hey, this is pure intellectual chic," James retorted, his eyes twinkling with mischief behind round spectacles.

Marcus cracked a smile as he glanced around the crowded bar. The air was thick with the scent of stale beer and youthful ambition, a stark contrast to the sterile corridors and suffocating silence of the library where he spent most days poring over texts. Here, life was vibrant and unscripted—a welcome reprieve from the structure of academia.

"Intellectual chic, huh?" Marcus echoed, taking a slow sip of his drink. "I guess that's one way to describe it."

"I haven't fully succumbed to the establishment like you," James said, raising his glass in a mock salute. To my chic armour, may it shield me from the slings and arrows of outrageous fortune."

"Or at least the occasional bar brawl," Marcus said with a wry grin.

Their laughter mingled with the bar's din. In this small corner of the world, they were just two more dreamers adrift in the tide of change, their futures as uncertain as the melodies carried on the smoky air.

Marcus leaned in, his voice a conspiratorial whisper over the clinking of glasses and the jangle of guitar riffs. "You know, Nixon's whole debacle—it's like watching a modern-day tragedy unfold. The hubris of it all."

James nodded the furrow in his brow deepening. "A Greek play for the television age. And what will be our takeaway? The erosion of trust in government? Or maybe the recognition that power, unchecked, corrupts absolutely?"

"Perhaps both," Marcus said, swirling the dark liquid in his glass. "And then there's Vietnam. An entire generation is questioning the very fabric of society, the validity of the American Dream."

"War has a way of tearing through the veil of innocence. It's not just the physical toll, but the psychological scars it leaves behind," James said. They were no strangers to the nightly news reports detailing the latest horrors from across the globe, the images of conflict juxtaposed against the carefree tunes spilling from the jukebox.

Their conversation meandered through their dissertations; the essence of their futures distilled into academic prose. Marcus's thesis on the impact of war on cultural identity seemed more relevant with each passing day.

"I want to teach, James. To share the lessons of history so we don't repeat them," Marcus said. "There's something about the exchange of ideas, the spark of understanding in a student's eyes—that's what I'm chasing."

"That's admirable," James said. He took a slow sip of his beer, considering. "Me, I crave a position where I can contribute to policy, maybe—a place at the table where decisions are made."

"One of those Think tanks?" Marcus ventured.

"Perhaps. Something that allows me to apply what we've learned, to shape the course rather than simply observe it." James's hands moved animatedly as he spoke, sculpting his aspirations into the smoky bar air.

"Whatever path we choose, let's make sure it's one with purpose," Marcus reflected, feeling the gravity of their shared ambition weighs him between them.

"May we find it," James toasted, and they drank to the unknown road ahead.

The clink of glasses and the low murmur of conversations meshed with the strains of a Led Zeppelin classic emanating from the jukebox. Marcus, elbows resting on the worn bar top, found his gaze wandering away from the intensity of their historical debate. Across the room, amidst the haze of cigarette smoke, stood a girl. Her blonde hair cascaded in loose waves over her shoulders, catching the light as she moved between patrons with an easy smile.

"Marcus," James nudged him, a knowing smirk playing lips. "You're staring."

He was caught, but the corners of Marcus's mouth twitched upward despite himself. His eyes lingered a moment before retreating to his friend. "She's... perfect," he said, the words tinted with a mix of admiration and something deeper—an echo of longing.

"Then go on, ask her out," James encouraged, leaning back in his chair with a casual air that Marcus both envied and appreciated.

"James, look at her," Marcus protested, but the words were hollow as they left his mouth. He knew it wasn't just about her looks; it was the ease with which she floated through the room—a stark contrast to his methal approach. "She's way too good for me."

"Too good for you?" James's laughter was a warm sound, tinged with affectionate incredulity. "Marcus, you forget who you are—one of the brightest minds in our program." His gesture encompassed the intellectual battleground they had carved within these walls. "If anything, I'd wager you're too good for her."

"Academics and real life are worlds apart," Marcus countered as if confessing a closely held secret. "I can navigate a library or deconstruct theories, but this..." He gestured toward where the girl worked, an embodiment of all the unpredictable variables outside the realm of books and dissertations.

"Sometimes, my friend, your intellect is a barrier you construct around yourself." James's tone was gentle yet unyielding. "You deserve happiness beyond these scholarly pursuits. Take a chance, Marcus. Let yourself live a little outside the footnotes and bibliographies."

"Sit down, you're making a scene," Marcus said under his breath, the heat of embarrassment creeping up his neck as James half-rose from their rickety wooden table. With a chuckle that didn't quite mask the underlying tension, James resumed his seat just as the subject of their earlier debate made her approach.

"Can I get you guys anything else?" she asked, her voice cutting through the rumble of classic rock.

Marcus was caught in the silent storm of her presence; up close, she shimmered with palpable energy. Her hair fell in golden cascades, framing features that seemed to defy the dim lighting, giving her an ethereal glow amid the mundane surroundings.

"Your name, for starters," James chimed in, his words slicing through Marcus's reverie with the precision of a well-aimed arrow.

"Julia," she said, her lips curving into a smile that seemed to hold a secret kinship with the Mona Lisa's.

"Julia," Marcus echoed, tasting the melody of the syllables. It was a name that felt like a discovery—a missing piece to a puzzle he hadn't realized was incomplete.

"James," said his friend, extending a hand which Julia shook with a firmness that contradicted the delicate nature of her fingers. "And this is Marcus."

"Nice to meet both of you," Julia said, her gaze settling on Marcus with an openness that unnerved him.

"Likewise," Marcus managed, forcing the word past the knot in his throat. Something about how she held herself—assured yet unassuming—made him feel as though he was standing at the edge of a precipice, teetering between the safety of solitude and the dizzying potential of connection.

"Anything else for you guys?" Julia prompted, her blue eyes scanning their nearly empty pint glasses.

"Another round, please," James said before Marcus could muster the courage to speak. The moment lingered, suspended in the bar like a note held beyond its measure, before Julia turned on her heel, leaving a scent of citrus that seemed to hang long after she'd gone.

"See? She's just a girl, Marcus," James said, leaning back in his chair with a look that bordered on smug satisfaction. "A very beautiful girl, but still just a person, like you and me."

"Yeah, she's beautiful," Marcus said, nursing the remnants of his beer. He couldn't shake the feeling that there was more to her—a depth that beckoned him to cast aside his usual caution and dive into uncharted waters. But the fear of drowning in the unknown depths held him back, tethering him to the safety of familiar shores.

Julia returned with a fresh round, the glass bottles clinking softly against one another as she set them down with practiced ease.

"Need anything else?" she asked, her tone lilting, expectant.

"Actually," James said, his voice cutting through the hum of conversations and the distant wail of a guitar solo from the jukebox. "My friend Marcus here, he's not just any grad student. This guy's the future of academia—a rising star destined to be a professor and an author. And he'd like to ask you out."

Marcus's cheeks flushed, a mixture of embarrassment and irritation bubbling up inside him as he shot James a pleading look. He turned to Julia, trying to salvage the situation. "James enjoys his beer a little too much," he said, his words rushed.

Julia's gaze shifted to Marcus, her blue eyes holding a hint of mischief that seemed to pierce through his facade. "So, you don't want to ask me out, then?" she queried, her head tilting to one side. Her straightforwardness was disarming, unsettling Marcus in a way he couldn't quite explain.

"Uh, no—that's not what I meant," Marcus said, his hands fidgeting with the label on his bottle. He could feel the weight of her stare, inviting yet challenging. It was as if she could see the layers he had carefully constructed over the years, each a defence against the vulnerability she was now coaxing to the surface.

"Because, Marcus," Julia said, the corner of her mouth lifting into a playful smile, "if you want to ask me out, all you have to do is ask."

The statement's simplicity and confidence with which she delivered it left him breathless. Here was a woman who knew her worth and seemed unafraid to confront life head-on—a stark contrast to the calculated caution that had always governed his choice. It was both intoxicating and terrifying, and for a brief second, Marcus envied that freedom.

"Would you like to grab a drink sometime?" he managed, his voice steadier than he felt.

Julia's smile ignited something akin to courage within Marcus. "I'd like that," she said, her voice smooth as the amber liquid in the glasses around them. I'm off at ten if you're still here." The words hung between them before she turned, the simple act transforming her into the epitome of grace in motion.

Marcus watched her retreat, her blonde hair catching the low light, sending glimmers dancing across the room. He hadn't realized he'd been holding his breath until she was out of earshot, and he released it in a silent sigh.

"Look at you, Dempsey," James said, slapping Marcus on the back. "I think you may have caught a good one."

Marcus glanced at the clock above the bar; its hands were nearing ten. The chatter around them seemed to fade into a dull murmur as he contemplated the gravity of what was about to happen. He had always been more at ease amongst dusty books and ancient texts than in the unpredictable throes of human connection.

"Maybe," Marcus said, though doubt clung to the word like ivy to old stone.

"Time for me to head out," James said, his voice pulling Marcus back to the present. He stood, the legs of his chair scraping against the worn floorboards. "Give you some space to work your magic."

"Thanks," Marcus said, though magic was foreign—a concept best left to storybooks and fairy tales. He offered James a tight smile, the kind that didn't quite reach his eyes.

"Good luck, Marcus. She's a catch." James wove through the tables with a final nod and disappeared into the night beyond the bar's entrance.

The silence that followed was filled with anticipation. Marcus could feel the steady rhythm of his heart; each beat a drumroll leading up to the unknown. He had spent years analyzing the past, dissecting events long since etched into history, yet now it was his future unfolding before him—one that held the potential for both profound joy and unforeseen loss.

It would be easy to slip back into his shell, to bury himself in academia where the risks were intellectual, not emotional. But Julia's laugh, tinged with warmth and unspoken promises, echoed in his memory, coaxing him towards a trust he was unsure he possessed.

As the minutes ticked by, Marcus wrestled with the facets of his identity that had brought him to this juncture, the intersection of who he was and who he might become. Was he the man who sought refuge in the safety of knowledge, or was he the one willing to embrace the thrill of the unknown?

The vinyl on the booth squeaked as Marcus shifted, his gaze tracing the condensation dripping down the glass of his nearly empty beer. The bar's noise turned into a distant hum, punctuated by the occasional clink of glasses and the unmistakable scratch of the needle against the record as another classic rock anthem burst forth from the jukebox.

He was alone now, James's chair opposite him vacant, its absence echoing the sudden solitude that wrapped around Marcus like a shroud. The anticipation in the pit of his stomach had grown roots, tangling with nerves and an unfamiliar longing for the clock to hasten its sluggish pace.

Then she appeared, her presence slicing through the haze of loneliness—Julia. She moved with a fluidity that seemed to defy the chaos around her, her hands balancing two frosted beers with practiced ease. Marcus felt the air shift as she approached and slid into the seat where James had been.

"Julia Davidson," she said, her voice a melodic contrast to the roughness around them. She offered the beers to Marcus like a gesture of truce between strangers. He took it, the chill of the glass a welcome shock against his warm fingers.

"Marcus Dempsey," he said, the words strange and heavy on his tongue.

Her smile bloomed slowly, a sunrise of recognition spreading across her features. "Professor Dempsey," she said, her blue eyes glinting with a spark of joy that seemed to dance in the dim lighting.

Marcus chuckled, a self-deprecating sound that scratched at his throat. "Not quite there yet. Still wading through the marshlands of graduate school."

"Ah, but you'll get there." Her confidence was unwavering. "I can tell."

A laugh threatened to bubble up within him, incredulity mingling with the tiniest seed of pride. Could she see something in him that he dared not acknowledge?

"Thank you," he managed, the words sincere despite their brevity. He sipped the beer she'd brought, letting the bitter coolness settle in his chest, a counterpoint to the warmth spreading from the core of his being—a warmth kindled by her unexpected faith in him.

The clinking of glasses and the low hum of conversation had dwindled as midnight approached, the bar's energy ebbing away with each passing moment. Chairs were upturned onto tables, their legs silhouetted against the fading light. He turned back to Julia, her face illuminated by the lamp above their table.

"Sometimes, I dream about the future," she said. "A little house with a boy and a girl running through the sprinklers... and a pool for hosting friends on warm summer evenings."

Marcus nodded, his eyes tracing the earnestness that lit up her features. "That sounds nice," he said, allowing himself a rare glimpse into a future unburdened by the weight of dissertations and academic rigour.

Julia leaned forward slightly, her hands cradling her beer like a crystal ball, revealing visions of what could be. "You know," she said, a wistful tone threading through her words, "I think I'd work, even if just part-time. But my kids would be my world."

"Work?" Marcus echoed, intrigued by the layers unfolding before him. "What kind of work?"

"Real estate," she said, her eyes brightening. "There's something about meeting new people, seeing their dreams of a home take shape. It's... it's like piecing together a puzzle where every piece is someone's hope or memory."

"Sounds fulfilling," he said, his tone genuine. The word hung between them, a bridge of understanding that spanned far beyond the scope of their casual encounter.

Julia's smile was soft as she looked down at her hands, now absentmindedly tracing the rim of her glass. "It is," she said, "or at least I think it will be."

The low hum of the jukebox had faded into a quiet backdrop as the last patrons shuffled out of the bar. Julia gathered empty glasses with a grace born of routine.

"Hey," she said, catching his gaze, "when do you plan on writing that first book of yours?"

"Ah, right after my dissertation," he said, pushing up the sleeves of his button-up shirt.

"Would you let me read it?" Julia's voice was tentative yet eager, contrasting her confidence behind the bar.

"Of course," Marcus said, brushing off the gravity of his work with a wave of his hand. She turned away to tend to her closing duties, but the small smile playing lips betrayed her pleasure.

With the last call long past, time seemed to have thinned, drawing the night to a close with hushed urgency. They made their way to the exit, the door creaking a protest as Marcus held it open for her. The cool night air enveloped them, a refreshing contrast to the stale warmth they left behind.

"Which way is your place?" Julia asked, adjusting the strap of her purse on her shoulder.

"Back towards campus," Marcus gestured, his eyes following the deserted street as it stretched before them. "But I'll walk you to your bus stop first."

"Are you sure? It's not too far, but still..."

"Positive," he said with an assuring nod. They stepped into the street, their shadows mingling on the pavement under the sparse glow of streetlights.

As they walked, their conversation flowed from fleeting passions to distant dreams. Julia spoke of her ambitions and how she envisioned her future children laughing in the summer sun by the pool.

"And what about you, Marcus?" she asked, her eyes searching his face for the untold chapters of his life. "What's your future look like?"

"Books and lectures, at least for the time being," he said, his voice trailing into the quiet surroundings. "It seems simple when I say it out loud."

"Simple isn't bad," she countered, her tone gentle. "Sometimes, it's exactly what we need."

The bus stop emerged ahead, a solitary bench bathed in the pale light of an overhead lamp. The evening's momentum paused.

"Here we are," he said, stopping beside the bench. The schedule posted on the pole promised a bus in minutes, the inevitability of their parting suddenly looming tangible and near.

"Thank you, Marcus," Julia said, her words wrapped in layers of newfound intimacy. "For walking me here, for the talk, for making this night... different."

"I had a great time," he said, his voice steady despite the tremor of realization that their brief intersection might fade into memory with the coming dawn.

They stood there, two silhouettes framed by the glow of the bus stop, their futures untold but, for a moment, intertwined.

The low rumble of the arriving bus echoed the quickening pulse that thrummed through Marcus's veins. He turned to Julia, her face illuminated by the soft glow of the streetlamp above, her eyes reflecting a quiet certainty.

"Tonight was unexpected," she said, her voice steady but betraying a hint of wistfulness.

"Unexpected in the best way," Marcus said, feeling a connection stretching beyond the few hours they'd shared, reaching into a past he could almost remember living with her.

As the bus door creaked open, inviting the night's end, she lingered on the precipice of departure. "I had a good time, Marcus," she confessed, offering a smile that was both an ending and a beginning.

"Me too, Julia," he said, and the simplicity of the exchange carried the weight of unspoken promises and dreams yet to be chased.

Something fragile and bold took root in the space between them, growing with each heartbeat that passed. Then, as if compelled by force greater than their sum, Julia leaned forward. Her lips met his in a kiss that felt oddly familiar.

Marcus wrapped his arms around her, bringing her closer, melding into the warmth of her embrace. Time became a distant concept; the world was reduced to the tender pressure of Julia's mouth against his, the soft sighs that escaped them, and the mingling of their breaths.

"Alright, lovebirds, break it up," a gruff voice intruded, laced with impatience and a hint of amusement. The bus driver stood in the doorway, eyeing the pair.

They parted, and the air between them buzzed with the electricity of a beginning. The laughter that bubbled up within Marcus was natural as if it had always been a part of their dialogue.

"Until next time," he said, the words an anchor thrown into the future, promising more moments like this one.

"Until next time," she echoed, stepping onto the bus with a backward glance that spoke volumes. The doors closed behind her, sealing off the scene like the final paragraph of a prologue, leaving Marcus alone with the echo of a kiss and the certainty that the story they'd started writing tonight was far from over.

"Goodnight," Marcus's soft voice carried the weight of newfound affection as he stood at the curb, the bus's diesel engine idling in the background.

"Goodnight, Marcus Dempsey," Julia said with a playful tilt of her head, her words wrapping around his name like a secret only she could unravel. She climbed aboard. Settling into a seat by the window, she glanced out, her eyes catching the streetlight that painted half her face in a golden hue.

The bus grumbled to life, pulling away from the curb, but not before Julia raised her hand, waving through the glass. Marcus lifted his own, his wave a silent vow in the space between them. His fingers lingered in the air even as the bus turned the corner, her silhouette blurring with distance.

He remained there, anchored by the echo of her laughter, the ghost of her touch still warm on his lips. Then, turning on his heel, Marcus began the walk back to campus. His mind replayed every moment of the evening—the sound of Julia's voice, the depth of her blue eyes, and the way she leaned into the kiss as if she had been waiting for it all along.

A big smile broke across his face. The gravel crunched beneath his boots with each step, a steady rhythm against the quiet campus murmurs. The night air carried the scent of autumn leaves, a reminder of cycles and seasons, of things ending and beginning.

Marcus walked alone, yet the solitude didn't weigh heavy; it was filled with the buoyancy of possibility, the knowledge that someone saw him—not just as a future professor or author, but as Marcus, the man with dreams and doubts, smiles and stories. Tonight, he had shared those stories, and in return, he had glimpsed the outline of another's dreams, the sketches of a shared future, however uncertain.

"Until next time," he said to the empty street, a promise hanging in the cool night air, an invisible thread stretching from his heart to the window where Julia had sat, somewhere out there in the moving cityscape, taking with her a piece of the night they had woven together.

Part 5

1983

Chapter 13

The insistent buzz of the clock radio tore through the silence, signally the arrival of morning. As the opening chords of "Sweet Dreams" filled the room, Marcus lay in the last remnants of his sleep. A wry smile tugged at his lips—the song's promise to travel the world and the seven seas was like a private joke to the man whose life was firmly anchored in the routines of suburbia.

"Julia," he said. His hand reached out, brushing against her shoulder in a tender nudge. "Time to wake up," he said, preserving her peacefulness as long as possible. He got up and went to the bathroom, leaving Julia to slowly wake up.

He grabbed the safety razor and swept the blade across his jawline, the steady scrape grounding him in the present. The sting of Old Spice aftershave was a brisk slap to the senses, chasing away the last cobwebs of sleep. As he dressed, he studied himself in the mirror, noting the broad shoulders that filled out the suit—and the sandy blonde hair that never quite behaved.

Marcus left the bedroom and wandered down the hall, avoiding tripping on Jamie's newest Transformer. He rounded the corner and stepped into the kitchen, which was quintessentially suburban with its harvest gold appliances and linoleum floor. The laminate countertops were cluttered with a ceramic cookie jar shaped like a mushroom and a matching canister set, all adorned with the same earthy colour palette. He navigated past the avocado-green refrigerator, which hummed in a comforting, continuous drone.

He filled the glass carafe with water and measured out the Maxwell House coffee grounds, their rich aroma overpowering the lingering scent of last night's meatloaf. As the drip coffee maker gurgled to life, he leaned against the faux-wood panelling of the cabinets, cupping the warm mug in his hands.

Julia slowly stirred from their bed, her movements fluid despite the early hour. She padded softly across the carpet to the bathroom, where the fluorescent light flickered, casting harsh lines across her face in the mirror. Yet even under the unforgiving glare, her vibrancy shone through—her long blonde hair fell like cascading rays of morning sunlight.

She moved with practiced efficiency, brushing her hair until it framed her face in soft waves. Her fingers applied makeup, just enough to enhance her natural beauty without masking it. "Julia," Marcus said, not wanting to startle her but feeling the pull of time as morning pressed on. "The kids will be up soon."

"Almost ready," she said.

Julia emerged from the bathroom dressed in a light blue robe and went to the kitchen. Marcus eyed her blue robe, which hung mid-thigh, revealing strong but smooth legs. He gave a quick whistle and pulled her in close to him. "Marcus!" she said, "the kids will be up anytime." Marcus laughed and released her from his grip. Her hands moved with maternal precision, lightly tapping the countertop as she reached for the skillet. The sizzle of eggs in the pan beat a soothing rhythm while the aroma of frying butter curled into the air, mixing with the earthy scent of coffee that lingered from Marcus' earlier ritual. She adjusted the flame beneath the skillet.

The toaster clinked, springing to life, and soon, two slices of bread began to transform into golden warmth. Julia poured the orange juice from a glass pitcher.

With breakfast underway, Julia focused on the day's next responsibility. Her footsteps were soft as she went down the hallway to Jamie's room, where childhood fantasies played out on the walls. Star Wars posters stood guard, their edges curling as if reaching out to the real world from their faraway galaxy.

"Jamie," she said, touching his shoulder. "Time to wake up, sweetheart. Remember your school project?"

A groan echoed beneath the star-speckled bedcovers as Jamie buried himself deeper into his dreams, seeking refuge from the morning's advance. Yet, Julia's hand remained steadfast, her touch a tender insistence that the day wouldn't wait.

"Five more minutes," Jamie said, but the veil of sleep was already retreating.

"Alright, five minutes," Julia said, allowing him this small rebellion.

The quiet hum of the Vic 20 computer on the desk was evidence of Jamie's emerging passions. The blinking cursor on its screen perpetually called to him. Julia's gaze lingered there, pride mingling with concern for the unknown.

From the kitchen, the sound of toast popping up signalled breakfast's readiness, and Julia called once more over her shoulder, "Come on now, or it'll get cold."

She left the room, the door ajar, light spilling across the entrance, a silent invitation to face the day. Jamie, his will succumbing to the inevitable, threw back the covers and sat up, his eyes blinking against the intrusion of the morning.

Julia's fingers swept across the smooth pastel surface of Nicole's bedroom door before pushing it open. The room was a sanctuary of whimsy, where Care Bears smiled down from shelves and Rainbow Brite promised adventures far beyond the four walls. Sunlight was held back at the window until Julia's hands parted the curtains, flooding the space with warmth.

"Morning, sunshine," she said, her voice soft. Nicole, wrapped in dreams beneath a quilt, stirred. Her eyelids fluttered, resisting the morning's call.

"Time to get dressed," Julia encouraged, easing a brush through Nicole's tangled locks. Nicole's eyes opened fully now. Julia selected a lavender dress.

"Is this okay?" Julia held the dress up for approval, receiving a tired nod.

In the kitchen, the clink of cutlery and the hiss of the coffee maker filled the air. Marcus had already established his territory at the head of the table. With the paper unfolded before him like a sacred text, he skimmed through the headlines, pausing to absorb the latest in politics and economics.

"Stock market's still recovering from that slump in March," he said without looking up, his voice carrying over the sizzle of eggs in the pan.

"Is that so?" Julia said, not needing to look at the furrow of concentration on his brow. She placed plates heaped with scrambled eggs and golden toast before Jamie and Nicole, who had now joined them at the table.

"Star Wars isn't real, but the 'Evil Empire' is right here," Marcus said, referring to President Reagan's recent speech. The term lingered in the air, mingling with the aroma of breakfast.

Jamie's gaze flickered to his father, absorbing more than just the words. He was learning the language of the world — Nicole, too young to grasp the gravity of such discussions, concentrated on buttering her toast.

"Remember," Julia said, her tone light but laced with the undercurrent of life's lessons, "we can always choose to be kind, even when the world around us isn't."

Jamie's spoon clattered against his plate, a triumphant punctuation to the crescendo of his morning chatter. "Then, after soccer practice, Scott said we can trade comics. I've got the new Batman issue he hasn't read yet!"

With a furrowed brow mimicking concentration, Nicole held up her reading book to Julia. "Mom, what's this word?" Her small finger pointed at a string of letters that danced beyond her grasp.

" 'Adventure,' sweetheart," Julia said, her voice a gentle melody in the chorus of morning routines. She leaned over Nicole's shoulder, pointing to each letter as they sounded together.

"Ah-d-ven-ture," Nicole said, her face lighting up with the victory of conquered syllables.

"Exactly," Marcus said from behind his newspaper fortress, his eyes peering over the top with a hint of pride. "Life is full of them, and each teaches us something new."

The clock on the wall ticked in agreement, its hands inching toward the time of departure. Marcus folded his newspaper, placing it beside his now empty coffee mug.

"Time to brave the day," he said, stretching his arms above his head, his suit jacket pulling taut across his shoulders.

Julia nodded, her hands working to clear the plates, the remnants of breakfast evidence of the family's morning ritual. "Make sure you take your raincoat, Jamie. The forecast said there might be showers later."

"Aw, Mom, it'll ruin my look!" Jamie protested, but his grin belied the mock indignation.

"Your mother's right," Marcus said, retrieving his briefcase from its resting place by the door. He approached Julia, kissing her cheek—his daily affirmation of gratitude. "Thanks for breakfast, love."

"Anytime," she said.

With youthful exuberance, Jamie and Nicole rushed to their backpacks strewn by the entryway. Jamie stuffed his Superman lunchbox inside, vibrant colours against the canvas, while Nicole cradled her Strawberry Shortcake box.

"Ready?" Marcus asked.

"Ready!" they chorused, an echo of unity and anticipation.

As they filed out the door, the kitchen fell silent, the stage cleared of its actors.

The Ford Country Squire's engine hummed as Marcus navigated the suburban streets, its wood panelling gleaming in the early morning light. Inside, the car was filled with the familiar sounds of childhood anticipation and the soft crackle of the radio DJ's voice extolling the virtues of Michael Jackson's "Thriller" soaring at number one.

"... And folks, if you're not already feeling the magic in the air, let me tell you about a once-in-a-lifetime event tonight!" the gravelly voice of the DJ crackled through the car speakers. "That's right, David Copperfield, world-renowned illusionist, is set to perform his greatest feat yet. You won't want to miss it, listeners! Tonight, he will make the Statue of Liberty disappear before our eyes! Can you believe it? Tune in at 8 p.m. sharp for a show that'll leave you speechless."

The DJ's excitement permeated the car. Marcus glanced at Jamie in the rearview mirror, catching a glimpse of wonderment in his son's eyes. The magic of possibility hung in the air, a tantalizing promise on the horizon.

"Can we stay up to watch it, Dad?" Jamie said from the backseat, his eyes sparkling with the same enthusiasm that animated his words.

"Please, Daddy?" Nicole said, her gentle plea floating above the radio's din and the road's thrum.

Marcus glanced at them through the rearview mirror, their eager faces searching his for an answer. "I'll talk with your mother," he said, his voice measured yet warm, bridging authority and affection. "It's a school night, but we'll see."

"David Copperfield is so cool!" Jamie said, kicking his feet with excitement. "He's going to make the Statue of Liberty disappear!"

"Disappear? Really?" Nicole's question was tinged with wonder, her belief in magic undiminished by the mundane realities of life.

"Only on TV, sweetie," Marcus said to her, the corners of his mouth lifting. In their innocence, they could still believe in impossibilities, and he envied them that purity.

The station wagon pulled to the curb outside the school, children spilling out of cars and buses. Marcus turned to Jamie, noting the crease of determination etching his young brow. "Remember to be respectful to Mrs. Jenkins," he reminded him, aware that the boy's enthusiasm could sometimes spill over into defiance.

"Always am, Dad," Jamie said, shouldering his backpack with a confidence that seemed too large for his slender frame.

"And Nicole," Marcus addressed his daughter, her quiet presence contrasting her brother's exuberance. "Try to find someone new to play with during recess, okay?"

"Okay, Daddy," she said, her small fingers already fiddling with the strap of her Strawberry Shortcake lunchbox as if clinging to a piece of home.

"Love you both," Marcus said, the words carrying the weight of unspoken fears and hopes for their futures.

"Love you too, Dad!" they chorused, and with one last wave, they were off—two small figures threading their way through the crowd, each step a tiny assertion of their growing independence.

As the car door closed behind them, Marcus lingered for a moment, watching until they disappeared into the building. The radio echoed a reminder of the world's persistent turning—and the boundless trust his children placed in him to navigate it.

The Ford's engine hummed a soft farewell as Marcus shifted into drive, leaving behind the bustle of school morning farewells. He steered through the suburban streets, the car's wood panelling glimmering under the early sun. With its manicured lawns and peaceful streets, the neighbourhood seemed to nod in silent approval of the routine, a backdrop unaltered by time.

The University loomed ahead, not just a place of employment but where his identity had been forged and was about to be redefined. A promotion—once a distant ambition, now a tangible prospect—whispered opportunity and upheaval. It promised advancement yet demanded a toll, extracting more hours from the finite treasury of his life, hours that would be spent away from Julia, Jamie, and Nicole.

A pang of guilt tugged at him, countered swiftly by the pride that swelled in his chest. Hadn't he always strived for this? To be a pillar for his family, to offer them stability and a future bright with possibilities? Yet, Marcus questioned whether his pursuit of academic success might come at the cost of his family.

"Responsibility," he said to himself, tasting like a vintage wine, rich with complexity and hints of bitter undertones. With it came an inventory of his life's ledger: lectures prepared with meticulous care, papers graded with an even hand, and office hours igniting the sparks of curiosity in young minds. And then, there were the dreams deferred, the quiet moments with Julia eclipsed by the promise of tenure and the relentless march of academic achievement.

Pulling into the faculty parking lot, he killed the engine and sat for a moment, enveloped in the hush of the car's interior. He allowed himself a rare indulgence—a momentary surrender to the tide of introspection. Would the children understand the necessity of his absence and the sacrifices made in the name of their collective future? Or would they one day look back, their memories tinged with longing for a father whose presence was often more spectral than substantial?

With a slow exhale, Marcus gathered the fragments of doubt and locked them away. Work was to be done, futures to mould—including his own. He stepped out of the car, straightening his tie, and strode towards the hallowed halls awaiting him.

Chapter 14

Marcus admired the university's imposing, ivy-draped brick and stone buildings as he walked along the path. He approached the history department building and climbed the worn steps to the entrance.

Inside, the corridors were alive with the youthful energy of students navigating their way to early classes. Marcus moved among them, seamlessly blending in with the academic tapestry.

When he entered his office, Marcus closed the door behind him, sealing off the ambient murmurs of the corridor. The familiar scent of his office enveloped him as he settled into his morning routine.

His gaze swept over the room—a landscape of scholarly chaos. Bookshelves strained under the burden of their contents; amid this mess of history lay his desk, a vast wooden expanse where stacks of papers and manuscripts rose like miniature skylines, each a testament to the ceaseless grind of academic pursuit. And in the middle of his desk rested his typewriter—the steadfast companion to his thoughts, its keys worn smooth from his fingertips.

Marcus approached the desk with reverence. His manuscript lay open, its pages splayed like a bird mid-flight, yearning for the freedom of completion. With a sigh, he leaned forward and, with a careful hand, began to mark the margins. Each stroke of his pen was a delicate incision that crafted a narrative.

Perched high on the shelf, the clock ticked away the minutes. Marcus glanced at it before reaching for his schedule—today's itinerary printed in the crisp, clean lines on the school's academic letterhead. He shuffled through his notes, pages filled with scribbled insights and meticulous reminders. As he organized them, his mind wandered. There were expectations to meet, pressures to withstand, and, of course, the impending promotion.

"Focus," he said, a mantra to dispel the encroaching shadows. Marcus straightened the piles on his desk, aligning them with the precision of someone who seeks control in the details. The notes, now ordered, formed a map of the day's discourse—a path he had walked countless times.

He paused, his hand hovering over the neat array of papers, and with a final glance at his manuscript, he sat at his desk, ready to begin his day. The door to Marcus's office swung open, revealing the queue of students lining the corridor. They trickled in, each carrying their ambitions and uncertainties. Marcus leaned back in his chair, gesturing toward the seat across from him with assured ease from years of mentoring burgeoning minds.

"Let's hear where you are with your thesis," he said, his eyes steady on the young woman who sat down first. Her topic was ambitious: a detailed analysis of the socio-political impacts of the French Revolution on modern democracy. As she spoke, Marcus listened, nodding occasionally, his fingers tented under his chin.

"Consider Robespierre's transformation from visionary to tyrant," he said, "It's a poignant reflection on the seduction of power." Her eyes lit up with understanding, and she scribbled notes. Marcus felt a warm satisfaction at the spark of inspiration he could ignite in his students.

As the hours passed, each student left his office with a clearer vision, imbued with Marcus's patient wisdom. He did not simply impart knowledge; he crafted scholars, shaping their inquiries.

With the last student's departure, Marcus glanced at the clock. Office hours had ended, so he rose from his desk, stretching the stiffness from his limbs. The hallway was deserted now, the earlier burst of academic life reduced to a hushed stillness.

He went to the faculty lounge, pushing open the door to a space infused with the aroma of brewed coffee. The room was a capsule of history, with walls adorned with framed photographs of past graduating classes, esteemed professors, and University events.

"Marcus, how goes the battle?" said Professor Thompson, his voice buoyant amidst the subdued conversations.

"Advancing on all fronts," Marcus said with a wry smile, pouring himself a steaming cup. He took a sip, the bitterness a brief respite, before returning to the fray.

"Ever the tactician," said Thompson, leaning against the counter.

"Strategy is nothing without purpose, isn't what we teach?" Marcus quipped back, feeling the familiar camaraderie that tethered him to this world of intellect and inquiry.

Amidst the lounge's hum, Marcus found peace, an interlude between the demands of his profession. Marcus rinsed his cup with the final drop savoured and placed it on the rack. It was time to return to the stage and don the educator mantle again.

Marcus stepped out of the faculty lounge and spotted Richard leaning against the wall, a file tucked under his arm. The hallway was abuzz with the sound of students shuffling to their next class, their youthful exuberance creating a stark contrast to the seasoned calmness Marcus carried with him.

"Congratulations are in order, I hear," Richard said, straightening up as Marcus approached.

"Thanks, Richard," Marcus said. "My years of toiling away may have finally paid off."

They began to walk, their steps synchronizing as they navigated through the crowd of students. The familiarity of the path to the meeting room did little to ease the fluttering anticipation that danced in Marcus's chest.

"Department Head," Richard said as they entered the spartan meeting room, its walls lined with accolades of those who had shaped the minds of generations. He closed the door behind them, sealing off the chatter of the world outside. "A deserved recognition, but make no mistake, it will come with a cost."

"I know," Marcus said, easing into one of the chairs that flanked the long wooden table. "The balance shifts, doesn't it? More administrative chains to tie me down."

"Chains can be forged into tools, though," Richard countered, seating himself across from Marcus. His eyes held a knowing glint, the shared understanding of the sacrifices their roles demanded. "But remember, what's important is that you keep your passion for teaching, the raw connection you have with the students... How do you keep that alive when you are faced with all the demands of research and publishing? That's the real challenge."

Marcus leaned back. "I suppose," he said, "it's all about prioritization. As Department Head, I can shape the curriculum and, at the same time, teach it to the students."

"But your lectures, Marcus, are more than just a dissemination of knowledge. They're an art form," Richard said. "The University needs your administrative guidance, but your students need your inspiration."

"Inspiration," Marcus echoed. It was true; each lecture was a performance, a composition of history and humanity woven together by his narrative thread. Yet, with this new position came the fear of losing himself to the burden of leadership.

Richard leaned back in his chair, the light from the window casting a glow on the golden streaks in his hair. "So, Marcus, how about we get a jumpstart on the celebrations? Drinks after work today?"

Marcus looked up from the scattered papers on the table. His gaze settled on Richard's expectant face before drifting toward the window, where the late afternoon sun heralded the end of another academic day.

"Thanks, Richard," he said, the corners of his mouth lifting into a polite smile, "but I'll have to decline. Julia and the kids are expecting me tonight."

"Ah, family man to the core," Richard said, his voice warm with admiration. "Always keep your priorities straight. But come on, one drink won't hurt?"

Marcus folded his hands, "I appreciate the sentiment, Rich. But this promotion... it's not just mine." He paused, his voice softening. "It belongs to them too—the sacrifices they've made, the evenings alone while I graded papers or prepared lectures. I owe them this time."

"Ok, I understand," Richard said, nodding slowly.

Richard stood, clapping a hand on Marcus's shoulder. "Then go. Be with them," he said, his voice a blend of command and encouragement. "And when you return, we'll all be here, ready to raise a glass to Department Head Marcus Dempsey."

With a final nod, Marcus turned and left the room.

"Family first," he said to himself, a mantra to steady the palpable longing for connection, for the laughter of his children and the knowing smile of his wife that awaited him beyond the confines of academia.

Marcus strode back to his office and sank into the chair, its leather creased from years of scholarly contemplation. Marcus's fingers scrutinized the pages as he laid out his lecture notes. Visual aids lay aligned images of ancient artifacts and yellowed maps that promised to bridge the chasm between past and present. The clock ticked, a metronome to his preparations. He reviewed his points, the cadence of his thoughts arranging themselves into the melody of discourse.

In the lecture hall, Marcus took to the stage. He gazed out over the assembly, young faces aglow with the luminescence of curiosity.

"History," he said, "is not just the study of what has been. It is an exploration of the human soul, a journey through the trials and triumphs that have sculpted our identity."

The words flowed from him, each sentence imbued with the passion of a man who had devoted his life to unravelling time's intricate tapestry. He spoke of empires risen and fallen, ideologies birthed and buried, and ordinary people whose extraordinary deeds transcended the ages.

"Consider the fall of the Roman Empire," he said, gesturing to a slide of crumbling aqueducts. "It wasn't just brick and mortar that collapsed; it was a collective belief in invincibility, trust in unassailable power."

His students leaned forward, captivated, drawn into the narrative as though they walked the Appian Way and felt the tremors of a civilization quaking beneath their feet. Marcus moved among them, a shepherd guiding his flock through the annals of history.

"Ask yourselves," he challenged, "where do we see the reflections of Rome's hubris today? In our leaders? In ourselves?"

Questions arose, tentative at first, then surging with the tide of engagement. Marcus fielded them with the ease of a seasoned academic, yet each answer was delivered not as a mandate but as an invitation to delve deeper, to question further.

"Professor Dempsey," a student ventured, her voice threading through the discussion. "Do you believe history is destined to repeat itself?"

Marcus paused, considering not just the query but the inquirer, recognizing the earnest desire for truth that lay behind her eyes.

"History," he said, "is a mirror held up to our collective face. Whether we acknowledge our reflection or look away—that is where our destiny lies."

As the lecture drew close, the once-vibrant discourse faded into silence. Marcus stepped down from the podium. The last student filed out of the lecture hall, their faces alight with newfound understanding. Marcus lingered by the podium, gathering the remnants of his presentation, when a few stragglers approached, their eyes earnest and hungry for more.

"Professor Dempsey," one said, clutching a worn notebook. "Could you recommend any further readings on the cultural impacts during the decline of the Roman Empire?"

"Of course," Marcus said, his voice bearing the texture of old parchment and wisdom. "Look into 'The Fall of Rome: And the End of Civilization' by Bryan Ward-Perkins. It's a poignant analysis that will offer you a more nuanced perspective on the socioeconomic ramifications of that period."

"Thank you, sir," the student said, scribbling eagerly.

"Also," Marcus said, "don't overlook the primary sources. There's nothing quite like reading the words from the era itself to understand the human element behind the historical events."

The students nodded, their pens dancing across the paper to capture every syllable that fell from the professor's lips. With a final round of thanks, they departed, leaving Marcus alone amongst the empty chairs and desks.

Retreating to his office, Marcus settled into his chair once again. He reached for the manuscript—the culmination of years of research and reflection—its pages brimming with potential. His fingers grazed the text, poised to chart its course further, when his gaze was deflected by a photo standing upright on his desk.

There they were—Julia, her smile as warm as a sunbeam breaking through an overcast sky; his children, echoes of joy frozen in time. The image, contrasting with the formal academia surrounding it, captured a moment of unbridled happiness.

For a moment, Marcus allowed himself to be anchored by their faces. His eyes lingered, pupils dilating with the affection and quiet yearning that the photograph evoked. Then

Marcus closed the manuscript. The soft thud of the cover meeting the opening page was a silent admission of his inner conflict—a historian torn between the realms of the world he studied and the world he had created.

He stood, his frame casting a long shadow across the room as the dying light of day wrestled with the encroaching dusk. In that dimming office, surrounded by the ghosts of the past and the echoes of future promise, Marcus Dempsey acknowledged the delicate balance he strived to maintain—a scholar's mind and a family man's heart.

Marcus snapped the brass clasp of his briefcase with a decisive click. He paused, hand on the door handle, and allowed himself a moment of introspection. He felt a satisfaction from a day steeped in academia's rigour. Yet within that chest swelled a longing and anticipation for the familial warmth awaiting him beyond these walls. It was a daily reminder, this push and pull of his dual devotions.

"Balance," he said to the empty room, a word meant to steady the scales.

Marcus turned away from his office and stepped out into the corridor. The fluorescent lights flickered overhead, casting an uneven glow that danced across the polished floors in an erratic rhythm.

As he walked, his thoughts meandered through the day's successes—the insightful questions posed by bright-eyed students, the weight of his pen as it caressed the margins of his manuscript, and the friendly nods shared with colleagues.

A smile etched itself onto Marcus's face, invisible to all but the lingering spirits of academia, as he contemplated the honour of his impending title. Department Head—words that carried the gravity of responsibility and the sheen of recognition. The corridor stretched ahead, and Marcus could feel the very pulse of the university, a steady heartbeat that thrummed against his own.

Marcus paused once more as he approached the heavy doors marking the divider between his worlds."Tomorrow," he said, not as a promise but as an acknowledgment of the endless cycle, "we begin again."

Pushing open the doors, Marcus stepped out into the evening air. As he approached the faculty lot, the fading light of day cast long shadows that retreated before him. It was time to return to those who anchored him to the life awaited with open arms and unconditional love.

The Ford's engine hummed steadily as Marcus merged onto the tree-lined boulevard leading out of the university. The car, an old wood-panelled relic that had ferried him to countless lectures and meetings, now bore him homeward through the quiet streets.

With each mile that unfurled behind him, the tension in his shoulders unwound, his grip on the steering wheel easing into a gentle hold. There was solace in this transition, the soft purr of the Country Squire's engine a comforting undertone to his thoughts.

Marcus's gaze was drawn to the sliver of pink and orange sky peeking through the branches overhead. The sunset painted a serene tableau against the encroaching twilight, its fleeting beauty a daily performance he too often missed, buried in manuscripts and lecture notes. He savoured the sight today, letting the colours wash over him.

As the car glided past familiar landmarks—corner stores with flickering neon signs, rows of houses with porches veiled in the dimming light—he pondered the faces that awaited him. Julia's wavy hair was likely pulled back after a long day. And the kids are always eager to share their day's adventures with him. He imagined their bright eyes and animated gestures, the unfiltered joy that only children possess.

"Almost home," he said, a smile tugging at the corners of his lips. Home, where his titles and achievements shed their weight, leaving behind just Marcus—the husband, the father, the man who loved and was loved in return.

The streetlights flickered on as dusk settled in, their amber glow guiding him through the quiet neighbourhood. He turned into the driveway, the familiar creak of the garage door welcoming him back to the refuge of family life.

Shutting off the engine, Marcus sat in the gathering silence. His hand found the picture tucked into the sun visor—an old snapshot of Julia and the kids, their smiles forever captured in a moment of unguarded happiness. He traced a finger over their faces.

He stepped out of the car, the weight of his briefcase a tangible reminder of the world he left behind. With each step toward the front door, anticipation quickened his heartbeat, a crescendo building to the moment he'd push open the door to be enveloped by the warmth of his family's embrace.

"Julia," he said as he entered, his voice heralding the end of the day's solitude and the beginning of an evening filled with connection and love.

Chapter 15

Julia's fingers spread out the towels with precision. The backyard popped with the neon pinks and yellows of plastic flamingos staking their claim on patches of green. She draped the string lights, their bulbs like captured fireflies, in a looping embrace around the fence.

"Looks good, Mom," Jamie said. He hopped from one foot to the other, restless energy coursing through him as he dragged the volleyball net across the lawn, setting it up at the pool's shallow end where the water shimmered.

"Careful with that. It's older than you are," Julia said, half-glancing over her shoulder as she unfolded another chair with a metal snap against metal.

Jamie chuckled, "It looks like it's older than Dad." His fingers fussed with the net, tying it to the poles.

"Your friends will have a blast. You've done well," she said.

"Hey, look at this old thing!" Jamie said as he unearthed an inflatable beach ball from the storage box. Its colours were faded but cheerful. With a few more breaths, he brought it back to life and, with a playful toss, sent it towards Julia.

"Still got it," she said, catching the ball with surprising agility.

The doorbell rang, and Jamie's heart skipped with anticipation. He brushed his hands on his shorts, ridding them of water, and strode toward the front door. A grin spread across his face when he flung it open to reveal Trevor, clutching a plate wrapped in tin foil, and Janice, whose smile was as warm as the afternoon sun.

"Hey, Trevor! " Jamie said.

"Hey Jamie," Trevor said, matching Jamie's energy.

Janice extended the plate towards Jamie, the scent of freshly baked cookies wafting between them. "I hope chocolate chip is okay. It's all I had time to whip up this morning."

"Chocolate chip is the best," Jamie said, nodding and accepting the offering.

Julia emerged from the kitchen. She tucked a stray lock of hair behind her ear and approached Janice.

"Janice, those cookies smell divine," Julia said, allowing the corners of her mouth to rise just enough to be considered a smile. "You'll have to give me the recipe sometime."

"Of course, Julia. It's no secret—just a little extra vanilla and a lot of love," Janice said.

Together, they made their way to the backyard. Without missing a beat, Trevor and Jamie dropped their pretense of decorum and bolted for the pool. Their bodies sliced through the air before plunging into the water with the carefree abandon unique to youth, their laughter bubbling to the surface.

As the afternoon progressed, more kids arrived. The air was full of the high-pitched glee of children at play. Jamie and Trevor queued up for their turns on the diving board. With each spring-loaded launch, they sought to outdo each other, their bodies suspended in a gravity-defying challenge before crashing into the pool with sprays that reached for the sky.

"Look at them," Julia said, her voice a hushed marvel, as she settled into a lawn chair beside Janice.

"Who would've thought?" Janice said, her gaze tracking her son's every move. "It's like they've known each other for a lifetime," Julia said.

"Jamie..." Janice said, turning towards Julia. "He's been such a positive influence on Trevor. After the move, I worried, you know? New place, new friends can be hard on a child."

"Jamie knows what it is to be the new face," Julia said. "He sees himself in Trevor think."

The boys emerged from the water, droplets cascading from their limbs. As they shook themselves like young pups, the sun caught in the spray, creating prisms that danced around them.

"Your family has been so welcoming, Julia," Janice said, her words infused with gratitude. "This neighbourhood is more than I dared to hope for."

"Community," Julia intoned, "it's so important to have a support system. We've all felt like we're about to unravel, right?"

"More than you know," Janice confided, leaning back into the embrace of her chair, allowing the sounds of the party to envelop her.

The shadows grew longer, and the sun dipped lower in the sky, casting a warm golden hue over the scene.

Water dripped from Jamie's hair, mingling with the beads of sweat on his sun-kissed skin as he and Trevor clambered out of the pool. The chlorine scent was strong in their wake. They left wet footprints across the warm flagstones, each step pulling them further from the other children.

"Race you to the slide!" Trevor said, breaking into a run that had more to do with excitement than any real competition.

Jamie laughed and bolted after him.

They reached the playground set; its wooden fortresses and plastic tunnels faded by years of sun and storm. The jungle gym loomed before them, a monument to childhood adventures. "The Last one to the top is a rotten egg!" Trevor said.

Jamie followed, feeling the texture of the ropes against his palms. At the top, they sat side by side, feet dangling over the edge, surveying their kingdom of green grass and azure water.

"Hey, Jamie," Trevor said, his voice tinged with the enthusiasm that endless possibilities only youth could entertain. "At camp, we played this game of capture the flag. We should make a course in the forest back there." He gestured toward the line of trees that bordered the property.

"Really?" Jamie said, turning to look at Trevor, his eyes reflecting a spark of intrigue.

"Yeah, it'd be awesome! We can make two teams, hide the flags, and set boundaries..." Trevor's words spilled out faster than his thoughts could keep up, painting a picture of camaraderie and playful warfare.

"Okay, let's do it," Jamie said.

"Sweet! It'll be like our secret project. We can start planning tomorrow," Trevor said, and Jamie nodded, buoyed by the warmth of acceptance and the thrill of anticipation.

As they descended from their perch and slid down the slide in tandem, their laughter cascaded through the yard.

Jamie's fingers danced across the page, tracing the borders of their imagined battleground with a stubby pencil. The afternoon sun cast long shadows over the paper as he and Trevor hunched over it, sprawled on the grass still damp from the pool. Lines intersected, and circles were drawn, their crude map growing more intricate by the minute.

"Here," Jamie pointed to a shaded area representing the thickets bordering the forest, "could be one base. And the other..." He looked up, surveying the yard before returning to the map, "across, by the old oak tree."

"Perfect! The woods are split in two, just how we need it." Trevor's voice was alight with excitement, his eyes bright. "And we can use the creek as a boundary line."

"Now, where do we hide the flags?" He chewed on the end of his pencil.

"Somewhere hard to find... but not too hard that we never find it," Jamie said, drawing an 'X' on either side of their heads. They were close as they sketched out the details of their game.

Meanwhile, Julia sat by the poolside, her wavy blonde hair reflecting in the sunlight. She watched the boys from afar, her heart swelling with pride.

"It's so beautiful here," Janice said, a contented sigh escaping her lips as she entered the flower-filled backyard. "I can't thank you enough for welcoming us into the neighbourhood. Trevor's taken to Jamie."

"Friendship can be such a gift, especially at their age," Julia said. "It's important they have each other."

"Absolutely," Janice nodded, her gaze following the boys. "Trevor talks about Jamie all the time. Says he's the brother he never had."

"Moving can be hard on a child," Julia said, "but it seems he's finding his way."

"I really think so," Janice said.

"I think their adventures today will be the beginning of many," Julia said, her smile genuine yet tinged with a quiet longing.

"Here's to new beginnings," Janice raised her glass of iced tea in a toast, clinking it against Julia's.

"New beginnings," Julia echoed softly, her eyes drifting back to Jamie, whose laughter mingled with the rustling leaves.

The sun had begun its slow descent towards the horizon, casting long shadows across the Dempseys' backyard, when Jamie and Trevor, invigorated by their shared plans, dashed back to the pool's edge. Their feet slapped against the warm concrete as they joined the children's chorus in a water volleyball game.

While the children orchestrated their watery spectacle, Marcus Dempsey arrived home. The familiar grind of gravel under his tires signalled his return. He stepped out of his car, the lines of academia smoothed away by the sight of the lively gathering in his backyard.

"Looks like I've missed quite the party," he said.

"Dad!" Jamie called out, his voice winded from the exertion. "Just in time!"

"I hope so," Marcus said, acknowledging his son with a nod.

"Hello, Marcus," Janice said, offering a hand. "Thank you for having us. It's been delightful."

"Janice, it's our pleasure," Marcus said, shaking her hand.

"It's great to see the boys getting along so well," Marcus said, gesturing towards Jamie and Trevor, who were now strategizing their next play, dripping wet and entirely absorbed in the game.

"Jamie has been a wonderful friend to Trevor," Janice said, her voice full of gratitude.

Marcus retreated into the house. Inside, he stripped off his work attire and slipped into his swim trunks.

The back door clicked shut behind him as he stepped out, and the vibrant energy of the party swelled to meet him. The children's laughter hit him like a wave, flooding the empty spaces within him with something warm and unfamiliar. Marcus moved with a vigour that disguised his age, his limbs propelled by the sudden urgency to witness the joy and be part of it.

"Watch out, kids!" he said, a playful warning in his voice that caught the attention of every young face around the pool. Without hesitation, he launched into the air, tucking his knees to his chest before crashing into the water with a thunderous splash. The resulting wave rose high, showering the nearby squealing children who had scrambled to dodge the tidal onslaught.

Cheers erupted from the pool rim, where Jamie and Trevor stood dripping and wide-eyed. For a moment, Marcus allowed himself to bask in the adoration, the simplicity of being the hero in their eyes.

"Alright, Mr. Dempsey, that was cool and all, but you've got nothing on my cannonball!" challenged one of the kids, a spark of competitive fire lighting up his youthful expression.

"Is that so?" Marcus said, eyebrows raised in mock surprise. "I suppose we'll have to make this a contest then."

One by one, the children thurled themselves into the pool with various degrees of success, their excitement fueling their attempts to outdo the last. Laughter filled the yard, intermingling with the splashes and the footsteps racing for another go.

"Your turn, Jamie!" Trevor said, nudging his friend forward.

With a breath, Jamie ran and leapt. The water enveloped. "Nice one, Jamie!" Marcus cheered, clapping his hands, pride swelling in his chest.

The contest continued until it reached its natural conclusion, with no clear winner but a collective sense of triumph. As the sun dipped lower, painting the sky in hues of loss and hope, Marcus pulled himself out of the pool, water streaming down his body. Jamie and Trevor shook off the excess droplets, their eyes alight with the simple happiness of childhood—a treasure he wished he could protect forever.

"Hey, Dad," Jamie said, breaking through Marcus's reverie, "That was awesome!"

Marcus smiled, a rare and genuine curve of his lips. "You boys made it awesome," he said. Marcus wrapped a towel around his waist, the fabric clinging to the last remnants of dampness as he strode towards the picnic table. The smell of sunscreen mingled with the aroma of barbecue, and the clatter of plastic plates underscored the laughter that still danced in the air. Julia was there, her hands fluttering as she arranged the snacks and poured lemonade into cups with practiced grace.

"Make sure you get some food, Jamie," she said, her voice the gentle nudge of concern wrapped in the warmth of maternal instinct. She handed him a plate piled high with chips and a hot dog, the ketchup bleeding into the bread in a familiar, comforting way.

"Thanks, Mom," Jamie said.

The kids swarmed around the picnic table, their wet footprints evaporating from the sun-warmed concrete. Marcus watched them. They were so vibrant, so alive, and filled with energy.

"Trevor!" Janice said, her words a signal that the day was winding down.

"Wait, before you go," Jamie beckoned Trevor over to a quieter spot by the now-gentle waves of the pool. The two boys huddled together; their heads bowed as if in conspiracy. "So, about that game," Jamie said, his fingers tracing patterns in the air as though they could sketch out their plans.

"Yeah, we can use the old fort as a base," Trevor said, his eyes shining with the excitement that only childhood games can inspire.

"Perfect," Jamie said. "I'll bring some old flags from the garage. We can set up the boundaries first thing."

"Deal," Trevor said, extending his hand. Their handshake was firm, a pact sealed in friendship and the shared sanctuary of imagination.

As parents ushered their children away, voices softened by distance, Julia leaned back in her chair, observing the exchange between Jamie and Trevor. "Looks like Jamie's found a good friend in Trevor," Marcus said, joining Julia at the table. Julia nodded, her gaze lingering on the figure of her son against the backdrop of twilight. "Yes, he has; seeing him so happy has been great."

The sun dipped lower. For a moment, the backyard was silent. "Another day," Marcus said, his hand finding Julia's. Their fingers intertwined. Marcus and Julia sat together in the dwindling light, watching the stars emerge. They spoke not of grand plans or distant dreams but of the quiet hope that bloomed in the simplicity of connection—a family, pieced together by moments like these, under the watchful eye of the coming night.

Janice approached Julia, her arms wide as if to embrace the entire day. "Julia, Marcus," she said, a warm smile spreading across her face, "I can't thank you enough for today." The setting sun cast a rosy glow on her cheeks, and her eyes sparkled with the sincerity of her gratitude. "Trevor had such a wonderful time, and it's been so nice to spend this afternoon together."

Julia returned the smile with an ease that belied the effort it took. "We're just glad everyone enjoyed themselves," she said, her voice a soft echo of the joy around her.

"Janice, it's our pleasure," Marcus chimed.

As Janice gathered her son and their belongings, Jamie and Nicole appeared from the shadowy corners of the yard, their forms animated by the task at hand. They moved through the backyard, overturning the day's fun into neatly stacked chairs and folded towels.

The last guests waved goodbye, their shadows stretching long across the lawn. The Dempseys stood for a moment, watching the world retreat into twilight.

Jamie flicked off the last of the switches, plunging the backyard into a softer darkness. The only light now was the soft glow from the kitchen spilling out onto the patio. The once vibrant pool party had simmered down to a quiet hush.

In the living room, Julia swept up the last crumbs of the day, the soft swish of her broom a familiar rhythm in the quiet house. Marcus paused at the doorway, watching her with a tenderness that belied his broad-shouldered frame.

"Julia," he said, the name itself a caress, "let's leave the rest for the morning, shall we?" His hand extended towards her, an invitation.

She looked up from her task, the corners of her deep-set eyes crinkling as she placed the broom aside and took his hand. Together, they stepped out onto the patio, leaving the warmth of the house for the cool embrace of the evening.

The garden chairs creaked as they settled in, side by side yet wrapped in their thos. Above them, the sky blossomed into a tapestry of stars, each a witness to the world below.

"Today was good, wasn't it?" Marcus finally broke the silence, not seeking confirmation but simply voicing a shared truth.

"It was," Julia said, allowing herself to absorb the simplicity of the statement. "Seeing Jamie so... alive."

"Our family," Marcus said, the word enveloping them like a blanket. "It's everything to me."

They leaned back, hands finding each other in the darkness, fingers intertwining—a physical manifestation of their lifelong journey together. In this quiet space, they allowed themselves to dream of a future where the fractures might mend, where trust could blossom anew, and where their identities could be reclaimed from the shadows of the past.

"Let's have more days like this," Marcus said.

"Yes," Julia said, her heart daring to agree. "Let's."

And there, under the watchful gaze of the stars, they found contentment in their connection, a sense of peace in the collective heartbeat of their family, pulsing beneath the chaos of life.

With the kids put to bed, Marcus and Julia retreated to their bedroom. They shed the layers of the day, baring themselves to each other with a vulnerability that felt almost weightless. Marcus's hands reached out to touch Julia's face, his fingers tracing lines of love and longing etched by time.

Julia's breath caught in her throat as she met his gaze, a silent understanding passing between them. The years melted away at that moment, leaving only two souls laid bare in the quiet space they had carved out for themselves.

Marcus climbed on top of Julia and gripped her hands with his, anchoring them over her head. With a swift motion, he entered her as he kissed her deeply. They moved in unison. Marcus's pace quickened, and Julia gripped his body with her legs. He came inside her with a shudder and released his grip. Julia gripped his back with her hands and pulled him close. They lay like that for a time until Marcus rolled off her onto his back. With heads turned, they looked at each other, and Marcus traced Julia's cheekbones with his finger.

"I love you," Julia said.

"I love you too, Julia," Marcus said.

Chapter 16

Marcus and Julia Dempsey parked their sedan along the curb and walked to James's front door. "Sounds like he's playing our old favourites," Marcus said with a rare, boyish grin. Julia smiled, "It will be nice to let loose for an evening." They ascended the steps to James's porch, touching their hands before knocking on the door. When it swung open, the sight of the wood-panelled living room greeted them.

"Marcus! Julia!" came James's boisterous welcome, his arms open in a gesture that pulled them from the doorway and into the heart of the party.

"James," Marcus said, allowing himself to be absorbed into the embrace of an old friend.

"Look at you two, escaping the quiet life for a night," James said, dancing between jest and genuine delight.

"Sometimes, the quiet life needs a little shaking up," Julia said.

As they stepped inside, the buzz of conversation and laughter enveloped them. Couples clustered near the fondue pot, its contents bubbling like liquid gold, while chunks of bread and crisp vegetables awaited their submersion. "Ah, the infamous fondue," Marcus said.

"Infamous?" James echoed, feigning insult. "I'll have you know this recipe is a family treasure."

"Treasure indeed," Julia said with a smile, reaching for a skewer, piercing a piece of bread and dipping it into the melted cheese.

"Can you believe how long it's been since we've all been together like this?" James's wife chimed in.

"Too long," Marcus said.

Marcus took in the lively scene as he and Julia navigated through the clusters of guests. Laughter bounced off the wood-panelled walls. They stopped at a bar cart in the corner. "Old fashioned for me, please," Julia said, her eyes scanning the choices before they settled on Marcus with an expectant look.

They carried their drinks into the heart of the living room. The group they joined was engrossed in a debate over television's latest offerings—"Magnum, P.I." or the opulent "Dynasty," which unfolded in their living rooms every week.

"Marcus, you've seen 'Return of the Jedi,' right? What did you think?" asked one of the guests.

"I think the Ewoks stole the show," Marcus said.

"Speaking of shows," James said, looping an arm around Marcus's shoulder and drawing him away from the group, "everyone, Marcus here is about to become the new head of the history department."

A chorus of congratulations rose among the couples. Marcus accepted the adulation with a modest nod.

"More paperwork than you can imagine, buddy," said a colleague, the jest softened by a genuine smile. "And let's not forget the joys of endless faculty meetings."

"Wouldn't miss it for the world," Marcus said, his laugh belying the creeping tendrils of doubt about balancing the scale between professional demands and the personal toll it might exact.

Julia watched the exchange, pride swelling within her. With a gentle nudge from Julia's elbow, Marcus found himself drawn towards the fondue pot, its aroma weaving through the air like a warm invitation. The cheese bubbled and glistened, a golden pool around which the guests congregated, skewers in hand, laughter cresting in waves. He speared a piece of bread, watching it emerge cloaked in the velvety cheese.

The turntable crackled slightly before giving way to the familiar beat of a rock anthem. The room's chatter dipped as a few guests hummed along, their voices mingling with the rasp of the singer's voice. Marcus caught himself tapping his foot, the rhythm pulling at a thread of youthfulness he seldom felt anymore.

Julia leaned close as the song reached its crescendo, saying, "You used to sing this in the shower."

"Guilty," he confessed, a twinkle of mischief dancing in his eyes. Refilling their glasses with a practiced hand, Marcus chose a smooth red wine for Julia and a more robust scotch for himself. They shuffled over to a cluster of friends engaged in an animated discussion about popular music, the circle opening to accept them.

"Have you heard about the CD player?" Marcus chimed in, the question more rhetorical than not. "Supposedly, it'll change music forever."

"Only if computers don't take over the world first," someone countered, sparking a round of chuckles and nods of agreement.

The subtle undercurrents of the conversation washed over Julia. Though indulging in a few drinks, Marcus remained remarkably composed, his stature commanding yet affable. "Here's to progress, then," Marcus toasted, raising his glass. "And to technology, may it always be one step behind our ability to enjoy life."

"Cheers," they echoed, their voices united. Marcus stood by the fireplace, the warmth of the flames a gentle counterpoint to the lively discussions that filled the room. James, his posture relaxed yet attentive, leaned against the mantelpiece and looked at Marcus with the easy camaraderie of old friends.

"Marcus, I've been meaning to ask you," James said, his voice rising above the hum of background chatter. "How are you feeling about your promotion? It's a big step, isn't it?"

The question hung in the air as Marcus took a moment to gather his thoughts. The excitement of professional advancement wrestled with an underlying current of trepidation.

"It's an honour," Marcus said, his voice steady but revealing a hint of the pressure he felt. "The weight of new responsibilities is daunting, though. There's so much to consider, especially when giving time to Julia and the kids."

Standing close enough to catch each word, Julia allowed herself a small smile. Her eyes brimmed with pride. She reached for Marcus's hand, a silent testament to her unwavering support.

"Your dedication has never gone unnoticed, Marcus," she said, her words laced with affection and assurance. "You've always found a way to keep us and your work part of your life, no matter how demanding work gets."

Around them, their friends raised glasses in a toast, the clink of crystal an affirmation of Marcus's achievements and the bonds that held them together through every twist and turn of their shared history.

"To Marcus," David pronounced, his voice rich with sincerity.

"Cheers," they echoed, a chorus of goodwill reverberating through the room.

As conversations ebbed and flowed, the guests naturally splintered into smaller groups, each absorbed in the nuances of the year's events. Marcus found himself drawn into a discussion with James, their voices low and earnest as they contemplated the future of academia.

"Change is on the horizon for the University," Marcus said, his gaze distant as if envisioning the landscape of tomorrow. "We have to stay ahead, carve out a place for innovation without losing sight of our traditions."

"Agreed," James nodded, his expression one of contemplative agreement. "It's a delicate dance, Marcus. But if anyone can lead the department through these times, it's you."

Across the room, Julia's conversation carried a different weight, one of motherhood and its myriad complexities. She listened intently to Laurie, whose parenting tales were familiar and comforting.

"Sometimes, it feels like we're juggling more than we can handle," Julia confided, a rare admission that slipped past her usual guard.

"Ah, but look at what resilient creatures we've become," Laurie said, her laughter tinged with empathy. "Our children grow stronger because of the strong example we set."

Julia's wrist flicked, the silver of her watch catching the light as she glanced at the time. Jamie and Nicole hovered in her thoughts, their lives a constant hum in the back of her mind. "I'm just so glad we found Debbie," she confided to Laurie, who was swirling her wine glass.

"Steady hands on the home front make nights like these possible," Laurie said with a knowing nod. She leaned in closer, dropping her voice to a theatrical whisper. "Last week, our sitter dressed up as Wonder Woman just to get the kids to eat broccoli. Called it 'superfood for future heroes.'"

Julia excused herself from the group and made her way to the kitchen. She reached for the cream-coloured rotary phone mounted on the wall. She dialled the familiar number of home. After a few moments, the line connected, and a soft voice floated through the receiver. "Hello?"

"Hi Debbie, it's Julia. I'm just checking in to see how things are going." Julia said.

"Everything's been great," Debbie said. "The kids went down over an hour ago. They seemed pretty tired after the games we played."

"That's great, Debbie," Julia said. "We're leaving soon, so if you need to run, that's fine. I think the kids will be fine for a bit. I'm sure your parents will be happy to have you home."

"Oh, ok, that's great, Mrs. Dempsey. I'll just finish cleaning up and then be on my way. Hope you had a good evening." Debbie said.

"Everything was great; thanks again, Debbie," Julia said.

"Bye, Mrs. Dempsey." The line clicked, and Julia returned the phone to its cradle. Satisfied that the kids were in good hands, she returned to the living room and rejoined the party.

The room pulsated with the crescendo of voices and music. Marcus stood amongst his peers, a half-empty glass cradled in his hand, his posture relaxed yet commanding. When Julia's eyes met his, there was an unspoken agreement about the hour.

"Darling, are you certain about driving?" Julia's question cut through the din, her tone light but underlined with concern.

Marcus turned. "I've been keeping count," he said to her, his voice steady despite his spirits. Just a couple of glasses throughout the night. We'll be fine."

"Let's savour these last moments then," Julia said. The clink of glass on glass chimed through the room as James, with his customary vigour, stood at the head of the gathering. "To friendship," he said, his voice wrapping around each syllable, "and to the roads ahead, may they rise to meet us."

"May they be ever in our favour," Marcus said, his glass raised in salute.

"Cheers!" The word was a shared breath among the crowd, glasses touching with the softness of old memories and the promise of new ones. Julia's hand found Marcus's, their fingers entwining with a familiarity that spoke volumes of the years weathered together.

"Thank you, James, for a wonderful evening," Julia said, her gratitude genuine as she leaned in for an embrace, her voice a whisper lost in the warmth of the goodbye. "And please thank Laurie for us."

"Will do, Jules," James said, his eyes crinkling with affection. "You two don't be strangers now, hear?"

The farewells continued, punctuated by hugs as Marcus and Julia retrieved their coats from the heap of outerwear. They slipped into them, the leather and wool a gentle armour against the night's chill.

"Ready?" Marcus said, his brows arched in that way that signalled his readiness to depart and his reluctance to end the comfort of good company.

"Let's," Julia said, a smile playing on her lips despite the tug of apprehension that now laced her words.

They stepped out, the door closing with a soft click behind them. Night had draped itself over the world, the cool air kissing Julia's cheeks and rousing goosebumps along her arms beneath the coat.

Marcus took her hand again, his grip firm and assuring. The gravel crunched beneath their feet as they moved towards their car, parked under the watchful gaze of an oak tree whose branches swayed in the breeze.

"Did you enjoy yourself?" Marcus asked, breaking the silence that had surrounded them.

"I did," she said, allowing herself to lean into the contentment that bubbled up from the depths of her heart. "It's been too long since we've simply... let go."

"Too long," he echoed, his thumb brushing over the back of her hand.

"Home then," Marcus said, unlocking the car with a soft click.

Chapter 17

They settled into the car, and Marcus adjusted the dial to a Top Forty station. As he drove, the headlights cut a swath through the darkness. "Did you see James trying to moonwalk?" Marcus asked, a smirk playing on his lips. Julia let out a laugh. "It was more of a stumble, if anything."

"Stumble," Marcus said, laughter bubbling from his throat. He glanced at Julia, her wavy hair catching the light as she shook her head, still amused by the memory.

"Remember when we used to dance like nobody was watching?" Julia said.

"Used to? My dear, I still do." Marcus reached over, squeezing her hands. "Granted, my moves aren't what they used to be."

"Neither is mine," Julia confessed. "But for tonight, it felt good to let go."

"Life's too short not to dance badly at parties," Marcus said.

"Or to laugh at your husband's terrible jokes," Julia retorted, nudging him.

"Terrible? I'll have you know my students find me quite humorous," he defended,

"Of course they do," Julia said, her voice a mix of sincerity and sarcasm. "They're grading on a curve."

The road unfurled before them. The trees lining the road were part of the same forest bordering their backyard. "Almost home," Marcus said, feeling the car's hum beneath him. He glanced at Julia; her profile softened by the glow of the dashboard.

Julia nodded, her eyes tracing the silhouette of the trees as they passed. "It's always so peaceful here. Like the rest of the world doesn't exist."

Marcus felt the ease of the steering wheel under his hands, the slight buzz from the evening's festivities lending buoyancy to his thoughts. The forest was like a silent passenger along for the ride.

Then, without warning, a shape dashed onto the asphalt, a blur caught in their headlights.

"Watch out!" Julia's voice pierced the tranquillity.

Marcus responded with immediacy. His arm tensed, and his hand swivelled the wheel as the car veered, tires protesting against the sudden betrayal of direction. A thud resonated through the chassis.

"Damn it!" Marcus said, foot slamming onto the brake, the vehicle lurching to a stop that clawed at their seat belts.

"Is it...?" Julia's question hung between them, fragile and unspoken.

Marcus's breath came in short, sharp gasps as the laughter that had once warmed the car's interior chilled into a thick silence. Beside him, Julia was motionless, her eyes reflecting the faint glow of the dashboard. Her hand found him on the center console.

"Are you okay?" Marcus finally managed. Julia nodded, but her gaze remained locked on the windshield. "I think so," she said, her usual composure fraying at the edges.

Outside, the world was as still as a held breath. Tall trees lined the road, branches reaching out above each other, forming a canopy obscuring the moon and stars. Marcus strained to hear beyond the soft hum of the idling engine, but there was no sound of approaching vehicles. This late, the forest road was deserted, void of life save for the occasional nocturnal creature that dared cross it.

"Nobody's around," he said, almost to himself, the words falling dead in the air. It was both a statement of fact and a realization of their isolation. They were alone with the consequence of what had just happened.

His mind raced with thoughts of what needed to be done next, yet his body remained frozen, caught between action and the paralysis of shock. The quiet between them stretched and warped, a tangible sign of the shift in their reality. In the distance, an owl hooted. As they sat there, the gravity of their situation sank in.

Julia's voice, a fragile whisper that seemed to crack the night's stillness, nudged Marcus from his daze. "I hope it wasn't a dog," she said, her words quivering with a mix of fear and the onset of sobriety.

Marcus's response was a mere nod; his fingers white-knuckled on the steering wheel as if it were a lifeline anchoring him. The familiar leather felt foreign under his grasp. "We need to take a look," he said, his voice steadier than he felt.

With a collective breath held between them, they exited the car, the door hinges creaking in protest. Their footsteps crunched on the gravel shoulder of the road. Julia's silhouette, usually so composed and unwavering, wavered now like a reed in an unfelt breeze.

As they rounded to the front of the car, the headlights cast long shadows across the asphalt, grotesque caricatures of their unsettled forms. Marcus's gaze fell upon the bumper—a small dent marred the otherwise smooth surface, a blemish on the car's polished facade.

"Look at this," Marcus said, tracing the indentation to confirm its reality. It was a minor wound on their vehicle, but its implications loomed large, stewing in the back of his mind where logic warred with primal guilt.

Marcus's eyes darted from the dent to their surroundings, his nostrils flaring as he swallowed unease. The night air was silent except for Julia's shallow breaths beside him; each exhaled a quiet echo of shared tension. They scoured around the car, searching for any sign of movement or life, but found only shadows dancing in the headlights' periphery.

"Anything?" Julia's said, her words dissipating into the night.

"Nothing here," Marcus said, his throat tight. He straightened up and peered down the road, where the beam of light from the headlamps met the oppressive dark. Something caught his eye—a shape, an anomaly in the landscape. A lump in the gully.

"Over there." He pointed; his finger unsteady.

Julia followed his gesture, squinting into the darkness. "I can't—"

"Stay close," Marcus said as they began to walk toward the gully, their steps hesitant, weighted with dread. The trees that lined the road closed in on them, their branches reaching out like gnarled fingers, casting eerie patterns on the ground.

The closer they got, the clearer the outline became, and Marcus's heart thrummed against his ribcage with a ferocity that belied his years. His mind raced, every beat a drum of possible scenarios, none of which he dared to vocalize.

"Be careful," Julia said, her hand finding his arm, her grip firm despite the tremor that ran through her fingers.

Marcus nodded, more to himself than to Julia. He descended into the gully, placing each foot, wary of the loose stones that threatened his balance. He crouched beside the indistinct shape; it lay still beneath the cover of night.

"Is it...?" Julia's question trailed off as she remained at the edge, the drop too steep for her frayed nerves.

"Wait," Marcus said to her. He reached out, the truth of the situation unfurling before him. He touched the shape, gasping as the reality set in—a reality far graver than any stray animal they had feared.

"Marcus!" Julia's voice penetrated the heavy shroud of dread enveloping him. His hands were unsteady as they reached towards the figure in the gloom, his breaths short and sharp against the silence of the night.

When his fingers brushed against the fabric, something cold and unyielding met his touch — skin, but not the warm flesh of life. He recoiled for a moment, heart hammering, then forced himself to roll the body over with a strength he did not feel.

A strangled scream tore from his throat, raw and terrified. "It's a person! Julia, it's a person!" His cry pierced the stillness of the forest.

Julia gasped from the gully's edge; her silhouette framed by the moon's ghostly light. Without a word, she scrambled down the incline, her movements fueled by adrenaline and fear. The loose stones gave way under her feet, but she kept her balance, propelled by an urgency that overshadowed the fragility of her age.

"Marcus, what—" Her question died on her lips as she reached his side, her eyes widening in horror at the sight before them.

His face drained of colour; Marcus looked up at her, his features twisted in shock. "It's Trevor," he said, the name feeling like a betrayal on his tongue.

Julia's deep-set eyes shimmered with tears that refused to be held back. She fell to her knees beside the lifeless body, her hands reaching out, hovering over the form of their long-time friend as if she could somehow bring him back to life.

"Trevor," she said, her voice breaking through the silence that had once again settled over the woods. Her cries filled the space around them, a haunting lament for a life cut short and for the innocence they had just lost.

The moment's gravity pressed down upon them, a tangible weight that seemed to constrict Marcus's chest, making it hard to breathe. In his broad-shouldered frame, a vulnerability now shook him to his core.

"God, what have we done?" he said, his charismatic facade crumbling as he looked down at Trevor's pallid face, now illuminated by tragedy.

Marcus scrambled out of the gully, his mind a whirlwind of panic and disbelief. Each step felt leaden, as if he were wading through the aftermath of a nightmare. His heart hammered against his ribcage, a relentless reminder of the grim reality awaiting him in the quiet forest.

"An ambulance," he said to himself, a futile attempt to impose some semblance of order on the chaos that threatened to engulf him. "We have to call an ambulance."

His hands trembled as he fumbled for the car keys, the metallic jangle sounding loud in the still night air. The familiar weight of responsibility bore down on him, yet he was unprepared to shoulder it in this dire moment. As a professor, he had always prided himself on remaining calm under pressure and guiding others through their uncertainties. Now, he stood there, adrift in his sea of doubts.

Julia's fingers sought the pulse she prayed she would find. Her touch was gentle, almost respectful, as if acknowledging the sanctity of the life in her trembling hands. She leaned over Trevor, the boy whose laughter had often filled their home, now silenced forever.

"Please," she said. There was no response, no reassuring rhythm beneath her fingertips—only the cold, still flesh that refused to yield any sign of life.

"Marcus," Julia's voice rose from the gully, carrying the weight of irrevocable loss. It was a sound laced with the kind of grief that hollowed out the soul, leaving behind a shell of a person who once was. "He's... he's gone."

The words struck Marcus with brute force, each syllable a blow to the world they had known. He turned towards her as if seeing Julia for the first time. "Dead?" he asked, though he knew the answer. It was not a question but a confirmation.

"God, Julia," Marcus said, his voice breaking as he ran a hand through his hair. "What do we do now?"

The forest held its breath in the silence that followed, and the darkness pressed around them like an unwelcome shroud. On this lonely stretch of road, the couple stood at the crossroads of their lives.

Marcus's steps faltered on the uneven ground beneath his feet, contrasting the stability he had always sought. His tall frame cast a long shadow in the beam of the headlights as he made his way toward the vehicle, the weight of Trevor's death anchoring him to this grim moment.

"Julia, how can you be sure?" he asked, his voice barely above a whisper, yet it cut through the night air with urgency.

She met his gaze, her deep-set eyes pools of sorrow under the moonlight. "I felt for his pulse, Marcus," she said, her hands trembling despite her composed tone. "There was nothing."

Marcus's expression crumbled. The cold scholarly detachment that had served him well in lecture halls seemed frivolous now. This was not an abstract moral quandary to be debated; it was raw and painfully real.

"We have to call someone. We can't just—" He choked on his words, the responsibility of what lay before them heavy on his shoulders. Turning toward the car, he imagined the sirens, the flashing lights, the questions.

"Wait," Julia said. Her hand, which had just searched for the absent beat of life, grasped his arm with surprising strength.

"Wait for what, Julia? We can't—" His protest died in the stillness between them.

"Marcus," she said, her grip on his arm unyielding, "we need to think."

"Think?" The word echoed in his mind. Think about what? There was no denying the gravity of their situation. But to Marcus, the path was clear. The implications of their next actions would ripple outwards.

"Julia," he started again, but she interrupted him with a look that spoke volumes. In her eyes, he read an unspoken plea for understanding, support, and a decision that would not be made lightly.

"Marcus," she said, "Marcus, listen to me," Julia's voice was firm, her hands still clasping his arm. Her eyes held a piercing clarity that rooted him to the spot.

"Julia, we have to—" he tried again, but the words felt hollow even as they left his lips.

"No," she cut across his fumbling speech. "Trevor is gone. Our calling anyone... it won't bring him back."

His heart pounded against his ribcage, loud in his ears. Confusion clouded his judgment, and distress etched lines into his forehead. He looked at her, his mouth dry, his eyes searching her gaze. "What are you saying?" he said.

She released his arm, stepping back to see him more clearly. The moonlight filtered through the leaves, casting dappled shadows over her features, softening the years etched into her face. "We have built a life, Marcus. A family. You're on the cusp of that promotion"

"Julia." His voice cracked. "Are you saying we should just leave him?"

"Think about what could happen," she pressed on, stepping closer again, her voice a hushed plea. "One mistake, one moment, and everything we've worked for could crumble. We could lose it all."

"Is that what our integrity is worth?" he asked, his struggle spilling out.

"Integrity doesn't provide for our family or secure your position. This could ruin us, Marcus." Her words were like stones in his stomach, heavy with the truth yet hard to swallow.

He knew she was painting a picture of their reality—one where reputations were fragile, and the consequences of a scandal could be dire. But the image before him shattered, replaced by the cold, still form of Trevor lying abandoned in the gully.

"Julia..." he said, but the protest died on his lips. He knew in that instant that the man who had once stood behind his podium, inspiring young minds, was far removed from the man contemplating the unfathomable in the darkness of the forest road.

Marcus's legs trembled as he stood by the gully; the soft murmur of the forest around them contrasted with the chaos within him. He turned towards Julia, "What are you saying? We can't just...we've killed someone, Julia."

Julia's gaze never wavered from Marcus's face, her eyes pooling with resolve amidst the turmoil. She stepped toward him, her movements deliberate and sure. "We can't change what has happened," she said, her tone laced with a firmness that seemed to anchor him amidst the storm of guilt. "But we need to think of our family now."

Her hands reached out to cup his face. Her thumbs brushed his cheeks, and for a moment, he was transported back to their early years, when her touch meant comfort, not complicity.

"Look at me, Marcus," Julia said. "Our family, everything we've built, is not just about us anymore. Our children depend on the life we have built."

The gravity of her words pressed down on him, the realization that their actions tonight would ripple through the lives entwined with theirs. In Julia's eyes, he saw the reflection of his conflict and the glint of a painful resolution.

"How can we live with this?" His question hung between them, a fragile thread in the fabric of their morality.

"Together," she said. "We can deal with this together, just like we have everything else that has come our way?"

Marcus's tears began to carve silent paths down his cheeks. His broad shoulders, once a symbol of strength and stability, now seemed to bear the weight of the night sky. He looked at his hands, those of a scholar who had spent years shaping minds with words and wisdom but found them shaking, incapable of reshaping this grim reality.

"Marcus," Julia said, her tone laced with a pragmatic edge. "You've been drinking. You know what that means, right? If they test you..."

The implication hung heavy between them, an unspoken verdict that could tear away the life they knew. Marcus's gaze met hers; he imagined the cold bars of a cell and the sound of a gavel sealing his fate.

"Our kids...," she said, her wavy hair catching the ghostly glow from the car's headlights, casting shadows on her face that deepened the lines time had etched there. "Do they need to suffer their whole livers because of our mistake?" The thought of his children, their lives upended by a scandal, their inheritance—their very futures—dissolved into uncertainty, clawed at him more fiercely than the grip of the law ever could.

Marcus's hand trembled as he reached for his face, the roughness of his skin unfamiliar to his touch through the haze of tears. His fingers came away wet. The last barriers within Marcus crumbled, his resistance washed away by the relentless tide of Julia's conviction. The choice in front of them was grim, but as the moments ticked by, the path she drew became the only one he could see.

"Okay," he said; the word was a surrender that bound them irrevocably to the course Julia set. With her hand still on his face, a pact was forged on the darkened road, forever changing their lives direction.

She took his hand, her grip firm, and led him back to the car. The night was still around them; the hum of the forest life contrasted with the storm raging in their souls. Marcus moved as if in a trance, absorbing the reality that the world they knew had forever changed.

He settled into the passenger seat. Shock clung to him like a shroud, and he stared straight ahead, his gaze unfocused. Outside, Julia cast a vigilant eye over the road, the shadows of the trees playing tricks on her vision as she searched for any sign of movement.

"Is anyone there?" he heard himself ask, not recognizing the sound of his voice.

"Nobody," Julia said. She slipped into the driver's seat; her hands deliberate as they closed around the steering wheel. Her gaze lingered on the rearview mirror, ensuring the path behind them was as empty as the one they faced ahead.

Marcus leaned back in the seat, the car's contours moulding to the shape of his despair. Julia placed a hand on his knee, a silent message of solidarity, before shifting her focus back to the road.

"Let's go, Julia," Marcus said.

She nodded more to herself than to him and inserted the key into the ignition, the metallic click a jarring note in the still evening air. The engine stirred, a growl breaking the forest's hush. Julia gripped the steering wheel, its familiarity a cruel reminder of the normalcy they'd just shattered. Her knuckles whitened with the force of her hold as she guided the car forward, away from where Trevor lay unseen.

Marcus sat beside her; his gaze lost to the road unwinding. The car's gentle rumble contrasted with the screaming silence that enveloped them.

"Julia…" He said, fracturing the quiet.

"Shh," she cut him off, her voice a threadbare blanket meant to cover the chill of their actions. "Just… don't."

The car seemed to shrink around them as the house appeared, signalling their return to the world they knew. The space between them grew dense with the enormity of their choice, a barrier as tangible as the darkness they left behind.

"We're home," Julia said.

Chapter 18

As the vehicle glided into the driveway, Julia cut the engine, and the sudden quiet felt deafening. She swallowed hard, a lump forming in her throat. Beside her, Marcus sat motionless, his gaze fixed on the darkened house. The two of them remained in the car, suspended in time, neither daring to break the stillness surrounding them from the reality awaiting inside.

Julia finally opened her door and got out. She moved around to the passenger door and opened it, signalling Marcus to get out. Together, they moved towards the house. Marcus fumbled for his keys, finally retrieving them and unlocking the door. The front door creaked open, and Julia winced at the noise, a silent prayer lifting that it wouldn't disturb their children.

Marcus and Julia stood opposite each other inside the kitchen, separated by the kitchen island, where remnants of daily life lay scattered—a newspaper, a pair of reading glasses, and a forgotten coffee mug. Julia's eyes met Marcus's. "Julia..." Marcus's voice broke the silence, but it was a mere whisper, trailing off as if he couldn't bear to give his thoughts sound.

"Marcus," she said, her voice equally fragile.

Words were unnecessary; their expressions spoke volumes of their shattered trust. They had crossed lines that could never be uncrossed, and the ghosts of those decisions lingered between them, unspoken accusations hanging heavy in the air. A clock ticked somewhere in the house, marking time that seemed irrelevant now. With every passing second, the weight grew, the realization of their choices settling upon them.

The silence was oppressive as they walked down the hallway towards the bedrooms. Marcus entered the master bedroom, and Julia quickly checked on Nicole and Jamie. She peeked into their rooms, trying not to wake them. Satisfied, she followed Marcus into the room. Julia slipped beneath the sheets without changing clothes, and Marcus followed suit.

They lay in the darkness, side by side, yet worlds apart. The faint glow from the streetlight outside traced the contour of Marcus's face, highlighting the tightness around his mouth and the furrows of worry etched deep into his forehead. His eyes were fixed on the ceiling.

Julia's breaths came in hushed gasps, her body trembling with silent sobs that Marcus could feel rather than hear. Her fingers clutched the linen pillowcase as though she sought to anchor herself against the guilt that threatened to pull her under. Her tears glistened as they fell upon her pillow. Time passed—an hour, perhaps two—and still, sleep remained an elusive spectre, flitting just beyond their reach.

The light was beginning to seep into the room when the stillness shattered. The sound of desperate pounding on their front door and Julia and Marcus jolted upright, hearts thundering against ribs that felt too constricting. They exchanged a glance, a wordless acknowledgment of the new dread blooming within them.

"Stay here," Marcus said, his voice hoarse. It was not a command but a plea, born of a desire to shield her from whatever lay ahead.

Julia nodded as Marcus left the room. The knocking grew more insistent and frantic. When he pulled open the door, Janice stood before him, her face pale, eyes wild with fear. Her words tumbled out in a torrent, each a hammer blow to Marcus's conscience.

"Trevor... he's gone. My baby is gone!" Her hands clawed at his sleeve; her desperation palpable.

"Come in, Janice. Let's sit down," Marcus said, his voice steady through sheer force of will. He led her inside, his mind racing. Each step he took was heavy, burdened by the enormity of the secret he carried. Julia's pulse hammered against her wrist as she emerged from the bedroom.

"Janice," Julia said, her voice a hushed whisper that rose above Janice's frantic sobs. The woman before her was dishevelled, her nightgown clinging to her like a second skin.

"Julia... I—I can't find him!" The words were choked, strangled by the terror that clutched at Janice's throat. Her eyes, wide and pleading, sought Julia's, finding there not the calm assurance they so desperately needed but a reflection of their horror.

"Come and sit down," Julia said, stepping aside. Her practiced composure was a thin veneer over the turmoil roiling within her.

"Please, we—we need to call the police," Janice begged, wringing together until the knuckles blanched white.

"Of course," Julia said, her mind racing with the implications of that call. Let's get you back to your house, and we will make that call." They crossed the lawn between the houses and entered Janice's home. Julia guided Janice to the cordless phone on the kitchen counter.

"Go ahead, Janice," Julia nudged, her hands folded tightly before her to still their trembling.

Janice dialled with shaking hands, and the room filled with the mechanical trill as the line connected. "My son, he's missing. Trevor... Trevor is gone," Janice said into the receiver, each syllable laden with dread.

Julia stood by, her heart sinking with each detail Janice eked out—the open window, the empty bed, the untouched toys. As she listened, guilt pressed down upon her, a physical force that threatened to buckle her knees and crush her spirit.

"Julia?" Janice's voice cut through the fog of self-reproach that enveloped Julia, her hand reaching out to grasp Julia's arm. "You'll stay with me, won't you? Until they come?"

"Of course," Julia said to her. It was a promise made of necessity, born of a desperate need to cling to any semblance of normalcy, even as the ground crumbled beneath their feet. The kettle had just boiled when Julia saw the lights of the police car pull into Janice's driveway. The police came to the door and rang the bell. Janice's face, pale as milk under the fluorescent glow of the kitchen light, crumpled into lines of worry and grief. Julia, her expression a carefully constructed mask of concern, watched the officers approach with measured steps, their uniforms dark blots against the encroaching dawn.

Julia let them in, and they sat in the living room opposite Julia and Janice."Ma'am," one of the officers addressed Janice, "Can you tell us what happened?"

Janice nodded, her words tumbling out in a breathless torrent. "I—I put Trevor to bed around seven. He was so tired from playing outside all day. I read him a story, and he fell asleep so quickly." She clutched at her cardigan, fingers tangling in the knit. "I went to bed early, around 9:00, and when I woke up this morning, his window was open and—"

"Open?" The officer said.

"Yes. I always keep the windows shut. I don't understand how—" Her voice broke off, strangled by the unsaid fears between them.

Julia remained silent; her arms wrapped around herself to ward off the chill seeping into her bones.

"Mrs. Dempsey?" Another officer, a woman, turned towards Julia. "Is there anything you might have seen or heard last night? Anything at all that could help us?"

Julia's throat felt dry; each word she considered weighed heavy with consequence. "No, nothing," she said. "We were at a dinner party and got home just before midnight."

"Ok," the officer said, jotting down notes on a small pad. "And you didn't notice any unusual activity around your property or Mrs. Harlow's here?"

Julia's reply was a single shake of her head, the robotic motion rehearsed: "Not a thing. We're such a quiet neighbourhood."

"Thank you, Mrs. Dempsey. We'll need to ask more questions later, but we appreciate your cooperation." The officer turned her attention back to Janice. "Did Trevor have any friends that he may have gone to see?"

Janice's voice quivered as she spoke, her words tumbling out in a rush. "Trevor—Trevor always talked about Jamie. They were close, you know?"

The detective nodded, scribbling something in his notebook before looking up. "Would it be possible to speak with Jamie?"

Julia felt a chill run down her spine. Her hands gripped the edge of the couch until her knuckles turned white. She managed a tight-lipped nod, conscious of how her acquiescence might betray the turmoil swirling within. "Of course," she said.

Back at the Dempsey household, the morning routine unfolded with tension. Marcus checked in on Nicole, her cheery disposition untainted by the night's events, as she hummed a tune and crunched on her cereal.

"Jamie," he said, knocking on the door. "Time to get ready for school."

There was no response from Jamie's room, just the muffled sound of shifting bedsheets. Marcus pushed the door open and found his son lying face-up, his eyes closed and breathing as though willing the world away through sheer force of will. Jamie's expression was unreadable.

"Come on, son," Marcus said, his voice soft but insistent. "You can't stay in bed all day."

Jamie turned his body towards the wall. Marcus stood, watching Jamie, then closed the door and returned to the kitchen. Nicole had finished her breakfast and was gathering her things for school. The house was filled with the ordinary sounds of the morning—a stark contrast to the chaos of emotion that roiled just beneath the surface. Marcus knew they would soon face the questions, suspicions, and unbearable truth of what had happened.

But for now, there was only the pretense of normalcy, a fragile veneer that threatened to crack with each passing second. Julia returned to the house, accompanied by two police officers. After introducing them to Marcus, she explained to him that they wanted to speak with Jamie. "I'm not sure how an eight-year-old boy will help you with this," Marcus said. "We're just trying to get a picture of his life to help us narrow down where he could be," the office said. "We'll be quick."

Julia let them down the hallway to Jamie's door. The female officer opened the door and went inside. "Jamie?" she said.

Jamie propped himself up on his elbows, his hair dishevelled and his eyes betraying a glimmer of fear. "Yeah?"

"Your neighbour, Trevor, is missing," she said, without the cushion of comfort. "He wasn't in bed this morning, and there's a concern for his whereabouts."

A visible shiver ran down Jamie's spine as he shook his head, his hands clenching into fists atop the quilt. "I don't—I don't know where he is," he said, each word seeming to take a herculean effort.

"Can you think of anywhere he might go? Anyone he might be with?" the second officer chimed in, a notepad at the ready.

"No..." Jamie said, choked by the tightness in his throat. "I... I don't know."

Marcus watched with a pained expression, his towering frame leaning against the doorframe as if it were the only thing keeping him vertical. He said, "Could we have a moment, please?"

The officers exchanged glances before nodding and stepping out, their footsteps receding into the distance. Marcus approached the edge of the bed, his hand outstretched toward his son's shoulder.

"Jamie..." His voice broke the silence that had settled over the room like a shroud. "We can get through this. You know that, right?"

But Jamie turned away, pulling a pillow over his head to block out the world and its piercing questions. "Just leave me alone," he muffled through the fabric, a plea layered with desperation.

"Son, I—" Marcus started, but the words lodged in his throat. He stood, observing Jamie's rigid body beneath the covers. With a heavy heart, Marcus left the room and closed the door.

"Janice?" Marcus's voice was tentative as he emerged from the shadows of the hallway. "Is she—"

"Ryan's mother is with her," Julia said. "She won't be alone."

Marcus nodded, his brow furrowing. A silent understanding passed between them, heavy with things unsaid, questions unasked.

Together, they retreated to their bedroom, where their facades crumbled away. As soon as the door clicked shut, sealing them in their private world, Julia's legs gave way, and she sank onto the edge of the bed. Her hands clasped each other, seeking solace in their grip.

"Julia..." Marcus's voice quivered as he sat beside her. His arm encircled her shoulders, a gesture meant to bridge the distance that had grown between them. "Marcus, what have we done?" Julia's words spilled out, choked by a sob that fought its way up from her chest. Her eyes brimmed with tears that streaked down her cheeks.

Tears welled in Marcus's eyes, the first he had allowed himself in years. His usual charismatic mask fell away, revealing the raw turmoil beneath. He pulled Julia close, and together, they succumbed to the grief that had been gnawing at their hearts. Their bodies shook with sobs, each cry a testament to the pain they bore, the enormity of their actions enveloping them like a shroud.

They clung to each other desperately, but there was no absolution in their embrace, no words that could erase the past or undo the damage wrought by their decisions. At that moment, they were trying to hold onto the fragments of a life that felt like it was slipping through their fingers. And outside, the world continued to turn, oblivious to the quiet devastation unfolding within the walls of the Dempsey home.

In the stillness of their bedroom, Marcus ran a trembling hand through his hair. His shoulders now seemed to bear the world's weight. He turned to Julia, his voice barely a whisper as it fractured the silence. "How could we have...?" He choked on the words, his face contorted by grief. "If it were Jamie..."

Julia's breath hitched at the mention of their son's name. She sat beside Marcus on the edge of the bed; her hair fell around her face like a curtain, trying to hide her torment.

"Marcus..." she said her voice a ragged thread of sound. "It's done. We can't undo it." Her hands clutched at the sheets, seeking something solid to hold onto. "We have to think of our family now," she said, her eyes meeting his.

"Julia," he said, "I'm not sure I can live with this." Julia reached out, her fingers brushing against Marcus's cheek. "We have to live with it, for them," she said, her mental fortitude wavering under the strain but not breaking. "For Jamie, for Nicole... they need us to be strong."

Their confessions hung heavy in the air, mingling with the lingering traces of guilt that seemed to seep into the very walls of the room. They were held captive by the unspoken pact between them, bound by the desperation to protect their family.

They grappled with the unbearable weight of their decision, finding a fragile solace in the shared burden of their secret.

Marcus lay still on the mattress. His gaze fixed on the ceiling, where a single crack snaked across the plaster. Beside him, Julia's body shook with silent sobs. Her hair spilled across the pillow, hiding her face. The tears that wet the fabric were not just for what had been done but also for the chasm it had carved between her and Marcus. Love had tethered them together, but now that bond was frayed by the jagged edges of guilt.

In another room, Jamie lay curled in the fetal position. His breathing was uneven, punctuated by stifled sniffles. Down the hall, Nicole sat at the kitchen table, her spoon clinking cheerfully against the bowl as she scooped up another bite of cereal. Her long brown hair fell around her shoulders, framing her face in a picture of blissful ignorance. She paused, her warm smile fading into confusion as she glanced around the empty chairs.

"Where is everyone?" she said, the question lingering in the morning air.

Chapter 19

Marcus sat at the edge of the bed, his gaze distant and unfocused as he clasped his hands together. Julia's heart ached with a mix of fear and uncertainty. The room was filled with a silence that seemed to press down on them, heavy with the weight of unspoken thoughts.

Suddenly, a burst of voices from outside sliced through the stillness. Julia turned her head towards the sound, her eyes narrowing as she tried to discern the cause of the disturbance. Marcus looked up; his charismatic features clouded by concern. "What now?" he said.

Without a word, Julia rose from the bed and walked to the kitchen to get a better look. She paused at the window, her fingers gripping the sill as she peered into the morning light. She looked toward Janice's home, where a new upheaval was unfolding.

The police cruiser parked at the curb was an ominous sign. A tall officer stood before Janice's door, his cap held in his hands—a gesture of respect and gravity. Julia's breath caught in her throat as she saw Janice emerge, her neighbour's face crumpling like paper in the fire.

"Marcus," Julia said, her voice laced with urgency, yet he did not respond. He remained frozen, trapped in the entrance to the kitchen, and unable to move forward.

Janice's knees buckled, and she fell to the ground, her grief spilling out for all to see. The officer reached down, offering a steadying hand. Julia's heart twisted. She felt a surge of something she couldn't name—perhaps empathy or a reflection of her hidden sorrows.

Julia remained at the window as Janice was helped to her feet and led back inside her home. The scene outside had unfolded with the stark clarity of a photograph, capturing a moment of raw humanity that would be etched in her memory forever.

"Julia?" Marcus's voice finally broke through her reverie. He stood in the kitchen doorway, his tall frame seeming smaller somehow, diminished by the weight of their shared burden.

She turned to face him, her eyes meeting his. In that look, there was a wordless understanding. This was their life now—a series of moments caught between heartbeats, each a reminder of the fragility of the world they thought they knew.

Julia's knees weakened, her body folding into the grief that had been chasing her since dawn. The tears she'd been fighting broke free, carving hot trails down her cheeks. She backed away from the window, her hands trembling as if she'd touched something sacred and scorching.

"Marcus," she said between sobs, "the police... Janice..."

He entered the kitchen, and his eyes locked onto her face, reading the silent language of her despair. Without a word, he crossed the room, his broad shoulders casting a shadow that seemed to envelop her.

"Come here," Marcus said, his voice a low rumble of concern. He reached out, his large hands guiding her away from the stark reality framed by the kitchen window. He wrapped an arm around her shoulders, drawing her close and leading her to the living room.

They settled onto the couch. Julia leaned into him, her head resting against his chest where she could hear the steady beat of his heart—a rhythm that spoke of life going on, even when it felt like it shouldn't.

"Marcus, I can't... How do we..." She struggled to find the words, the enormity of everything pressing down on her.

"We'll find a way," he said to her, though his voice betrayed the uncertainty they both felt. His hand stroked her hair, strands slipping through his fingers like time.

"We need to create normalcy for the kids," Julia said, her voice barely audible. "You need to go back to work. We need to keep moving forward."

"Julia, I'm not sure I can..." Marcus said, but she cut him off with a fierce determination that belied her fragile state.

"You need to go back. It's why we made this decision." Her eyes met his, conveying a plea for them to cling to the remnants of the life they'd built.

He nodded slowly, a reluctant agreement. "I'll try." His words hung in the air, heavy with a promise that felt like a thin veil over the gaping wound of their current existence.

"Good," she said, her voice steadying. "We have to act as normal as possible for the kids and police."

"Julia," he said, taking her hand, feeling the strength that pulsed beneath her weathered skin. "We'll get through this together."

She gave a nod, more to convince herself than to reassure him. Together, they sat in the quiet living room, two figures holding onto each other amidst the turmoil of an unravelling world.

"The kids," she said, voice steadier, "should stay home today."

"Yes, I think you're right," Marcus echoed.

Julia's hand hovered over the doorknob to Nicole's room, a faint tremor betraying her stoic façade. She pressed down, easing the door open with a soft click that seemed to ripple through the house's silence. Inside, Nicole sat on the floor, surrounded by an array of photographs she was organizing into albums, her brow furrowed in concentration.

"Mom?" Nicole looked up, her eyes reflecting a calm that felt like a foreign language to Julia.

"Everything is okay, dear," Julia said, her voice a practiced lullaby of normalcy. "Just stay inside today, alright?"

Nicole nodded, a gentle smile gracing her lips as she returned to her task, shielded for a moment longer from the harsh truths lurking just beyond her sanctuary.

Julia closed the door, the soft snick of the latch whispering finality. As she turned, Marcus's gaze met hers, a silent understanding passing between them. They moved together toward Jamie's room.

The door to Jamie's room creaked open to reveal his form, a shadow amidst crumpled sheets. The curtains cast bars of light across his withdrawn figure as if nature was trying to coax him back into the world. Marcus cleared his throat, a small sound that seemed to echo off the walls.

"Jamie?" Julia's voice was feather-soft, but it landed heavily in the dim room.

There was no response, just the rise and fall of Jamie's chest beneath the blankets. Marcus stepped forward, the floorboards protesting under his weight.

"Son, we're here for you," Marcus said, reaching out a hand to rest on Jamie's shoulder. The gesture meant to bridge the chasm of grief hung suspended in the half-light.

"Jamie, please," Julia implored, her heart clenching as she watched the stillness that had claimed her son. "Talk to us."

But the words seemed to dissolve before they could reach him, absorbed by the thick air of loss that filled the space. Julia's hand fluttered to her mouth, her breath catching on a sob that threatened to escape.

Marcus gave Jamie's shoulder a final, gentle squeeze before letting go. "We'll give you some time," he said, his voice heavy with unspoken promises and regrets.

Back in their room, the door clicked shut behind them, a barrier against the world that continued to turn despite their lives have come to a standstill. Julia leaned against the cool wood, her eyes searching Marcus's face for something—anything—that might resemble a plan, a way to navigate this new reality where every step felt like a betrayal of the life they once knew.

Marcus turned to Julia; his back pressed against the solidity of their bedroom door. His eyes, usually a fortress of composure, betrayed a turbulence that had been churning since the night before. "Julia," he said, his voice unsteady, "Maybe we need to tell someone. I'm not sure we can carry this on our own."

Julia's hand, resting on the dresser, curled into a fist. The room felt suddenly smaller, her breath heavy with the scent of aged wood and Marcus's cologne, a reminder of normalcy that now seemed like a distant dream. "No," she said sharply, her eyes flashing with a fierceness that belied her years. "We can't afford to unravel now."

"Julia—" Marcus stepped toward her, the plea in his voice wrapping around her like a shroud.

"How?" Her voice rose, each word a shard of glass. "How do we explain this to anyone?"

"I don't know, but it will eat us alive!" Marcus countered; his broad shoulders tensed as if bracing against an invisible storm. "Look at Jamie—look at us. We're a step away from breaking."

"We can't break, not now," Julia said. "We need to bury this, Marcus. Move forward. That's how we survive."

"That's how we survive?" Marcus's hands reached out, imploring. "By burying everything? How can you just forget what happened?"

The question hung between them. Julia staggered backward, her heart thundering against her ribs. "Forget?" she screamed, her voice cracking under the strain of suppressed agony. "I haven't forgotten!"

Her hand flew out, striking Marcus's chest with a force that reverberated through the silent house. It was more than a physical release; breaking a dam within her held back a lifetime of guarded emotions.

As the echo of the impact faded, Julia's knees buckled, and she found herself sobbing, her body wracked with sobs that seemed to tear at the very fabric of her being. Her tears were a river bursting its banks, spilling over with the pain of the past and the terror of the unknown future.

Marcus, his face etched with lines of helpless despair, hovered over her. He wanted to reach out, to encircle her with his arms and shield her from the storm. But the space between them remained, filled with the words left unsaid and actions undone.

"Julia," he said, but the tide of her grief carried away his voice, lost in the waves that crashed against the shore of their shared life, threatening to pull them both under.

Marcus, his chest still echoing from Julia's anguished blow, watched her crumple like a discarded playbill beside the bed. His heart ached to envelop her in comfort, yet he felt his arms were weighted down by lead, incapable of offering solace. He took a step back, each movement feeling like a betrayal. The air between them had grown thick with unshed confessions and silent screams that clung to the room's walls.

"Julia..." he said, but no more words came. She was folded into herself, her hands buried in the waves of graying hair, her body heaving with sobs that seemed to pull her deeper into the ground. Marcus stood, paralyzed by the tableau of her despair, the very image of helplessness.

Unable to bear the sight, Marcus turned and left the room. He moved through the house with the ghostly presence of a man who had lost his place in the world. Stepping into the dimness of the garage, the musty scent of old memories and neglect greeted him—a fitting shroud for what awaited.

The car, once a symbol of their comfortable life, now loomed before him like an accuser on the stand. He reached out, his fingers brushing over the cold metal, stopping at the dent marred on the right-hand side passenger front. The imperfection, so small in the grand scheme of things, held the weight of a thousand sins.

His breath hitched, a dizzying wave of faintness threatening to topple him. He gripped the edge of the car to steady himself, the coolness of the paint a stark contrast to the heat rising in his cheeks. A single thought churned in his mind:

this dent, this physical mark, was the manifestation of their unravelling lives.

"Dammit," he said under his breath. His fingers traced the dent again to confirm its reality, affirming that this nightmare was their new truth. But no touching could undo what had been done; no amount of wishing could erase the damage inflicted—not on the car and their souls.

As Marcus stood there, the garage's silence bore down upon him, a silent witness to the turmoil that seeped from every pore of his being. He knew he would have to return to Julia to face the aftermath of all that had transpired.

Marcus' hand collided violently with the car's cold metal skin. A shock of acute pain shot up his arm, a primal grunt escaping his lips. The sting was sharp and immediate—a welcome respite from the slow, suffocating ache of guilt that had taken residence in his chest.

For a fleeting second, his mind was clear, focused on the throbbing in his hand, the redness blooming across his knuckles. But as the physical sensation waned, the tide of remorse rushed back in, threatening to drown him again.

He turned away from the tainted vehicle and returned to the house. Inside, the atmosphere was thick with unspoken words and unshed tears. Julia lay on the bed, her body a landscape of exhaustion, every line and crease on her face etched with defeat. The wavy strands of hair splayed across the pillow.

"Julia," Marcus said, but she didn't stir. He reached out, touching her shoulder, the gesture a stark reminder of his need for her despite the chasm that had opened between them.

She blinked slowly, turning her eyes toward him.

"We have to get rid of the car," he said, the words tasting like ash on his tongue. "It's the only way to—"

"Eliminate any evidence," Julia finished for him, her voice a threadbare fabric, worn and fragile. There was no question; it was an echo of a plan already forming in the recesses of her meticulous mind.

He nodded, feeling the gravity of the moment settle between them. This was more than discarding a piece of property; it was an attempt to discard a fragment of their past, a desperate bid to sever the link to the tragedy that threatened to consume them.

Julia sat up, the sheets pooling around her waist. She looked at Marcus, and for a moment, the remnants of their shared life—the love, the challenges overcome, the identity they'd crafted together—flickered in her gaze.

"Okay," she said simply, the word a quiet surrender to their new reality.

Marcus stood, the keys to the car jangling with a hollow sound in his hand. He turned to Julia, his shoulders slumped under an invisible weight.

"I'll take it to a dealer today," he said, "trade it in for something else."

Her eyes, clouded with turmoil, met his. "Yes," she said. "Get rid of it."

The room felt small, the air between them thick with the unsaid. Marcus watched as she pulled the blanket tighter around herself, a futile shield against the reality that seeped into their sanctuary.

"What about your work..." Julia's voice trailed off as she looked up at him through lashes wet with tears.

"I've already called in sick," Marcus said, rubbing the stubble on his chin, a gesture betraying his unease. "I told them I needed time to deal with... a family matter."

"Is that what this is now?" Julia said her question more to herself than to him. "A family matter?"

Marcus could not answer. What were they but two people bound together by the need to protect their fragile sense of normalcy? Two souls are navigating the murky waters of consequence and morality.

He moved towards the door, each step resonating with the burden of the unspoken. As he reached for the knob, he glanced back at Julia, her form a still life framed by the bed's wooden headboard. In that frozen moment, he saw the woman he had loved at first sight at the bar so many years ago, her resilience woven into the fabric of their life together.

"Go," she said. "Before we lose the nerve."

"I'll be back after lunch," he echoed, nodding more to himself than to her.

"Marcus..." Julia's voice broke through the silence, a thread of vulnerability weaving through her words. "Are we going to get through this?"

He turned to face her, searching her eyes for an answer he could not find within himself. They reflected at him a strength that had weathered countless storms yet flickered with a fragility he had never seen before.

"Julia," Marcus said, the honesty in his voice cutting through the fog of uncertainty, "I don't know."

Her gaze didn't falter, even as the corners of her mouth twitched to maintain her composure. Unable to offer the reassurance they both sought, Marcus reached out, hovering over her arm before retreating. He watched as a single tear escaped the confines of her stoic expression, tracing a path down her cheek like a silent echo of their shared sorrow.

"Go," she said, her voice nearly lost in the stillness. "Do it."

Marcus opened the garage door, leaving behind the sanctuary that had become their purgatory. Each step away from Julia, from the life they had built, felt like an unravelling of the threads that bound him to her.

As the door closed behind him with a quiet click, Marcus allowed himself one last glance at the home that held their secrets, their love, and now, their deepest fears. With the keys clutched in his hand, he stepped into the uncertain day, the world outside unaware of the invisible fractures splitting the foundation of his existence.

Chapter 20

Marcus's alarm pierced the stillness of dawn, a shrill chirp that seemed too cheerful for the gray light filtering through the bedroom curtains. With a groan, he swung his legs out from under the covers and planted his feet on the hardwood floor. His toes recoiled at the cold touch, but Marcus paid it no mind; the chill was nothing compared to the heaviness that settled in his chest—a weight that had been his constant companion since that fateful night six months ago.

He rose and padded down the hallway. The door to Jamie's room creaked as he pushed it open, a sound he had grown accustomed to over the past few months. Inside, Jamie lay motionless, tangled in sweat-dampened sheets that bore the dark stain of another accident. Marcus sighed a deep, soul-weary exhalation. This new habit of Jamie's was a silent scream, echoing the trauma that lingered like a stubborn shadow.

"Jamie," Marcus said, though he knew better than to wake him. He reached out, resting a hand on his son's shoulder. No response came, just the steady rise and fall of Jamie's chest, a rhythmic assurance that life, in some form, continued.

Returning to his bedroom, Marcus found Julia just as he left her—nestled in bed, a figure swathed in blankets, her wavy hair splayed across the pillow. The sight tugged at something within him, a mixture of concern and frustration knotted together.

"Julia," he started, his voice barely above a murmur as if loud words might shatter the delicate morning calm. "You can't keep doing this."

Her eyelids fluttered, a sign she was not asleep, merely adrift in her sea of despair. "Can't I?" Her voice was a thread of sound, frayed at the edges.

"Look at you," Marcus implored, gesturing helplessly. "You're just... lying here. Day after day."

"Is there somewhere I should be going?" Julia's eyes remained fixed on the ceiling; her gaze as distant as her thoughts.

"Anywhere," he said with a firm nod. "Outside, around people. You need to start living again, Julia. For your sake... for our family's sake."

"Living," she echoed, a bitter twist to the word.

"Please, Julia." Marcus reached out, fingers brushing the back of her hand, seeking a connection that felt increasingly tenuous. "I'm worried about you."

"Are you?" Julia turned to look at him then, her deep-set eyes searching his. "Or are you worried about how this reflects on you?"

"Both," Marcus said, his voice softening. "This isn't us, Julia. We've never let life beat us down like this."

"Maybe we've never been hit this hard before," she countered, pulling her hand away.

"Maybe not," he conceded, the lines of his face deepening with concern. "But we've always faced challenges head-on. Together."

"Maybe before Marcus," Julia shifted, propping herself on an elbow. The motion was languid as if her body protested the effort. "Now we just sweep them under the rug, hoping they'd disappear."

Either way…" Marcus paused, struggling to find the right words to bridge the gap between them. "We can't keep hiding from the world. From each other."

"Can't we?" Julia's lips curled into a wry, sad smile. "Seems like that's all we're good at these days."

"Julia," he said again but stopped short, the plea dying on his lips. What more could he say? What words could lift the shroud of despair that had settled over her, over their once vibrant home?

"Go to work, Marcus," Julia said, settling back against the pillows. "Do what you do best."

He hesitated, watching her for a moment longer before he turned and walked toward the door. There were no adequate goodbyes or reassurances—just the silence that enveloped them both, a silence heavy with unsaid things and battles yet to be fought.

Marcus stood by the door, his hand lingering on the cool metal of the knob as if it were a lifeline to normality. He glanced back at Julia, her form barely denting the bed where she lay wrapped in sheets that hadn't felt the sun in weeks. His voice, when he spoke, was tinged with frustration.

"Julia, how do you think I manage?" he asked, almost pleading for her to understand. "I get up and go to work because we have to eat because life has to go on."

She turned slowly, eyes meeting his—a dull mirror reflecting the storm inside him. "How can you just carry on?" Her words were soft but laced with accusation. "Like nothing has happened?"

"Because sitting here, wallowing in what's done—it will drive us mad," he said, his voice rising, the words spilling like the pent-up waters behind a dam. "I've got responsibilities now, more than ever since being made department head. You know this."

"Ah, yes, the promotion." The bitterness in Julia's tone sharpened the air between them. "Living the good life while the rest of us drown."

Marcus's jaw clenched, his stoic facade beginning to crack. "Don't you dare," he said, his hands balling into fists at his sides. "We made our choices that night for the sake of the family, for my job—our livelihood. To throw it all away now... it would make everything pointless."

"Pointless?" She propped herself up, her voice a hiss. "Is that what you call it?"

"Julia, I was ready to pick up the phone—to call the police," he confessed, the memory of that night's terror and confusion flashing in his eyes. "But we decided. Together. We protected what we had built."

"But what's left to protect now?" Her question hung heavy in the room, festering like an open wound.

"Enough," Marcus said, his voice carrying a finality that echoed off the walls. "Enough."

"I don't want to talk about it anyway," she said, slicing through his intent with a precision that left no room for argument. Her voice was a whisper, yet it bore the weight of a shout.

"Julia," Marcus implored, softening his tone as he took a tentative step forward, the floorboards creaking beneath the burden of his plea. "You can't keep hiding in here. The world is still out there, waiting for us."

Her laugh, devoid of humour, echoed off the walls. "And Janice? Am I supposed to run into her at the market? Smile and chat about the weather?"

Marcus faltered, the spectre of their neighbour – and all she represented – looming large between them. "You can't avoid her forever," he reasoned or perhaps hoped.

"Like you do?" Julia countered, her eyebrows knitting together as she propped herself up against the headboard, a queen holding court over the ruins of her kingdom. "Working late, taking extra classes—"

"Those are obligations," he said, but she waved him off.

"Excuses," she said. "You're avoiding me, this," she motioned to the space between them, "our reality. We might as well be sleeping in separate rooms, Marcus."

The sting of her words settled like a lead weight in his gut. He moved toward the door, each step an effort against the morass of regret and unspoken grievances that filled the room. Pausing, he turned back, the need to share one last piece of their unravelling day pressing against his chest.

"Jamie wet the bed again," he said, the words falling into the space between them.

Julia's face crumpled, the edges of her resolve giving way to the tide of distress within her. "He's changed, Marcus. That boy... our boy before the incident," her voice broke, "I don't know how to fix him."

"Fix?" Marcus said the term foreign inadequate. Could they fix something that they barely understand themselves?

"Time, it's just time, Julia," he managed to say, though the word tasted bitter on his tongue. It promised healing but gave no solace for the wounds of now.

Without another word, he stepped out, closing the door to the sound of Julia's quiet sobs—a familiar sorrow that played on a loop in the Dempsey home.

Marcus left the room, the ghost of Julia's anguish trailing him like a shroud. The house was silent, except for the creaks that spoke of its age and the secrets it held within its walls. He moved through the hallway, his hand grazing the cold railing, feeling the familiar nicks and scratches in the wood—a topography of memories etched into their family home.

The children's rooms were silent; their doors ajar with the resignation of another day begun in disarray. Marcus lamented their routine—once punctuated by laughter and the clamour of breakfast dishes—now suffocated under the weight of shared loss. Jamie's door was open, and the faint smell of urine escaped into the hall, an intense reminder of the trauma that lay within the room.

A glance at the clock confirmed his suspicion; they would be late for school again. The thought scraped at him, but what more could he do? Julia was unreachable in her bed, her absence in the mornings growing as wide as the chasm between them.

He made his way to the kitchen, once the heart of their home. He caught sight of the pool through the glass door leading to the backyard. Once a vibrant blue oasis, it was now cloaked in a green haze—neglected and ailing, much like the family it belonged to. Marcus noted the need for cleaning with a mental sigh, filing it away with the other tasks that awaited his attention.

Stepping outside, he felt the crisp morning air against his skin, contrasting the stifling atmosphere within. He walked toward the newer model station wagon, standing in the driveway.

Marcus's gaze drifted to Janice's house as he backed out of the driveway. There she was, framed by the kitchen window, her figure static as she stared out into nothingness. Perhaps she, too, was lost in the maze of her thoughts, trapped by the same event that had ensnared his family.

He raised his hand with hesitant resolve, a slow, hopeful gesture of camaraderie in their shared pain. But Janice did not flicker with acknowledgment, no sign that she saw him or the olive branch he extended in the form of a simple wave. Her stillness mirrored Julia's; both barely living in their own homes.

Marcus's hand hovered in the air for a moment longer, suspended in the silent gulf between their houses. Then, letting it fall, he focused on the road ahead, to the day's demands that waited for none, not even the broken-hearted.

The university's ivy-laden brick facade was indifferent to the maelstrom of thoughts churning within Marcus Dempsey as he climbed the steps and entered his professional realm. The corridors echoed with the bustle of early morning energy, students navigating through the currents of their academic endeavours, unaware of the storm behind their department head's eyes.

"Good morning, Professor Dempsey!" A chorus of youthful voices greeted him, their faces alight with the anticipation of uncovered knowledge. Marcus offered a half-smile, the gesture not quite reaching the depths of his deep-set eyes, shadowed by sleepless nights.

He rounded the corner to his office, the click of his shoes on the polished floors a metronome against the erratic rhythm of his heartbeat. Before him, the custodian, a silhouette against the morning light streaming through the windows, was screwing in place a gleaming new placard that heralded 'Department Head.'

"Ah, it looks official now, doesn't it?" the custodian said without turning, sensing Marcus's presence.

"I guess it does," Marcus said, his voice betraying none of the turmoil beneath his composed exterior.

"Professor Dempsey!" His secretary emerged from her adjacent cubicle, her smile bright and expectant. "Congratulations again on your promotion. Mrs. Dempsey must be over the moon with pride."

"Thank you, Clara." His response was automatic; a learned script performed countless times to maintain the facade of normalcy.

Marcus stepped into his office, a sanctum of books and papers, where the weight of his title felt heavier than the leather-bound tomes lining the shelves. He closed the door softly behind him, an instinctive need for solitude overtaking him.

He allowed himself the luxury of vulnerability at his desk, his broad shoulders slumping as he surrendered to the moment's gravity. With a weary exhale, Marcus cradled his face in his hands—a man versed in the rhetoric of healing yet unable to mend the fractures within his own home.

A flask from the recesses of a drawer emerged—a tarnished silver companion bearing witness to the silent battles waged within these four walls. Its cool touch against his lips was a reprieve, the burn of the liquor a stark contrast to the numbness that pervaded his existence.

A single tear betrayed him, carving a path down his weathered cheek, an outward sign of the internal chaos he fought to quell. He wiped it away, the saltiness lingering like the unresolved tensions of a life divided between duty and despair.

With a deep breath that filled his lungs with resolve, Marcus straightened his tie—a noose of responsibility—and gathered the sheaf of papers that spelled out the day's obligations. Another day awaited, another performance to be given in the grand theatre of academia.

"Time to begin," he said to the empty room, his voice a mere echo in the chamber of his heart.

The morning sun cast a feeble glow through the half-drawn curtains, laying a pattern of light and shadow across the room where Julia Dempsey lay ensnared by her sheets. She turned her gaze, settling on the mélange of amber pill containers that sprawled across her bedside table like fallen soldiers. With fingers that trembled ever so slightly—a delicate tremor that betrayed her inner turmoil—Julia reached for a jar. The click of the cap echoed too loudly in the silent room as she palmed two small, oblong pills and brought them to her lips with a sip of stale water.

She lay back down, the motion mechanical, her eyes fixed upon the ceiling with a blankness that seemed to absorb the very light from above. Each pill carried with it the hope of numbness, a reprieve from the weight of six months' sorrow that anchored her to this bed, this room, this unbearable stillness.

A floorboard creaked outside her door, and though she did not turn to look, Julia's heart constricted with the knowledge of who walked there.

In Jamie's room, the distance between him and the wall was mere inches, but in his mind, he stretched that space into miles, continents, and oceans. He lay motionless, his eyes open and unblinking, staring at the wallpaper that had begun to peel in one corner—a physical manifestation of his unravelling.

The air felt thick with the remnants of a dream, or perhaps a nightmare, the kind that clung to your thoughts long after waking. The incident, a word that had come to define the abyss in which he now found himself, hovered at the periphery of his consciousness. Six months ago, he would have risen with the sun, eager to greet the day. Now, facing the world beyond these four walls was like being asked to breathe underwater.

As the Dempseys remained locked in their separate prisons of grief and guilt, the house itself seemed to hold its breath, waiting for a release that refused to come.

Nicole's small fingers fumbled with the crinkled plastic bag inside the cereal box, the sugary loops tumbling into her bowl in a colourful cascade. She had learned to be self-sufficient in these quiet mornings, the house often wrapped in an uneasy stillness. As she tipped the box further, more cereal spilled over the bowl's rim and scattered across the countertop like pastel confetti. She pursed her lips in mild frustration but left the mess untouched, her young mind already moving on to the next task.

With a slight grunt, she dragged the stool closer to the refrigerator. With a determined yank, she opened the fridge door, the light within casting a sharp contrast to the dimly lit kitchen. Her small hand found the handle of the milk jug, wrapping around it with care as she maneuvered it out onto the counter beside her cereal bowl.

Milk splashed into the bowl, some droplets escaping to join the errant cereal on the counter. Nicole watched the loops bob and dance in the white tide before steadying herself to transport her breakfast to the living room. She was careful not to spill anymore as she walked, her steps measured and silent.

As she settled onto the carpet, the vibrant colours of morning cartoons flickered to life on the TV screen, illuminating her earnest face. The animated characters moved with exaggerated cheerfulness, their voices chipper and bright, yet they felt worlds apart from the sombre atmosphere that clung like cobwebs to the Dempsey household.

She spooned cereal into her mouth quietly, occasionally shifting her gaze from the screen to the hallway as if half-expecting one of her parents to emerge. But the only sound was the faint hum of the television and the distant, muffled noise of the world waking outside their walls.

Nicole might not have understood the depth of the sorrow that had taken root in her home, but she sensed the shift in its energy—the way voices hushed when she entered rooms or how smiles seemed to falter and fade too quickly. It was in the way her brother's eyes no longer sparkled with mischief and how her mother's laughter, once the music of their lives, had all but disappeared.

She took another bite, the sweetness of the cereal a stark contrast to the bitterness that seemed to linger in the air. Her innocence shielded her from grasping the full scope of the family's anguish, but the weight of unspoken words and stifled emotions pressed against her small shoulders, as insistent and real as the chill of the tile floor beneath her.

Part 6

2023

Chapter 21

The bedroom door creaked open, a sliver of tension escaping before Julia and Marcus Dempsey stepped out. Their faces were stone-carved replicas of serenity, a practiced masquerade they had cultivated over the year. The silence in the living room hung heavy as Jamie and Nicole glanced up from their respective corners.

Marcus crossed the room with a gait feigned casualness, though each step betrayed an undercurrent of unrest. He reached the bar, his hands steady as they retrieved a glass, the clink of ice against crystal punctuating the stillness. He poured himself a drink, the liquid swirling into the glass—a temporary refuge in his argument with Julia.

Julia's movements were more tentative, a hesitance clinging to her like a second skin as she drifted toward the kitchen. She paused at the entrance, her gaze flitting over Jamie—her son, who seemed so distant—and Nicole, whose maternal fierceness stood in stark contrast to her faltering presence. Then, as if shaking off the weight of scrutiny, she continued into the kitchen, opening the fridge with a faint sigh. The light within cast her in a harsh, clinical glow; she reached for a bottle of water, the coolness of it grounding her trembling fingertips.

Jamie's posture was rigid as he surveyed the family's facade. Nicole watched him, her heart a knot of empathy and sorrow, knowing too well the fragile threads that held their unit together.

"Everything okay?" Nicole's voice was soft, yet it carried the weight of a thousand implications. It was not a question as much as an acknowledgment—a recognition of the simmering discord that threatened to boil over.

"Of course," Marcus said, his tone too smooth, teetering on the edge of believable. He took a sip, the alcohol a momentary balm to his frayed nerves. "Why wouldn't it be?"

But Jamie said nothing, his silence a loud echo, evidence of the chasm between what was spoken and what lay deep within the fabric of the Dempseys. The truth was a shadow that loomed, always present, always mysterious, and never truly faced.

Jamie's fingers lingered on the cold, glossy surface of the photo, tracing the outlines of forgotten contours as if they could summon the past from its hiding place. His unwavering gaze locked onto the image with an intensity that seemed to drain the colour from the rest of the room.

Nicole glanced over at her brother, her hands pausing mid-stroke on the keyboard. She recognized that distant look in his eyes—the one that seemed to see through the walls and years to a time long buried under layers of forced smiles and feigned ignorance. She sighed and returned to her computer; her attention split between the cursor blinking on the screen and Jamie's unnerving stillness.

Chase was oblivious. He was absorbed in the flickering images on the TV screen, unaware of the silent storm brewing around him.

Jamie's mind hurtled back across the decades to a night cloaked in the innocence of youth, now tainted by the corrosion of time. He recalled the thick and alive darkness around Trevor's house as he stood below the window, clutching pebbles that felt like ice despite the summer warmth. With a flick of his wrist, the first pebble kissed the glass—a gentle plea. Silence answered him. A beat passed, a second pebble took flight, and the window creaked open this time, revealing Trevor's bewildered face bathed in the faint glow of a bedside lamp.

"Jamie?" Trevor's voice was a hushed whisper carried on the night breeze, imbued with the surprise of an unexpected late-night visitor.

The memory was so vivid that Jamie could almost feel the gravel beneath his sneakers and hear the tentative excitement in his voice from all those years ago. The scene unfolded behind his eyes, playing out against his will, each detail etched with the precision of a well-loved nightmare.

And there he was again, a ghostly projection of his younger self, beckoning to his friend with the promise of adventure, the thrill of a game played under the cover of darkness. It was a time when consequences seemed as distant as the stars overhead when the world was vast and full of mysteries to unravel.

Nicole watched Jamie's face contort with the effort of remembrance, lines of pain etching themselves around his eyes. "Jamie?" she ventured, soft but insistent.

But he was lost to her, caught in the grasp of a memory that held him tighter than any embrace. He was back in that year when everything changed, the pivot point of their lives, where the path forked into before and after.

"Jamie, talk to me," Nicole pressed, reaching out to touch his arm, but he was a statue. Her heart clenched at the sight of him.

"Hey, Trevor," Jamie said, a mischievous glint in his eyes that belied the innocence of his lanky frame silhouetted against the moonlit window. "What are you doing here?" Trevor's voice held a mix of surprise and wariness as he peered down at his friend.

"Did you sneak out?"

Jamie nodded, a conspiratorial smile dancing on his lips. He held up a pair of brightly coloured flags, their fabric limp in the night air. "Are you ready to play some capture the flag?"

Trevor's eyes widened before retreating into a frown as he glanced back into the perceived safety of his room. The ghost of a smile teased the corners of his mouth, but apprehension pulled it away. "You want me to sneak out, too?" he asked.

"Come on," Jamie goaded with a light laugh, the sound carefree and infectious. "What are you, chicken?"

"Chicken?" Trevor bristled at the challenge but was visibly torn. The thought of being caught loomed over him. "But what if my mom catches me?"

"She won't," Jamie assured, his voice steady and confident—a contrast to the instability that would later define him. "We won't be gone long. Your mother is probably already asleep, and my parents are out for the night. They won't even know to check."

"Jamie..." Trevor hesitated, teetering on the edge of decision. His room beckoned him to stay, yet the allure of the forbidden game tugged at him.

"Trust me, Trev," Jamie said, sensing the victory within his grasp.

"Okay, okay," Trevor finally relented, adrenaline surging through him as he pushed aside the fear. "Alright," Trevor said, more to himself than to Jamie. "Let's do it."

Trevor's silhouette cut through the gloom, his figure clumsy as he tumbled out the window onto the dew-kissed grass. The moonlight glanced off his wide eyes, reflecting a cocktail of exhilaration and trepidation. He shakily found his footing and straightened up to face Jamie, who stood with an expectant grin plastered across his face.

"Let's go," whispered Trevor, as if speaking louder would shatter their midnight escapade's fragile veil of secrecy.

Without another word, they turned on their heels, their youthful energy propelling them toward the end of the back-yard. Their feet pounded the soft earth in unison, their breaths coming out in misty plumes that mingled with the night air. They reached the fence, its wooden slats a mere obstacle to their enthusiasm. With adrenaline-fueled limbs, they clambered over and vanished into the forest, where dark-ness swallowed them whole.

Once enveloped by the towering trees, Jamie dug into his pocket and produced two folded flags—one red, one blue. He handed the blue one to Trevor, whose fingers trembled as he accepted it. Jamie then retrieved a pair of walkie-talkies from his backpack, pressing one into Trevor's uncertain grasp. Finally, he passed Trevor a small flashlight and simulta-neously turned his on.

"Hide your flag, and don't make it easy for me," Jamie said, a mischievous glint in his eye that was visible even under the sparse light filtering through the canopy. "We meet back here by the fence in ten minutes."

"Got it," Trevor said.

They dispersed into the woods, each carrying the weight of their secret mission. Leaves crunched underfoot, and the occasional snap of a twig punctuated the stillness. Jamie watched Trevor's shadow recede before he turned to find his hiding spot. A hush fell over the forest again, save for the distant rustle of movement as each boy buried their banner in the wilderness.

Minutes ticked by, marked by the rhythmic chorus of crickets and the occasional hoot of an owl. Jamie returned to the meeting place first, his heart thrumming against his ribcage. Trevor emerged, breathless and flushed with the thrill of their covert operation.

"Ready?" Jamie asked, a smile playing at the corners of his mouth.

"Ready," Trevor said, his earlier apprehension washed away by the rush of the game.

The walkie-talkies crackled to life as they tested them, their static-filled voices confirming the final link in their nocturnal alliance. For a moment, everything else faded—the looming risk of discovery by their parents, the mundane drudgery of day-to-day life, the unknowable future. There was only the here and now, the bond of trust they shared, and the identity they forged within the forest's shadows.

"Okay, Trev," Jamie said through the darkness, the dim glow of his flashlight casting eerie shadows on their determined faces. We split up. Hunt for the flag. The first one to grab the others and return here without getting tagged wins."

Trevor's nod was barely discernible in the forest's twilight, but Jamie could sense the eagerness in his friend's stance, the readiness to dash into the night. The air was charged with the electric current of their mutual challenge.

"Go!" Jamie said, turning on his heel and sprinting away, leaving only the sound of his footsteps as evidence of his presence.

He darted between trees, the beam of his flashlight dancing over bark and leaves, sweeping across the forest floor in search of Trevor's hidden flag. The cool air filled his lungs, sharpening his senses and focusing his mind singularly on the task. The game was underway, and Jamie felt alive in a way that only these stolen moments of adventure could provoke.

Somewhere off to his left, he could hear Trevor's progress—the muffled steps, the occasional crackling of underbrush. The bobbing light of Trevor's flashlight flickered like a distant star through the thicket, beckoning Jamie toward the chase. But he resisted the urge to call out, taunt, or tease; this was a game of stealth, not bravado.

Jamie moved with intention, each step deliberate, avoiding the dry twigs and leaves that would betray his position. His heart pounded a rhythm that matched his pace, reverberating through his chest with exhilaration and trepidation.

The minutes stretched, time becoming as malleable and elusive as the shadows that played upon the ground. Each potential hiding spot he checked was empty, void of the sought-after flag, driving him deeper into the woods.

In the distance, Trevor's light stopped moving. A surge of adrenaline shot through Jamie's veins. Had he found it? Was he now racing back to the fence, victorious?

"Focus," Jamie said, eyes scanning the terrain with renewed urgency. He crouched by a fallen log, directing the flashlight beneath its bulk. Nothing.

"Keep looking," he urged himself. "It's here. It has to be."

Jamie's breath came in heavy gasps, the cold night air biting at his lungs as he hurtled through the underbrush. His flashlight danced erratically between the trees, casting long, sinister shadows that seemed to chase him just as he chased Trevor. Amidst his frantic footsteps, Jamie could hear the distant, muffled sounds of Trevor's triumph.

"I've got it! I've got it!" Trevor's voice, full of youthful glee, pierced the darkness ahead.

He's close, Jamie thought, a surge of adrenaline propelling him forward.

Eyes locked on Trevor's flashlight's bobbing light, Jamie felt a rush of the wild, a feral thrill that had nothing to do with the game and everything to do with the chase itself. As Trevor burst from a thicket, his silhouette framed by the ambient glow of the moon, he turned his head and saw Jamie barreling toward him. Their eyes met, two sparks of clarity in the chaos of the forest at night.

"Jamie!" Trevor's shout was part laugh, part challenge.

With an agility born of panic and play, Trevor pivoted, his sneakers digging into the soft earth as he changed direction. The sudden movement sent leaves swirling into the air like a flock of startled birds taking flight.

Jamie's smile broke through his determined expression, a rare and genuine display that reached his eyes.

The two of them were racing, a frenetic ballet among the pines. Jamie dodged a low-hanging branch, the rough bark grazing the skin of his forearm, but he hardly noticed. All that mattered was the space between him and Trevor, the gap he desperately tried to close.

"Can't let you win that easily," Jamie said, his voice tinged with a breathless laughter that had been silent for too long.

But there was no time to think beneath the canopy of trees. There was only the electric pulse of the present, his heart pounding synced to the rhythm of his feet against the forest floor. Jamie closed in on Trevor, no more than a hundred fleeting yards away now.

Up ahead, he noticed the landscape change. In that instant, he recognized the road cutting through the forest. "Turn around, Trevor!" he screamed, his voice ragged with desperation. But his plea evaporated into the void between them—the distance too great, the warning too late.

From afar, he saw the shape of Trevor emerge from the protective shroud of the forest, his figure illuminated by the car's harsh headlights for an instant before being swallowed by a collision that echoed like a gunshot through the woods.

Jamie's limbs turned to stone, his body instinctively retreating behind the nearest tree as he took in the calamity. The world narrowed to the sight of the halted vehicle, its red tail lights bleeding into the darkness.

Time stood still. There was a profound silence that seemed to consume the air he breathed. Then, the car's doors opened, spilling yellow light onto the pavement as two figures emerged—silhouettes against the glare, strangers cast as villains in Jamie's nightmare.

He strained his eyes, trying to make sense of the scene before him, but details remained elusive, masked by the chaos of his own pounding heart. He could only watch as the figures moved with purposeful haste to the front of the car, their actions obscured, intentions unknown.

Then, as if surrendering to some unspoken command, they drifted up the road, their forms growing indistinct before descending into the gully that ran alongside. It was as if the earth conspired to swallow any trace of the tragedy that unfolded, leaving Jamie alone with the ghosts of what had just occurred.

Hidden within the shadows, Jamie's chest heaved with each shallow breath, his pulse a frantic drumbeat against his temples.

But there, in the aftermath, amidst the deafening silence, all he could grasp was the paralyzing grip of shock, rooting him to the spot, a statue to the moment his world irrevocably changed.

A distant shout fractured the silence, a garbled cry that failed to form into words before the night snatched it away. Jamie's blood ran cold, and his muscles finally broke free from shock's icy clamp. He turned on his heel, the faces of the figures in the car blurring in his peripheral vision as he sprinted away.

His feet hammered against the earth, each thud a desperate plea for escape. The fence loomed ahead, a barrier between two worlds—the innocent pastures of his youth and the dark forest where innocence died. With a grunt, he vaulted over, the metallic clang of his landing echoing into nothingness. His backyard, once a canvas of childhood adventures, now felt alien under the moon's unyielding gaze.

He dashed past the pool, its still waters contrasting his turmoil. The pool seemed to mock him with its tranquillity, indifferent to the chaos that churned beyond its manicured borders.

The sanctuary of his room beckoned, a promise of solitude and shadows. He scrambled through the window, tumbling onto the floor before crawling into bed. The soft cotton sheets were no comfort as he buried his face into the pillow, his sobs muffled within its depths. They came in waves, a tide of grief and guilt that refused to ebb. He was lost, terrified, and pleading for the simplicity of a life unmarred by tragedy.

Nicole glanced around the living room, catching the framed semblances of happier times. The palpable yet unspoken tension clung to the air until Jamie's return sliced through it like a blade.

"Jamie, are you okay?" Nicole asked, her voice tinged with concern. Her eyes, twin pools of empathy, sought out her brother's. But Jamie's gaze was distant, his eyes glistening trails of unshed tears, windows to the storm that raged within.

Her heart clenched at the sight, recognizing the same tormented look that often stared back at her from the mirror—the inheritance of a broken family. She wanted to reach out, to bridge the gap between them, but the weight of their shared history held her back.

"Jamie?" she pressed, but he remained silent, locked in his world, a fortress of pain that no words could penetrate.

Jamie's hand trembled as he traced the car's outline in the photograph, a ghost from the past materializing before his eyes. The image was grainy, and the colours faded, but the shape was unmistakable. A chill crawled up his spine, his pulse quickening with the dawning horror of recognition.

"Nicole," Jamie said, barely audible as memories surged like a deluge through the levees of his mind, "this car... I've seen it."

Nicole shifted closer, her gaze flitting to the image that had trapped her brother's attention. "What about it?" she asked, her voice a feather on the tense air.

"It was there that night—the night Trevor..." His voice broke the words lodging in his throat like shards of glass.

"Jamie, what are you saying?" Nicole's brow furrowed in confusion, her fingers reaching out to touch his arm, seeking to ground him as his world spun out of control.

He didn't look at her, couldn't tear his eyes away from the damning piece of evidence that lay innocuously between them. "That's the car, Nic. The one from the accident. The one that hit him.".

"Jamie, what are you talking about? How do you know," she said, her voice wavering between doubt and the creeping dread of realization.

"Jamie..."

"Everything changed after that night." His words were a torrent now, unstoppable, each laced with venom and grief. "It wasn't just me or Janice—it was all of us. Mom and Dad, too. They knew."

"Knew?" Nicole echoed, disbelief etching her features.

"They knew, Nicole." Jamie's eyes finally met hers, and she recoiled at the raw anguish they held. "It was their car. They were the ones."

Nicole sank back, her breath catching in her chest. In her brother's gaze, she saw the crumbling edifice of their family— a structure built on secrets and silence, now exposed in the stark light of truth. And behind that revelation, the shadow of an even darker question loomed—could the people who raised them harbour such a monstrous secret?

"Jamie, this is—I can't believe it." Her voice was a murmur lost amidst the crashing waves of revelation.

"Believe it," Jamie said, his tone hollow. "Believe it because it's true. And it's been true for forty years."

As silence enveloped them, Jamie's eyes remained locked onto the photograph, the picture that spoke a thousand words of betrayal. It was more than proof; it was a testament to the loss of innocence, the death of trust, and the identity he thought he knew—an identity irrevocably altered by the wreckage of a single, tragic night.

Jamie's gaze lifted from the damning photograph, his eyes pooling with tears that coursed unchecked down his cheeks. His vision blurred, but not enough to obscure the sight of his father standing there—a man who had been a pillar of stoic strength throughout Jamie's life, now unwittingly unveiled as the architect of his deepest pain.

"You bastard," Jamie spat out, each word trembling with the weight of the years he'd spent entombed in guilt.

Julia reentered the living room just in time to catch the venom in her son's voice. Her heart clenched at the sight of him—her boy, so hollowed out by secrets and sorrow. The creases around her eyes deepened as she absorbed the tableau before her, the concerned look on her face a mask barely concealing her inner turmoil.

Marcus, taken aback by the accusation flung at him, could only muster a confused defence. "Jamie, why are you saying that?" His voice cracked, the scholarly veneer that had always defined him now peeling away under the moment's strain.

Jamie's head swivelled toward Nicole, desperation etched into every line of his face. "It was them," he said, the words like shards of glass in his throat.

Nicole's warm brown eyes, so often a source of comfort, widened in confusion. Her instincts as a mother kicked in, and she turned toward her son, Chase, who had been lost in the glowing screen of his smartphone, oblivious to the growing storm around him. "Chase, go to your room," she said, her tone leaving no room for debate.

With an adolescent huff, Chase stood up and shuffled out of the room, casting a last glance over his shoulder at the unfolding drama.

Nicole faced Jamie again, her expression a tangle of fear and uncertainty. "What are you talking about, Jamie?" Her voice sounded foreign even to herself as if she were hearing it from a great distance.

Jamie's hands shook as he pointed to the photograph still clutched between his fingers, the edges crumpled from the force of his grip. The image, once benign, now screamed its ghastly truth into the quiet of the room.

"Look at the car, Nicole," he said, voice strained. "It's theirs. It was theirs all along."

In the silence that followed, the chasm that had long divided their family seemed to yawn wider, threatening to swallow them whole. Nicole stared at her brother, seeing the little boy who had once chased fireflies in the backyard, now a man haunted by shadows stretching across the decades, eroding the foundation of their shared history.

The air was thick with unspoken thoughts, heavy with the gravity of truths too long buried. And within that silence, the delicate fabric of trust that had held their identities together began to unravel, thread by painstaking thread.

Jamie's voice was a low, hollow echo in the cavernous room as he uttered the name that had been etched into his soul. "Trevor..." The single word hung in the air, a spectre from the past summoned to witness the present turmoil.

Julia's heart plummeted, the blood draining from her face as she watched her son, the lines of sorrow etched deep across his brow. Her knees threatened to give way beneath her. She looked to Marcus for support but found only a reflection of her horror mirrored in his countenance. His hand trembled visibly as he struggled to place his whiskey glass on the mantel, the clink of crystal on wood sounding unnaturally loud.

"Jamie...what are you saying?" Nicole's voice was soft, almost pleading. The warm smile that so often graced her features was now quivering at the edges with fear. She leaned forward in her chair; hands clenched tightly in her lap as if to brace herself against the tide of revelations threatening to sweep them away.

"Marcus," Jamie said, turning his gaze from the photograph to his father. The accusation in his eyes was sharp and accusatory. "It was you all along. You killed him." Each word felt like a blow, tearing through the carefully woven tapestry of their family's life.

"Jamie!" Nicole's exclamation was a sharp crack in the strained atmosphere. "Why are you saying this?"

But Jamie was unyielding, an obdurate force confronting the frailty of their constructed normalcy. He knew, with a certainty that clawed at his insides, that the shadows of the past were finally stretching out to claim their due. And within those shadows, the faces of his parents loomed large—

protectors turned persecutors, their actions a betrayal that transcended time and memory.

"Answer me, Jamie!" Nicole's voice rose, tinged with the first notes of desperation. Her world, once so certain, teetered on the brink of collapse. Her eyes implored him, silently begging for some other truth than the one he wielded like a weapon.

Yet the truth, once unearthed, could not be buried again. It poisoned the air, colouring each breath with the metallic tang of guilt. For Jamie, the past was no longer a distant country. It was here, alive and demanding recognition. And in its wake, it left nothing but the echoes of a boy's laughter, snuffed out on a road long ago.

Jamie's gaze was unflinching. "You hit Trevor with your car that night," he said, his voice barely above a whisper, yet it carried the weight of years of silence. "And then you covered it up."

Nicole snapped her head toward him, her eyes wide with disbelief. "That's impossible," she countered, the edges of her words frayed with confusion and denial. She had known sorrow and shouldered the weight of a past that always seemed painted in shades of gray, but this accusation was a darkness beyond her comprehension.

"Look around, Nicole," Jamie implored, his plea etched into the lines of his weary face. "Everything changed that day. And now we know why."

The room held its breath, suspended in the gravity of his revelation. Nicole's gaze shifted to their parents, seeking an anchor in the storm of accusations. "No," she said, shaking her head to dispel the nightmare before her eyes. "You couldn't have done this."

Marcus and Julia, the architects of her childhood memories, remained silent, their faces betraying nothing. The absence of denial was louder than any protestation could ever be.

"No, no, no..." Nicole's voice cracked, breaking through the dam of her composure. Tears traced the contours of her face, mapping the terrain of her shattered certainties. "Tell me you didn't do that."

Her words hung in the balance, a desperate plea for a salvation that would not come. The ghosts of a thousand unspoken conversations whispered through the room in the stillness that followed, each a requiem for innocence lost.

Marcus's hand trembled as he set down his glass, the ice cubes clinking like distant bells foretelling doom. His voice, usually steady and imbued with academic authority, betrayed a hint of fragility. "Jamie, why would you say that? How could you possibly know that?"

The question hung in the air, but Jamie's response crashed through the room like a thunderclap. "Because I was there!" His voice rose to a yell, raw with the torment of hidden truths clawing their way out. "I was fucking there, damn it! I'm the one who convinced Trevor to sneak out that night—to play in the forest. And when I chased him, when we reached the road—I saw the car hit him!"

His breathing was ragged, punctuating the silence that followed his outburst. Marcus and Julia stood as if turned to stone while Nicole's warm eyes, always seeking to understand, now searched for something beyond comprehension.

Jamie's finger jabbed accusingly at the photograph of a silent witness on the table. "This picture—it's this car, isn't it? You got rid of it, didn't you?" The intensity in his voice belied the years of self-blame and secrets buried beneath layers of time.

"Please," Nicole's voice emerged faintly, a whisper torn from her throat. Her gaze flitted between Marcus and Julia, pleading for a sliver of hope in the darkness. But Julia's face, etched with the sorrow of decades, met her daughter's eyes.

"Oh, Nicole." The words were a mere breath, laced with an agony only a mother's heart could know. "I'm so sorry."

At that moment, the living room, filled with mementos of happier times—felt like a mausoleum, housing not just memories but ghosts of what they once were. Jamie's revelation had stripped them all bare, exposing the fault lines that ran deep beneath the surface of their collective identity.

Nicole clenched her hands into fists at her sides as if trying to hold onto something, anything, in the wake of the devastation wrought by the truth. The apologies and regrets were a thin balm, too feeble to heal the wounds that had festered unseen for so long.

And amidst the ruins of trust and the echoes of childhood laughter that would never reoccur, they grappled with the stark reality of who they were and what they had become.

Jamie surged to his feet, the muscles in his lean frame taut with a fury plaguing for decades. His fingers trembled as he stared across the room at Julia and Marcus, the architects of his torment. "All these years, I blamed myself," he spat out the words like they were poison, each syllable heavy with the weight of wasted years. "It ruined my life. It ruined our family. And all along—it was you. You could have fixed it. How could you do this!"

The air thickened around them, thick with the betrayal that spilled from Jamie's lips.

Julia, her gray hair casting shadows over her deep-set eyes, stood up slowly as if the act required a strength she no longer possessed. "We did it for you," she said, her voice barely rising above a whisper, yet it cut through the silence with the precision of a scalpel. "For the family. It would have ruined us."

Jamie's laugh was bitter—a sharp, jagged thing that bore no humour. "Ruined us?" he said, his gaze locked onto Julia's. "It did ruin us. More than you could ever know." His voice cracked, the sound of a soul splintering under the burden of a truth too heavy to bear.

Julia reached out a hand, frail and trembling, but Jamie recoiled as if her touch were searing flame. Her hand fell back to her side, useless.

In the space between them lay the remnants of trust and the spectre of identity, both now unrecognizable. Jamie's revelation had not only unearthed a past long buried but forced them to confront the reflection of who they truly were—a reflection marred by the shattered pieces of what could never be made whole again.

Nicole's hand was a steady warmth against Jamie's trembling one as she guided him back to the couch. She lowered herself beside him gently, her eyes never leaving the tattered photo clutched in his other hand. The image, faded and yellowed by time, seemed to pulse with an accusatory life of its own.

"I can't even remember that car," she said, her voice soft enough to be almost lost beneath the tension between them like a shroud.

Jamie, his face a study in anguish, turned toward her. "I do now. It's been there, somewhere deep inside." His voice broke, tripping over memories long suppressed, and he swallowed hard against the knot of emotion lodged in his throat. "I must have repressed it or...or just forgotten it." A tear traced a path down his cheek, cutting through the grime of the past.

Nicole followed the solitary track of his tear with her own eyes, feeling the weight of their shared history press upon her chest. She turned to their parents, who stood like spectres of their former selves, the facade of normalcy stripped away to reveal a core marred by unspeakable acts.

"You killed him," she said, the words tumbling out like stones from her mouth. "You fucking killed him. And buried it all these years."

Marcus and Julia seemed to shrink before her, their expressions leaden with the guilt that had festered in decades of silence. Marcus' lips parted, but no sound emerged—a pantomime of communication rendered obsolete by the gravity of truth.

"How can anyone live with this?" Nicole's voice rose, a crescendo of doubt and despair. "And you"—her gaze cut to Julia—"you fucking lived next door to Janice all these years and watched her suffer!"

Julia's eyes flickered, the merest flinch, but it spoke volumes of the chasm that had opened beneath them all. Her hands clasped together, knuckles white, as if trying to hold onto the fragments of a life that no longer existed.

The room was imbued with the raw scent of betrayal, the air so thick it threatened to choke them. Jamie leaned into Nicole, seeking solace in the proximity of someone who shared his heartache. His silent sobs were a testament to the years of pain that flowed unbidden and unchecked.

At that moment, they were not a family but a tableau of tragedy, each locked within their hell, bound together by the irrevocable threads of a single, devastating act.

Marcus stepped forward, his presence looming over the disarray of exposed secrets. The room, once a sanctuary, now felt cold and hollow—a mausoleum for their shattered pretenses.

"We did it for you two," he said, desperation tugging at the edges of his voice. His eyes searched Jamie's face, seeking absolution in the haunted landscape of his son's features. "For your future. We would have been ruined. I had my promotion, too."

"Who cares about a fucking promotion?" Nicole's words were sharp, slicing through Marcus's feeble justifications as if they were nothing but air. Her hands clenched into fists at her sides, her body rigid with anger. "You left a boy to die on the side of the road."

Julia's gaze flickered away, a silent flinch from the accusation. "He was already dead," she said, her voice a brittle thing that threatened to crack under the weight of its falsehood.

"Jesus, Mom, how could you?" Nicole's plea was a broken sound, a daughter grappling with the inconceivable.

Jamie's fists were clenched so tightly his knuckles shone white. Every line of his body spoke of betrayal, his lean frame vibrating with suppressed rage. "I fucking hate you," he said, the words tearing from him raw and unfiltered. Tears stained the photo in his hands, blurring the edges of a past now poisoned.

"Do you know what I've been through because of you?" His voice broke, the dam of his long-contained emotions finally breaching. Sorrow seeped into the room's fabric, settling heavily on their shoulders.

"All the lies have torn this family apart," Jamie said, his gaze locked with Marcus's. There was accusation there, but also an imploring—pleading for recognition of the pain that had plagued me in silence.

"Wh-what do you want us to do now?" Marcus said, his composure unravelling, revealing the frayed cords of his soul. He reached out as if to steady himself against the tide of Jamie's grief, but his hands found only space.

The room held its breath, every eye trained on Jamie, every heart hammering with the dread of truths yet spoken.

The photo album collided with the wall, its spine splintering from the force of Jamie's throw. Echoes of the impact reverberated through the silence.

"We're going to start telling the truth now," Jamie said, his rasp edged with decades of buried torment. His eyes, usually dulled by resignation, burned with an incandescent fury.

Nicole pushed herself to her feet, her movements mirroring the urgency in Jamie's stance. The protective mother, the mediator of their childhood squabbles, now faced her brother in a room where the air was thick with revelations. "What are you going to do, Jamie?" Her voice trembled, not with fear, but with the weight of impending change.

Jamie turned toward her, and in the hollows of his grief-stricken face, she saw the boy he once was—a boy burdened too soon with guilt and secrets. "I'm going to do what should have been done 40 years ago."

His words hung between them, a sentence passed on the life they had all been living, a life stitched together with half-truths and willful ignorance. Nicole reached out, her hand almost touching his arm, but she hesitated. Her touch could not undo the past and unbreak the trust that lay in pieces at their feet.

"Jamie," she said, her heart aching for her brother, who had carried this alone, "how can we fix this? How can we ever make it right?"

But Jamie was already moving, propelled by a resolve that seemed to lend him strength he hadn't possessed moments before. "We can't fix it," he said, pausing at the room's threshold, casting a last glance over his shoulder. "But we can face it. We can own up to it."

And with that, he stepped out into the evening, leaving the remnants of a family portrait that would never be whole again. Nicole watched him go, knowing that whatever came next, the facade of the Dempsey family had crumbled, leaving them all exposed to the harsh light of truth.

Epilogue

The porcelain cup was warm in Jamie's hands, contrasting with the crisp morning air swirling around the Willow Tree Café's outdoor tables. He sat there, an observer of small-town life, watching as tendrils of steam danced from his coffee into the autumn sky.

Jamie's gaze drifted across the street. It had been a year since his confession to Janice. His fingers traced the rim of the cup, the motion grounding him in the present. There was a newfound roundness to his cheeks, evidence of the nurturing he had afforded himself away from the chaos of his past. His hair, now brushing his shoulders, framed a face that seemed sculpted from contentment itself - the hard lines that once spoke of sleepless nights and inner turmoil had softened.

A smile touched Jamie's lips, a private acknowledgment of his journey—he had climbed out of the valley of addiction. He leaned back in his chair, allowing the morning sun to paint his features in a golden hue.

He glanced at the empty chair across from him, anticipating Janice and Nicole's arrival. The quiet anticipation evoked a palpable sense of serenity.

Janice's approach broke the soft murmur of the café. She waved as she navigated through the scattered tables and chairs, her smile reaching him long before her voice did.

"Jamie," she said, her voice warm as it wrapped around his name. The simple utterance held layers of history, a salutation that had weathered storms and emerged hopeful on the other side.

"Janice," he said, standing to welcome her. His chair scraped against the pavement. They embraced briefly; a tangible sign of the trust rebuilt over the year since truths laid bare had reshaped their lives.

"Look at you," Janice said, pulling back to appraise him. "You look great."

"Thank you," Jamie said, reclaiming his seat while gesturing for her to do the same. "Life's been different. Good different."

They settled into the rhythm of conversation, the kind that meanders through time and shared experiences. They spoke of small triumphs and quiet struggles, each word painting a vivid portrait of the year that had stretched between them, shaping their identities anew.

"Tell me about this new life of yours," Janice prompted, her curiosity sparkling. "The last email you sent mentioned a cabin?"

"Ah, yes," Jamie leaned back, the sun casting a lattice of shadows across his face through the café's awning. "It's not much, really—just a small place surrounded by nature. I've got solar panels, a rainwater collection system, and a garden that's more weeds than vegetables at the moment," he chuckled, but there was pride in his voice.

"Sounds like quite the transformation from city life. What made you decide to leap?"

"Solitude," Jamie said. "There's something pure about living where the only sounds are the wind in the trees and the birds at dawn. It's a life stripped down to its bones, just essentials, and somehow, through that, I found a fullness I never had before."

"Is it lonely?" Janice asked gently, her fingers tracing the rim of her coffee cup.

"Surprisingly, no," Jamie said, meeting her gaze. "Out there, alone, I'm finally learning who Jamie Dempsey is when he's not lost in the noise of everything else. And the dogs," he said with a smile, "are a great company."

"Always knew you had a way with animals." Janice's smile matched his. "Seems you've found a way to peace as well."

"Peace," Jamie said softly, letting the word linger between them like a delicate promise. "Yes, I think that's exactly what it is."

The chime of the café door announced a new arrival, pulling Jamie's attention from the remnants of his coffee swirls. Janice's eyes followed his to the entrance, where Nicole appeared, her long brown hair catching the sunlight in a warm cascade.

"Sorry I'm late," Nicole said with a buoyant stride as she approached the table. "The universe decided today was the day everyone needed extra love at the shelter."

She wrapped her arms around Jamie first, the embrace lingering enough to communicate years of unspoken support. Then she turned to Janice, her hug equally heartfelt. Jamie watched them, appreciating how effortlessly Nicole's presence seemed to dissipate the heavier air between the pages of their past.

"Tell me everything," Nicole said as she settled into the chair next to Janice, her smile an open invitation.

Janice, energized by Nicole's enthusiasm, leaned forward. "Well, volunteering at the community center has been... it's been transformative," she began, her voice tinged with sincerity. "There's this group of kids I've been mentoring, and you know, they remind me a lot of us when we were younger—trying to find our way."

"Has it helped?" Jamie asked, studying Janice's face for the subtle tells of her heart's truth.

"More than I could have imagined," Janice confessed, her eyes misting. "They've given me purpose again, a reason to look beyond my grief. And the other volunteers, we've become like a family, supporting each other through everything."

"Sounds incredible, Janice," Nicole said, her tone soft yet earnest. "Finding that sense of belonging is so important." A knowing look passed between the sisters, acknowledging shared struggles and the pursuit of healing.

The conversation flowed naturally afterward, with Nicole sharing snippets of her life at the shelter and the small victories that kept her days bright. Jamie listened, a contented observer to the ebb and flow of their stories.

Nicole brushed a stray strand of hair from her face; the smile never left her lips. She glanced across the table at Jamie, her eyes reflecting a life that suddenly had more light than shadows. "And can you believe it? Chase has snagged himself a job at that new tech startup downtown. Sure, he's just fetching coffee for now, but he's over the moon—feels like he's part of something big."

Jamie raised his eyebrows, a playful smirk tugging at the corners of his mouth. "Well, we all have to start somewhere, don't we? Good for him." He leaned back in his chair, arms folded, the warmth of pride swelling in his chest for his nephew.

"Exactly," Nicole nodded emphatically. "He's talking about coding and apps, not just scrolling through them. It's like watching him wake up to the world." Her gaze drifted, lost in thoughts of Chase's newfound spark.

"Seems like waking up is contagious in the Dempsey family," Janice said, a glint of admiration in her voice. "You're practically glowing, Nicole."

"Maybe," Nicole conceded with a laugh, "I've been reconnecting with old friends, diving back into the real world. And—I can't believe I'm saying this—I've even started dating again."

"Really?" Jamie couldn't resist the tease. "Should we prepare for someone new at next year's reunion?"

"Let's not get ahead of ourselves," Nicole said, her laughter mingling with the café's ambient chatter. "But it's nice to feel... hopeful, you know? Grounded."

Their cups sat empty, but the conversation was full, flowing from Chase's small triumphs to Nicole's cautious steps toward a future she was finally allowing herself to shape.

"Speaking of hope," Jamie said, voice softening as he shifted the topic. "Marcus and Julia—they've begun their community service sentence. Given their age and health, I suppose it was appropriate."

Nicole's hands paused mid-air, the stir of her spoon in her cup ceasing. "The court was pretty lenient," she said, her tone neutral.

"Maybe," Jamie said, his eyes darkening with the complexity of his emotions. "But maybe it's a chance for them to make amends in some small way."

"Community service can be humbling," Janice said. "It forces you to step outside yourself, to see the lives you touch—sometimes for better, often for worse."

"True," Nicole said. "And in their case, there's much touching up to do."

The air around them held a stillness. Each pondered the frailty of trust and the long road to redemption. But there was no bitterness in their silence, only a shared understanding that healing was a journey they were all walking, separately yet somehow together.

"Rebuilding isn't easy," Jamie finally broke the quiet, "but it's worth the effort. We're proof of that."

Nicole reached out, her hand covering Jamie's. "We are," she affirmed, her eyes meeting his with a resilience born from the trials they'd weathered.

Their collective gaze turned outward, where the sun began its descent, painting the sky with hues of hope and endurance—much like the path they had carved for themselves.

Nicole's gaze wandered to the street beyond their cozy circle, where the golden light draped over the town like a delicate veil. "They sold the house," she said, her voice tinged with relief and resignation.

"Sold it?" Jamie echoed, his brow arching in surprise as he set his coffee cup down with a soft clink against the saucer.

"Yep." Nicole nodded, watching a family of four stroll by, their laughter floating on the breeze. "They're living in separate apartments now."

"Separate after all these years." Janice leaned forward; her interest piqued.

"Completely apart," Nicole said. She glanced at Jamie, then Janice. "It's strange, but I think it's for the best. They've started walking their paths—paths to redemption, self-discovery...Have you met the new family?"

"Ah, they're lovely." Janice's smile grew genuine at the thought. "A young couple with two kids—a boy and a girl. They're always in the pool, splashing and laughing like their private ocean."

Jamie chuckled, the sound bubbling up deep within him, warm and sincere. "Kids have a way of breathing life back into a place, don't they?"

"Absolutely," Nicole agreed, her laughter mingling with his. "I hope they find joy in that home."

Janice nodded, her eyes reflecting the same sentiment. "Joy and peace."

The conversation drifted, settling around them like leaves from an autumn tree, each word a testament to change and growth. Nicole's next words carried weight, yet they did not sink the mood; instead, they offered a perspective steeped in the wisdom of hard-earned experiences.

"Mom and Dad, they're... well, they're working on themselves. Separately." Her voice was steady, the timbre rich with complexity. "They've been attending counselling sessions."

"Really?" Jamie's eyebrows rose, a spark of curiosity igniting in his eyes. "That's a big step."

"Massive," Nicole concurred, nodding solemnly. "The separation, the community service—it's all forced them to face the past, to look at themselves and the hurt they caused."

"Sometimes you have to be broken apart to find a way to mend," Janice said quietly, her gaze distant yet focused as if she could see the threads of their lives slowly knitting back together.

"Exactly," Nicole said. "They're trying, you know? Making efforts to atone for their mistakes."

As the three of them sat there, the weight of their collective pasts seemed to lift, replaced by a fragile sense of hope for the future—a future where yesterday's shadows did not shackle identities, trust could be rebuilt, and loss, perhaps, could find its counterpart in newfound strength.

Jamie reached into the bag resting by his feet and carefully drew a small, potted sapling. Its leaves rustled softly in the breeze, a gentle whisper amidst the clink of coffee cups and murmur of conversation around them. He placed it on the table, pushing his mug aside to make room.

"I brought something," Jamie said, his voice a low hum that seemed to draw Janice's attention more than any grand gesture might have. "A tree."

Janice's eyes widened slightly, her gaze dropping to the delicate green symbol of new life.

"Jamie, it's lovely," she said, her voice imbued with genuine warmth and surprise. "But why?"

He looked at her, his face open and earnest in a way that still felt unfamiliar even after all this time. "It's a symbol, I guess," he said. "Of growth, new beginnings. I was thinking. .. maybe we could plant it together, somewhere that matters."

The idea settled between them, a tangible offering of hope and renewal. Jamie watched as Janice considered the proposal, her fingers brushing against the rough texture of the bark.

"Somewhere meaningful..." Janice echoed. A softness entered her eyes, born from deep reflection and intimate knowledge of loss. "I know just the place."

"Where?" Jamie asked, sensing the significance of her tone.

"Right outside Trevor's window," she said, her voice steady but layered with emotion. "He loved to watch the seasons change through the glass. It'll be like he's still there, part of everything that grows and lives."

Jamie nodded, understanding without needing further words the sacred nature of such a spot for Janice.

"That's a great idea," he said sincerely, feeling an honour he hadn't anticipated being included in such a personal moment. "I'd be honoured to plant it for you."

Janice met Jamie's gaze, her eyes reflecting a quiet gratitude. "Together," she said gently. "We'll plant it together."

As they sat there, the small tree between them, it wasn't just the potential of what it would become that filled Jamie with a sense of purpose—it was the understanding that even when trust had faltered. Identities had been lost, but there remained a chance to create something lasting that spoke of resilience and the courage to grow anew.

Jamie set down his empty coffee cup. The afternoon sun cast an amber glow over them, wrapping their faces in warmth.

After a while, they rose from their chairs, the scrape of metal against cobblestone marking the end of their trance. Jamie picked up the small tree, its leaves whispering promises of growth as he cradled it in his arms.

"Ready to make this little guy part of the family?" he asked, nodding toward the sapling.

"More than ready," Janice affirmed, her voice carrying the weight of a mother's love and loss. She reached out to touch the tender green leaves, thinking of Trevor and the life he should have had.

"Let's plant some hope," Nicole said softly, her hand resting on Jamie's shoulder.

Together, they left the café and returned to the quiet cul-de-sac where their journey had begun.